"CHARLES JOHNSON IS A MAGICIAN, a skillful weaver of spells for healing broken souls and sick spirits." —Russell Banks

"Mixes good black magic with down-home wisdom, describes people so clearly you'd swear you knew them and weaves colorful words and phrases around you in such a fashion that they command the senses as well as the intellect to take part in the experience. . . . Charles Johnson does not play it safe in his first novel. He could probably have written at least three very simple books with all that he has in this multi-leveled one, but his bravery in mixing sense and non-sense . . . makes for a good thing."
—*Essence*

"THIS FIRST NOVEL IS SO ORIGINAL, SO IMAGINATIVE, AND SO EXCITING in what it has to say about the black woman's experience in America that it deserves major attention. A reading experience unlike anything else in a long time."
—*Publishers Weekly*

(For more extraordinary acclaim, please turn the page . . .)

CHARLES JOHNSON is the author of two other novels, *Oxherding Tale* and *Middle Passage* (winner of the 1990 National Book Award for Fiction and available in a Plume edition); a short-story collection, *The Sorcerer's Apprentice* (nominated for the 1988 PEN/Faulkner Award and available in a Penguin edition); and TV dramas that include the prize-winning PBS drama *Booker.* He is Pollock Professor of English at the University of Washington in Seattle.

"*Faith and the Good Thing* must be heralded as one of the great American novels of this century. In the vein of Saul Bellow's *Henderson the Rain King* and Flannery O'Connor's *The Violent Bear It Away,* it registers with flair and confidence a soul in quest of Nirvana. Charles Johnson spins a tale which moves from fact to fiction, from metaphysics to Black folklore, from side-bursting humor to wrenching pathos, from allegory to the one-dimensional. Yet subtlety rules the day. . . . *Faith and the Good Thing* is unqualifiedly good and extraordinarily beautiful."

—*Black World*

"If you're wondering what happened to all the great black writers in this country, I think Johnson is one of the best we've got, black or white." —*San Francisco Examiner*

BOOKS BY CHARLES JOHNSON

CHARLES JOHNSON

FAITH AND THE GOOD THING

A PLUME BOOK

PLUME
Published by the Penguin Group
Penguin Books USA Inc., 375 Hudson Street, New York, New York 10014, U.S.A.
Penguin Books Ltd, 27 Wrights Lane, London W8 5TZ, England
Penguin Books Australia Ltd, Ringwood, Victoria, Australia
Penguin Books Canada Ltd, 10 Alcorn Avenue, Toronto, Ontario, Canada M4V 3B2
Penguin Books (N.Z.) Ltd, 182-190 Wairau Road, Auckland 10, New Zealand

Penguin Books Ltd, Registered Offices: Harmondsworth, Middlesex, England

Published by Plume, an imprint of New American Library, a division of Penguin Books USA Inc.
This is an authorized reprint of a hardcover edition published by Atheneum Publishers.

First Plume Printing, October, 1991
10 9 8 7 6 5 4 3 2 1

℗ REGISTERED TRADEMARK—MARCA REGISTRADA

LIBRARY OF CONGRESS CATALOGING-IN-PUBLICATION DATA
Johnson, Charles Richard, 1948-
      Faith and the good thing / Charles Johnson.
        p.   cm.
      ISBN 0-452-26690-4
      I. Title.
      [PS3560.03735F35   1991]
      813'.54—dc20   91–22480
                                            CIP

Printed in the United States of America

PUBLISHER'S NOTE
This is a work of fiction. Names, characters, places, and incidents either are the product of the
author's imagination or are used fictitiously, and any resemblance to actual persons, living or dead,
events, or locales is entirely coincidental.

BOOKS ARE AVAILABLE AT QUANTITY DISCOUNTS WHEN USED TO PROMOTE PRODUCTS OR SERVICES.
FOR INFORMATION PLEASE WRITE TO PREMIUM MARKETING DIVISION, PENGUIN BOOKS USA INC.,
375 HUDSON STREET, NEW YORK, NEW YORK 10014.

TO THE MEMORY OF CHARLES A. GILPIN

Fides ergo est, quod non vides credere.
—ST. AUGUSTINE

Allah delights in many kinds of Truth
and Truth in many degrees, but even
Allah doesn't like the entire Truth.
—ARABIAN SAYING

FAITH AND THE GOOD THING

t is time to tell you of Faith and the Good Thing. People tell her tale in many ways—conjure men and old gimped grandmothers whisper it to make you smile—but always Faith Cross is a beauty, a brown-sugared soul sister seeking the Good Thing in the dark days when the Good Thing was lost or, if the bog-dwelling Swamp Woman did not lie, was hidden by the gods to torment mankind for sins long forgotten.

Listen.

The Devil was beating his wife on the day Faith's mother, Lavidia, died her second death. The first, an hour-long beating of bedsheets pierced by grating breaths, had been the day before, but a country doctor, Leon Lynch, came to the farmhouse where they lived and massaged Lavidia's heart. She returned from wherever it was she had been, both her legs pumping beneath the covers, her white eyes wide with terror. Lavidia raced like that the entire night, into the next day, and would have broken all long-distance records if she'd not been flat on her back. Finally she rested, counting her breaths. Faith, eighteen years old that day, stood at the window of her mother's bedroom, staring at a red sun as flat and still against the sky as moonlight on pond water. Light at first, like the sprinkle of baptism, yet steadily building, the dissolution of the clouds drenched the twenty acres of land left to Lavidia by her husband. Todd Cross had died in an odd way, so odd no one had spoken of him in Hatten County, Georgia, for twelve years. And now Faith's mother breathed her last.

Lifting the hem of her dress, Faith dried her eyes and turned from the window. She walked barefoot along the uneven wooden floorboards, circled an open-mouthed stove in the center of the room, and sat beside her mother's bed on an old fiddleback chair. Judging from the photographs on her dresser, Lavidia Cross, during the Great Depression, had been a handsome woman. She once had worn back her long brown hair, her skin sparkled from homemade lard, and her limbs were strong and sturdy. But at fifty-five, her figure was gray, both her arms spindly, and her swollen legs, drawn beneath the covers and quilts close to her breasts, were as soft as those of a toad. On the wall above her head swung a dull cross beside a calendar no one had changed for months. To Faith's right were Lavidia's wig stand, her lamps made from vinegar bottles, and a heavy maple-framed mirror, her mother's favorite heirloom. But Lavidia herself was slipping slowly out of time. Cockroaches lost their balance on the damp wall and fell along her face. These Faith quickly removed. Only light from the parted drapery of the room's single window lit the room. Water dripped from a ceiling sagging at its center. And the walls shuddered with each crash of thunder, the time between thunder rolls freighted with waiting. With mourning. Faith placed her fingers under the heavy covers to touch her mother's hand. It was cold.

"Momma," she said.

Lavidia's discolored eyes closed, her mouth sprang open, a web of spittle spread between her lips. "Don't ask me no questions," she said. ". . . Lord give me four hun'red million breaths to take, and I'm already on the three hun'red ninety-second millionth—I can't waste none on foolish questions."

Faith began to cry. "I called for Reverend Brown. He's outside. . . ."

Lavidia's eyes opened as though to drink in a vision. She stared sightlessly at Faith, and the blankets rose again with the kicking of her legs. Lavidia said, "Girl, you get yourself a good thing"; then she gulped once, whispered, "Four hun'red million," and died.

Behind her, Faith heard the bedroom door creak open. Through the doorway came the chubby preacher, Lucius Brown, and Oscar Lee Jackson, town mortician. Jackson, who wore a linty black suit and held his mottled hands folded in front of his paunch, stepped quietly inside the room and said, "Is she . . . ?"

Faith shook her head and quietly withdrew her hands from the covers. "Momma's resting."

Brown and Jackson went right to work. Jackson covered the empty eyes and open mouth on Lavidia's face with a bedsheet; Brown placed his arm around Faith's shoulders to lead her into the kitchen, blew his flat nose, and said, "I know she's gone to Glory. You believe that, Faith."

Faith, lowering her head to her hands, wept. "She couldn't be going to Glory the way she was running. Momma must have got where she was going the first time, turned around scared, and run all the way back."

"And," Brown said softly, "started runnin' straight for Glory."

From the table, they could see through the kitchen window that Jackson and his two assistants had straightened out Lavidia's legs and were carrying her on a stretcher to the open door of a hearse idling just yards from the front porch. Brown's eyes rolled toward the ceiling; he said something pious in a deep voice, reached across the table, and stroked Faith's hand. "What will you do now, child?"

Do? Faith paused, squinting her eyes to clear her head. The kitchen had changed. You could locate nothing misplaced, nothing out of the ordinary, for as a housekeeper Lavidia was meticulous; but the kitchen's former gloss of permanence was gone. Its smell was still that of the dry cotton fields just outside the open window above the sink, of browning bread Lavidia had baked just two nights before; yet Lavidia was gone. Though old, dissipated, sometimes evil, she had been the focus of the farmhouse since her husband's death, its most crucial node, surely its mistress. Without her the kitchen, the house, the world beyond fell apart. Fruit cabinets on the wall still held sweet jellies preserved in the odd-shaped bottles Lavidia salvaged like a scavenger from house and yard and rummage sales; her stiff mops and silver pail still rested in the corner by brooms she'd assembled by hand. Then what had changed? Certainly not the things themselves. Studying Lavidia's dresses heaped in a washtub by the door, her pipes in their dusty rack on the kitchen table, and dry lifeless wigs, Faith felt her answer emerge from the contours of these objects: none of them was for her; they belonged, related to no one. Even Lavidia, perhaps, had not made them her own, because —with her death—they seemed suddenly freed to be as they were. Empty things, cold, without quality, distant. Without order—it was evident—there could be no life, no sense to things, no way to awake in the stillness of morning and move from the day to and through the terror of eveningtime.

Her thoughts like wild animals fed upon themselves. Before her, *out there*, the wall stretched completely beyond all familiarity, possession, and warmth. She felt the urge to touch it, to reclaim it as the same wall against which Lavidia had measured her height across eighteen years. But if she touched it, might it not tumble away?

Faith looked down at her hand lying brown and crablike on the checkered tablecloth. Was it her hand? There was grave doubt, yes, of even this. She let it rest on Reverend Brown's blunt fingers, thought, "Spread your fingers," and was amazed at the result. The fingers spread, but between the command and the movement only a vague parallel held sway. Things had only a tenuous connection. The unreality of life without Lavidia melted even the gloss of permanence she felt enveloped her own life. No longer was she Faith, only child of Todd and Lavidia Cross, no longer was she what she believed herself to be; only a self-conscious pressure drifting about the empty, changing, charged-with-otherness kitchen, drifting through a cold space filled with shadows.

"Pray with me," Brown said.

Startled, she withdrew her hand. Brown's words had not come from his lips; like smoke, they had risen from the room itself, flowing from silence, returning to it, at first everywhere—surrounding them both—then gone. Her eyes in desperation sought familiar details in the smooth grain of the kitchen door where as a child she could often see the faces of jinn, mermen, and fairy queens that filled her father's make-believe world. Faith studied the room and held her breath ("You'll live longer holding your breath," Lavidia had often said). The kitchen remained beyond her: *out there*. Inaccessible to love, to need. *Out there*. Its chairs and tables appeared tiny, as though made for and by dwarfs. The walls receded from her, meeting at apexes a dizzy distance away.

The reverend stroked his squared jaw with sharp, mechanical motions and laughed uneasily, perhaps frightened, for Faith was said to have funny ways like her father. "It's always hard at first . . . always."

"Momma told me to get myself a good thing," Faith said softly. Then she asked, "What do you think she meant?"

Reverend Brown smiled as broad as a Halloween pumpkin and seemed to swell in her vision. He stepped around the table behind Faith, floorboards groaning against his weight, and placed both his hands on her shoulders. "Faith, you know what the good thing is. You've known ever since your father died." His fingers tightened, holding her hunched over the table. "Don't you remember what happened to you?"

Brown's hard calluses met her skin, the rough texture of his fingers squeezing from her the nightmare she had hidden from herself long ago. Faith closed her eyes against remembrance. But it ascended—the images, clear as crystal, hurtling before her mind, her ears filling with the words of the messenger: God called Todd Cross.

She'd heard it first while playing during recess in the schoolyard. Children were everywhere, fighting, laughing, exchanging frogs and funny-shaped stones, and Faith had thought someone, perhaps Alpha Omega Holmes, who'd said he cared about her, was trying to talk about her father in the cruel way of grownups. She turned toward the sound, expecting the next call to be about her mother's virtue or her own eyes, which people said were uneven, or her legs, often mocked by some children as skinny. Over the heads of the other children Faith saw fat Eula May Jenkins, her mother's neighbor, wheezing near her teacher in the doorway of the schoolhouse, her face drawn into itself like a prune, crying, "Death sneezed Todd Cross stiff as a board." The woman's huge frame shook, she wailed, she balled her fists. "Lavidia found him half an hour ago at the edge of the woods. Don't it figure the way he acted and all? Didn't I tell you them crazy ideas would catch up to him sooner or later?"

Faith broke away from the other children and ran. Eula May Jenkins called after her, but she pressed her palms to her ears and hurried home. Fifteen minutes later she stood breathlessly watching the farmhouse from afar. People crowded the small front porch and spoke in excited voices. A strange woman called to her from the yard, but Faith turned, her shoes flying from her feet, and raced for the woods. When she reached the crowd at the border of the woods she was barefoot and breathless. She shoved her way through a maze of legs and stopped, aware of her father's smell on the air: tobacco and sweat. Both his bare feet swung above from a pine tree. Caught from her waist from behind, Faith was carried away.

She had been only six then, and by nightfall most of her fear was spent. What truly upset her after seeing her father's dangling, ashy legs was that everyone now expected something from her. But no one said what it was. Many visitors came to the farmhouse and told her to be brave, to pray. Brave about what, pray to whom? Lavidia shaved her head and told her, "Your daddy sneezed his soul away— it's just." Faith accepted this without further questioning. It was believable, for life was filled with stranger things, as her father had repeatedly told her. She remembered his saying, "Everything that is is right, or it wouldn't be." During the wake Faith, thinking of this, even smiled.

Concern for Faith's peculiar reaction brought Reverend Brown, younger then and indefatigable, on regular visits to the farmhouse. He would park his old Plymouth close to the porch and sit late at night with Lavidia as she smoked and spit and rocked in the moonlight, telling her of the great spirit-man who would soon speak to sinners in their county. Faith would sit close to her mother, dozing after a big dinner, thinking of her father and Alpha, who made her laugh, and only half hearing the plans for her salvation.

The day after one such visit her mother dressed her in white and took her miles from home to an enormous tent in the fields behind town. Faith had been excited—it was a *circus* tent, tall as timber, with flaps that spread like wings. Big Todd, she remembered, had worked in a circus, had been part of its world and found what he called his calling there. Mightn't she, too? Before they reached the entrance Faith could hear singing inside and the clash of tambourines. But it struck her as they entered that this place held no entertainment. Old men and wasted women she recognized as tireless sharecroppers and maids sang from chairs lining the interior of the tent; some spoke hurriedly, biting their tongues, in the lost language, while others spun like tops through the aisles. They had not come to see an event; they had come to be one.

Faith pulled against Lavidia, who slapped her lightly and dragged her inside to the front row, where Eula May Jenkins—not a neighbor now, or a bearer of grief, or a whisperer of rumors, but a silent dancer—beat the soles of her bare feet against the ground. Beside her two women held Alpha Omega Holmes in his chair. He, the boy who loved her even then, was almost unrecognizable. His face was crimson, twisted, his lips parted, screaming emptiness, and his limbs jerked in all directions, blurred like fluttering batwings. Down the row, deep in meditation, a cripple mashed an off-key accordion; leathery old men in barley-stained overalls bent forward in their seats to hear Reverend Alexander Magnus, the spirit man, at the front of the tent. He stood head and shoulders above the others in the tent, over seven feet tall if a foot, intimidating them with his size and deep sonorous voice. When he gestured—raising his big square hands into the air and pointing toward the sky or shoving them out with his fingers curled back like claws—they could catch their breaths and hold them for what seemed like an hour. Magnus paced and pointed at people in the front row, his face shut and sweating. "Children, you are crooked and ulcerous, you are cancerous and weak. You are damned from birth and distant from the source of all good. You are as dust and excrement to Him. You are as the groveling mole and eyeless maggot before the power that pardons your trespasses and prevents your death. You are nothing! In due time, it is written, your feet shall slide and the unsteady floor of your life shall give way. Shall it be tonight?" He looked left, his eyebrows arched, toying with their fear. "Or tomorrow?"—looking right, his eyes wide, sly. "You are damned for delighting in this world. Your tongues savor fatback and burgoo, your flesh hungers for other flesh." Magnus stopped to stare into the face of a farmer and his wife. They shrank back, silent, and he shouted, "Worms will be your supper soon!

"Sinner, have you ever tortured a spider? Have you ever held it over a smoking fire on its silky web, sick of its slimy form, feeling—deep in your heart—that you'd let it drop and watch it burn? Have you ever stalked and cornered a fly for the trespass of buzzing in your ear? Brother Spider," he said to Alpha, "Sister Fly," to Lavidia, "Sinners!" to everyone in the tent, "your life is supported by a perfect being who watches you with disgust, just like you watch chinches and waterbugs, slugs and lice, knowing that if you have the cheek to go too far, then—*whop!*" Magnus slapped his hands together like a cannon shot. "But He loves you still (*I* don't know why!). Nothing else explains why you didn't drop into hell in your pajamas last night. Nothing you have done, do now or will do shall save you. Not even innocence can save you." (Herewith Faith shuddered and grabbed Lavidia's clammy hand.) "Witness crib death and the diseases of childhood. Witness the fury of storms, floods, droughts, lightning, hail, the dangers of machinery, earthquakes, plagues, famines and poisoned food, senseless slaughter, recessions, depressions, bloodshed, revolutions, civil wars and the eventual destruction that creeps closer and closer to your front door. It's here now. Can you *feel* it—death moving ghoul-like in the dark? Maybe tonight when you put out your candles, close your eyes, and start to sleep lightly, maybe then you'll feel death down your spine and come full awake with a start, sweat streaming in your clothes, your eyes searching the darkness of your bedroom until you see the red eyes of the Devil riveted on you; over there, brothers—in that far corner, tiny red eyes just to the right of your chamber pot." Magnus laughed at the thought of it. No one else said a mumbling word. "He'll shove his claw down your throat, fish up your soul and steal away, lame and hunchbacked, leaving no tracks for your family and friends to find you—the *real* you, brothers, because it'll be shoved, gibbering and pale, into Satan's big black traveling bag. Pay attention! My prayers can't save you then. He'll toss you like so much trash into rivers brimming with blood and burning corpses. All the filth and offal ever to pass through the bodies of birds and beasts and men will fill your mouths. The fire there is forever," he said in a hushed voice. "It boils the blood in your veins and bakes your brain like a biscuit; it blackens your skin so you'd think you're white right now. You'll smell your hair burn, brothers—light a strand right now and see how it stinks; you'll hear the howl of demons forever: '*Were you not saved*?' And you will call on Him. Who will not hear. Torment for eternity, brothers—because you loved this illusion, this fire-wheel we call the world!"

An old woman in a black bonnet and black shawl began to dance. To Faith she danced the way a snake writhed or maybe like something dead but newly risen—like something that had no business dancing at all. She snapped back her head and stepped a mad cakewalk through the aisles, screaming. Magnus smiled. "All that is given to man, to life and to this illusion is stolen from God. Who shall you serve? If Him, your salvation is assured. If the world . . ."

Magnus chortled so deep, so strange that it sounded like the earth moving and stiffened all who heard, ". . . woe unto you who would dare to love this world."

None would dare.

So the congregation thumped their feet in loud tattoos along the ground, clapped their hands, and called out. Air in the tent grew dense with dust, cries and smells released from the gathering. Distance between their bodies dissolved until all the raised voices in the tent echoed inside Faith's head. Inching slowly through the tent, Reverend Brown sought prey—the proud. He laid his fingertips on Eula May Jenkins' temples, lifting the big woman like a puppet. She quaked, shouted, screamed, and fell at Faith's feet.

Lavidia gestured to Eula May's empty seat. "You sit here by Alpha." Alpha's shirt was torn away, his chest was the color of fire. There, Faith did *not* want to sit. She backed away, aware of a sickness springing at the pit of her stomach, a stinging in her arms and legs. Seeing Faith and Lavidia, Reverend Brown spun on his heels and, from across the room, pointed his finger like a revolver at Lavidia. She froze, trembling once as if cold or being crushed by a great, invisible palm; then she left her seat, tearing at her throat. She collapsed, flailing the air. Faith went to her, tried to pin her arms and legs to the ground.

It was useless.

Faith's dark reflection sparkled in Lavidia's wide eyes; but her mother could not see. Lavidia's wig, golden in the lights strung overhead throughout the tent, burst from its pins. Veins corded in her neck. Beside Faith, knifing through the riot of the hymns and loud tambourines, she heard Reverend Brown whispering:

"Are you ready, child?"

Dark and triumphant, Brown's face was a mask of moving, proud expressions. He touched her arm and something inside Faith broke free. She tried to inhale, but the air was swirling, thick and weighted with invisible things. On her tongue strange words formed, and more vividly than before she saw her father's swinging feet as retribution for his terrible pride and passions.

"Call!" Brown demanded.

Pain rippled like electricity through her limbs, so intense she wanted to leap, to avoid it, from her skin. "Call," Brown whispered.

"Say 'Thank You,' child." It meant nothing to her. She would have said anything to extinguish the pain inside her. There on the ground, the earth at her ear humming with voices in the air, she saw it clearly—all the possible number of things in space, all forms that had ever existed in time reflected back into time like a man's image trapped in a room of mirrors—she, herself, Faith Cross, fading back and forth on the continuum of time until she could no longer be certain of the images of herself that shone in her father's eyes; those of Lavidia, the preacher, the undertaker, and Alpha were more real than she, if in that crazy complex of images she existed at all. Faith screamed it—"Thank Yooou!"—sang it—"Thank You"—and finally believed in its healing grace—"Thank You!"

But it didn't last. The silent kitchen said so. And so did the yard beyond.

She glanced over her shoulder at Reverend Brown, wondering if he knew how short-lived had been her salvation. An afterglow that warmed her and dissolved her intimations of a ghastly world without meaning or sense, save salvation and survival, had carried her through the remainder of her childhood. Time, though, did damage to it. For it often took the form of a hunger unsatisfied by further prayer meetings. Always these feelings possessed her, as a demon or jinni might, haunting her experiences to find a vision of complete freedom. It took in breaths beneath her own, moved with her limbs. Demanded its rights.

Sometimes she tried to ignore it, to grow up like other children. Ignoring it, though, was somehow akin to trying to forget one's own heartbeat; louder it grew with denial. Like a lover or lecher, the awareness came to her at night when she tried to sleep, stealing through her bedroom window like the scent of night-blooming flowers or the whispering rustle of wind in the trees. When it came, the world as it usually appeared . . . disappeared. Time was suspended, and tomorrow took its true form as illusion. Only the present was immediate and everywhere, disclosed to her as the miraculous—woven veins in a browning autumn leaf, in the minor miracle of an insect nature had fashioned like a twig—with legs!

Clearest were these feelings on the afternoons she spent spooning with Alpha Omega Holmes, her first and, she often thought, last love. It was more than a run-of-the-mill high-school affair; she was certain! Together they would lie in the tall grass, holding each other until their in and out breaths coincided, breathing as a single body; her shorter breaths would slowly slip beneath his own. And the grass and trees, it seemed, would bring their pulsations in line with them until the universe was a single heartbeat. Reality was a dream, or sometimes a nightmare, but no more than this: a rhythm. She felt herself at such times carried through the world as though she had wings, but not toward Glory, never toward Glory. Only back to earth, deep within its strange fabric. No personalities existed in such a pure world of feeling, just flashes of human outlines in the quilt of creation where plants had their place, and animals—all coexisting peacefully, lyrically, like notes in a lay.

"Well?" Reverend Brown said, removing his hands from her shoulders. "You and your mother both had it for a while. You can have it again."

Faith looked away. "I felt something back then, but I don't think that's what Momma meant." She looked at him timidly, almost afraid to say more. "I think Momma meant something like it . . . only more."

"More?" Brown grumbled, and again, "*More?*" as though the word were bitter. He stepped close to her, intimidating her with his size as his hands flexed at his sides. "What more *is* there? Honey, the world is just the way you saw it on the floor of that tent—there ain't no more—there couldn't be! People who look for more will be annihilated."

"She meant *some*thing," Faith insisted.

The reverend cleared his throat and towered over Faith, drumming his fingers on the tablecloth. "Sometimes family deaths can be disruptive. They take away someone who's been the center of your world for a long time, and you see how difficult it is to live without someone or something to hold on to. Death ought to start a person thinking—"

". . . About what the good thing really is?"

Brown's fist crashed on the table; Lavidia's pipes spilled from their rack. He glared at them, then at Faith. "Don't interrupt me! I'm trying to tell you something!" The reverend's lips curled back over silver-capped teeth, his brow wrinkled. Faith immediately wanted to take back what she had said. Brown had taken it personally. Bitterness laced his voice:

"I ain't gonna preach sin to you. There's more involved than that! Your momma, God rest her soul, was tryin' to tell you on her deathbed that you've got to have somethin' to hold on to now that she's gone . . . somethin' that'll pull the world together." Brown, Faith sensed, was no longer talking to her, but to himself, slamming his left fist repeatedly into his right palm and pausing for reflection. "This world we live in—it's like a shadowy cave fulla crazy sounds if you've got nothin' to light it up. There's no sun but the Saviour, y'see? There's no right or wrong, and nothin's clear-cut—there's nothin' but a lot of empty things that keep bumpin' into each other in the dark. . . ."

Faith thought of her father, of his stunning fictions and well-meant lies. "I've heard different."

"From who?" Brown sneered. "From the Swamp Woman? I've heard tell of the stories she tells kids stupid enough to believe them. You listen to me. Forget people like that." Brown winced and grabbed at his right side. "Even *talkin'* about her hurts me—happens every time I mention the old witch. People like her will have you believin' in haints and hoodoo and the walkin' dead if you let them." Brown seized a napkin from the table and wiped the wrinkles from his forehead.

"Pray with me," he said.

The bleating horn of Jackson's hearse drew Faith's attention. She went to the front porch, Brown at her heels, muttering almost under his breath, "I'll be back tomorrow and the day after and I'll keep comin' back until you start showin' some sense."

From the doorway she leaned against the railing of the stairs and watched as the reverend sprinted through the rain to the hearse and slid onto the front of the seat beside the undertaker. It seemed impossible the dark machine in the mud held her mother. Lavidia's deep, almost manly laughter would no longer awake her in the morning; silent was the voice that had called her from the fields. Though it was pointless, she forgave her mother for her selfishness; her will, spitefulness, and grudges; even for taking Alpha from her in the cruelest possible way. Forgiving, though, was not forgetting. Always she would remember resting her head on Alpha's chest as they sat on the front porch of the farmhouse, painting in broad, vague out-lines the possibility of a life together, only to look up and see Lavidia's gray face scowling in the window nearby. Always she would hear her mother say, "You'll *never* have *no*body that'll love you like your mother did! You'll cry for me when I'm gone."

Lavidia lived in fear of Faith's leaving her to a house full of memories that would become distorted and terrifying with the pas-sage of time. Therefore, she clung to her, screened every boy that drove up to the farmhouse to visit Faith, and browbeat each with questions: "Faith's been saved—she's married to God," Lavidia would say; then wryly, with squinted eye and twisted mouth: "Are you God?" Alpha found such competition unbearable. He never returned. Faith had waited for him each evening on the front porch until Lavidia informed her, "He won't be back no more. I was payin' him to court you 'cause you looked so lonesome all the time. Wouldn't no other fellah look at a girl as plain and backwards as you. I couldn't afford it no more. I guess he's gone for good."

It *must* have been a lie. Yet to this day Faith was uncertain. Others —the rowdy boys from the mill, the shy ones without a future, and the bold ones destined to die soon in fights or drink—came to the farmhouse after Alpha's disappearance, but Lavidia never confronted them. Faith herself turned them away, excusing herself to do school- or housework, or simply hiding from them in her bedroom. Did one ever really know another's affections? You could guess at them and live as best as you could in the shadow of uncertainty. That was Big Todd's way. He never asked, never doubted that haints and demons inhabited everything. He told her great love and hatred moved men to happiness and shame: it was that simple.

She looked at Reverend Brown beside the mortician and saw that his smugness, his strength came from knowing or thinking he knew with his heart the workings of other men, that they lusted, or felt lost and would be rewarded or damned proportionally for those longings. But was that true? Was all that really there? Concerning his feelings, Alpha's face told her nothing. His dark eyes were quiet, and his lips bent up at their corners whenever he saw her; but there was nothing about this, or his smooth hands, or his face and smoother words, that *really* told her what he was thinking. Love was a myth born in imagination, pieced together from the inferred softness of a stare, deduced, probably from false premises or undistributed middle terms, from his smile: it could have been deceit. Lavidia never ceased to make that clear when Faith found herself moping about the house. "Just *how* did you know he loved you?" she would challenge. No reply was possible. You could never know. And Alpha and the world of things, of kitchen furniture and hearses, came to her as cold, inaccessible things *out there*.

You couldn't fool yourself; you knew you wanted the smile to be love, and knowing that you knew completely ruined the feeling. How had Big Todd done it—lived in a world so full of magic that he could call pots and pans by proper names he'd given them? Seen from the floor of Brown's tent the world had been a wasteland; the one in Big Todd's tales, a dream. Could you choose?

Within herself Faith found no answer.

And now the hearse was at the road, hauling her mother to the halfway house between Hatten County and Hell. She jumped down the stairs and ran slipping through the mud. Jackson stopped the car, rolled down his window, and called:

"You go and stay with Mrs. Jenkins tonight."

They left her at the road. From the north the wind brought rain to pelt Faith. She suddenly feared re-entering the farmhouse. It rested on white stones her father had carried by mule from the forest. Lavidia's rocking chair creaked back and forth slowly in the wind. Tree toads were carping, harbingers of a storm, and the rain exploded like the report of rifles far away. Faith remained still, staring at the front porch, trying to imagine Lavidia sitting in her rocker, smoking and squeezing from the pores of her waxy nose white things she called worms. The cabin defied her memories, determined to remain . . . *out there*. Then came thunder, and in a way that frightened her—as though the noise would tear the thin membrane of the sky, rending it to the horizon like a run in cheap hosiery, and angels, God's throne, and heavenly host would tumble like leaves across the fields. Faith began running south until she fell. She looked back, still frightened by the cabin that appeared to descend into the soft ground. Alone, she cried, but kept walking, aimlessly and for hours. Her flight took her to the edge of the swamp. Then it was that Faith decided to seek audience with the werewitch at her shanty in the bogs.

esidents of Faith's county told rumors that the Swamp Woman was the Last Gnostic and hated visitors, that she had once been a diviner of dragon bones and dodo gizzards in Nubia before the coming of the Portuguese, French, and English. They said when her tribe was pillaged and its members shaved, manacled, and driven into the ships lining the west coast of Africa, she had chosen death over captivity and made herself one of the living dead to torment her people's captors forever from the dank swamps, cackling to herself, working hoodoo, and conversing with spirits. Those who believed in her said she was a midwife for the things hiding like tumors beneath a man's personality; others said she guarded forgotten mysteries and formulas lost to man. But everyone in southern Georgia attributed miracles to her—like the time before the Civil War when old Massa Furguson paid her eight hundred dollars in horses and slaves to make him young again. The Swamp Woman, if the story is true, was reported to be mischievous. She slaughtered cows and sacrificed virgin slaves that entire night, and by morning the witchery was done. The old Massa awoke and pulled back the covers of his bed. He was young again. And black. His wife screamed, awakening the entire plantation. Old Massa looked in his bedroom mirror and saw that he was in the body of one of his slaves, a healthy but stupid one named Jug. When he turned around, Jug was standing in the doorway, grinning in the Massa's old body. Jug sipped at a bottle of the Massa's best port, sucked at his long Cuban cheroot, and gave a strong, protective arm to the Massa's wife as defense against the raving nigger fingering his face before the mirror. That's exactly how they say it happened. Jug sold the Massa the very next day for two new muskets and a

mustang, freed all his slaves, and threw a party in the Massa's Big House every weekend for thirty years until he died.

Terrible was the Swamp Woman said to be in matters of vengeance. On the Thursday evening just before the evacuation of Atlanta to escape Sherman, the Algonquin boys from the Hollow drank themselves courageous with moonshine; they started out to capture the Swamp Woman with shotguns and hounds. P.T. Barnum would have paid quite a sum for featuring the hoary old hag, but—it is said—she exposed herself in all her otherworldly nakedness to the boys at the foot of the bogs. She drove them *mad*, children. The older folks all spoke of how the Algonquin boys came running back to town barking on all fours, their hair white as ash, while the dogs were leading them on ropes with toothpicks jutting from their muzzles.

But the tales of the Swamp Woman did not bother Faith. She had, in eighteen years, heard of stranger things. Although tired, she traveled all that evening, and by midnight, was slowly walking, guided by yellow moonlight cutting through the trees overhead, through the swamp. Beneath her feet, the moonlight forced shadows away from crawling vines, often causing them to look like serpents. Through these Faith stepped easily, remembering her father's eyes, for some strange reason, and his story of the snakes: long ago he had sat her at his feet before the hearth as he warmed his legs, telling her in an awe-softened voice how, when just a boy, he had wandered away from home and become lost in the woods. A snake by his foot had frightened him, but looking closer he discovered it wasn't a snake at all—just a vine. Life, he told her, would be like that—he told her that someday she would awaken from a life of everyday slumbers and realize all she considered familiar were just shadows. But if she began to look, to search with her mind fresh and her heart yearning for truth as a man weaned on sand thirsts, then she, like everyone in time, would find her way out of the woods. Beyond the shadows. Faith's search was at an end. In the clearing just ahead was the werewitch's dwelling.

The Swamp Woman's shanty was odd, children, squatting above the fetid swamp on wooden poles with a crazy hole for its door. The hole was circular and carved in the side of the shanty where the traditional Door of the Dead belonged, through which a deceased member of a family was carried so that his spirit could never find the proper entrance and thus haunt his own clan. The rear of the shanty was submerged in the swamp, half hidden under water rising as high as the window sill. Faith held her breath and swatted at bogflies circling her head. Something about the shanty held her still. Its windows seemed to be lit from within by fire. Shadows crept behind tarpaulin stretched across the triangular-shaped windows. Faith inhaled for courage and started across a rickety bridge of damp boards leading to the entrance. Sounds drifted from within —the whir of machinery, an eerie discordant music. She thought of running, of shouting, of balling her fists to calm herself. One could only guess at the bizarre things awaiting her within the shanty. She might not leave it alive. Faith had almost convinced herself to leave when she first perceived a presence behind her: the smell of something old and dry. Heavy breathing, not her own, filled her ears. Without thinking, she turned to face the origin of the labored breath; this she immediately regretted. Crouching at her heels was a hairless old woman whose face held features like those glimpsed in novel arrangements of vegetation, freak potatoes in the shape of cow skulls. It was horrible. *Horrible!* One tiny eye, the left one, was partially closed and had no pupil—clear it was and the color of egg yolk. The other, a disk, had a green cataract floating free in its center. Such a creature could never have been born—only spawned; never grown —only fermented in some ghastly cesspool. Like the swamp.

Faith jumped back a foot and lost her balance, falling along the moist boards of the bridge. Above her, draped over a burlap gown and resembling dual drops of water suspended in space, hung long, purplish breasts tipped with teats as sharp as nails. Faith glanced away, down, only to have her eyes light upon two misshapen feet gripping the edge of the bridge like fingers. She shivered, stricken by a heavy, sulfurous smell that grew stronger as the potato face drew near. Its lipless mouth moved without sound; the werewitch's words rang deep within Faith's mind as the old woman shouted in silence, "You're here to steal my secret, ain't ya?"

Faith cringed. "God, no!"

The mouth twisted into a sneer, brandishing teeth as keen as the files of a saw. "Then what'ya want? A potion? Yer boy friend can't get it up no mo' and ya wants a potion, right? Ya know what it takes to make a potion these days, girlie? Eye of newt and auric eggs don't come as easy as they use to!"

"No," Faith whispered, "nothing like that."

The emerald eye, dull and dilated, winked. "Revenge? Ya want to see me turn somebody ya don't like into a squirrel? Hee hee! That always was my favorite; but his astral body's gotta be in trine with the right planets before it'll work."

"No . . ."

"Then ya wants money? Sho! Ya wanna be rich and live forever!"

Faith fainted, the brief escape being pleasant, not quite like dreamwork, but similar to yet greater than reality, for her father was in it, and anything associated with Big Todd Cross had to be for real. She witnessed, as in times past, the occasion when Todd was threatened by the Weaver Clan, who terrorized Hatten County for six years. Or at least until the day they tried to take over Todd's farm. To a man, the Weavers were mean and ugly. They believed that men were base and the world was a jungle; therefore, they concluded it should be managed by the meanest, ugliest men around. For this, the Weavers all qualified—animals, for fear of being poisoned, did not bite them. And together the Weavers killed so many men that Oscar Lee Jackson had to expand his mortuary and work on Sundays just to keep the county serviced. It started to look like the Weavers were right about the world. They made a mistake, though; they threatened to take over Todd's farm and, perhaps, Faith, too—just for sport. Faith's father descended on their ranch like a storm, toting rifles so big they required two men to load them and a third to supervise. The Weavers saw him coming. They turned pale. So pale in fact their eyes turned pink, their hair colorless, and their flesh as pallid as dough. From that day forward the Weavers left Todd alone. Even they saw they'd been wrong. But that didn't turn them black again. The doctors said Todd Cross had frightened them so the melanin in their blood evaporated in their sweat. Simpler folks just told the truth: Fate had chosen Big Todd as the means to bring albinos to their little spot in Georgia.

"Yow!"

Opening her eyes, Faith realized she was stretched naked on a hard pallet in the shanty, a snow-white cat hissing on her stomach. In her head a thin voice said, "You was dreamin' about yer daddy—

that's always a bad sign that you've lost yer way and need some direction." Faith, looking across the room, saw the Swamp Woman squatting before a bubbling cauldron, drying her dress. The werewitch nodded toward the cat and said in Faith's head, "Don't mind him none. My familiar gets way too familiar sometimes." Her mouth widened in a silent smile. "Quiet as it's kept, he's really the imprisoned spirit of Joseph Arthur Gobineau . . . I just keep him around to vex every now and then."

The cat screamed—a bloodcurdling cry that sounded almost like swearing—jumped from Faith's stomach, rushed to the werewitch's left leg, and sank in its claws. The cat, receiving a shock of some kind, spun away to sulk near the circular door.

Chilled to her bones, dumb with fright, ready (almost) to die, Faith rose slowly, averting her eyes from the Swamp Woman. Like an enormous, half-human frog the werewitch sat herself in a hatha-yoga position and sipped at embalming fluid from a silver goblet. Around her, rusty wands and V-shaped divining rods littered the floor. Worktables in the room were covered with slide rules, sextants, Ouija boards, jugs filled with jelling dark fluids, and bizarre, useless inventions. The walls were plastered with anatomical and cosmological charts and unfathomable trigrams of the four elements sketched on curling brown papyrus. Book shelves held dusty volumes bound with large silver rings: *The Complete Demonomancer, Domino Divination in 10 Easy Lessons,* and *The Bedside Cartomancer.* Against the western wall, sunken into thigh-deep water beneath diagrams of the Adamic, Hyperborean, Atlantean, Aryan, and Lemurian Root Races (with lacunas left for two more to come), a large machine hummed and played music, its gears powered by the frantic racing of a green Gila monster along a treadmill.

"I'm gonna patent that." The werewitch giggled in Faith. "Everybody knows a mathematical nexus holds between the frequencies of tones in the musical scale; and any fool knows you can chart the planets in their orbits with similar calculations. Right?"

"Right," Faith gulped. "*Right.*"

The werewitch giggled again. "Well," she said, crafty, "not many people know the distance between the centers of the planets causes 'em to make music when they swing around the sun. Hee hee! And I've got the only machine in the world that figures out their frequency and tapes that music. Saturn's a basso profundo, Jupiter's a bass, Mars is a tenor, the earth's a contralto, Venus is a soprano, and Mercury—since it's got the shortest orbit—is a falsetto. Want me to turn up the machine so you can hear 'em?"

"I don't think so. . . ."

Words exploded in Faith's head. "Ya don't believe in the Music of Spheres, do ya?"

"Yes! Yes, I *do*!"

"No," the Swamp Woman sighed, "like everybody else ya need some kind of demonstration—as if *that* proved somethin' veritical." The werewitch made a cat's cradle with her fingers, and leaned toward Faith.

"What's yer full name, girlie?"

"Faith Cross. . . ."

"Faith's a good name," the Swamp Woman said. "Did ya know Saint Augustine said faith meant believin' in what ya can't see? No, I guess ya didn't know that. Never mind. Ya see that chart over yonder?"

Faith turned to a small chart just above the door. It read:

1 2 3 4 5 6 7 8 9

A B C D E F G H I

J K L M N O P Q R

S T U V W X Y Z

But she couldn't understand it. Or the Swamp Woman's hasty computations.

"The numbers in your first name add up to twenty-six, the numbers in your last name come to twenty, which is forty-six altogether. Four plus six is ten, and one plus zero is one. That makes you a Number One, girlie."

"Is that good?"

The werewitch sniggered. "What's in a number? A rose by any other—well, you know all that already. Number Ones are good people, but they have to be pointed on the right path, or they'll meet with disaster."

Considering this for a moment, Faith said, "What're you?"

"A thirteen."

"And that means—what?"

Sardonically, the Swamp Woman said, "The numbers all stop at twelve. . . ."

Faith paused. Then pursed her lips. "Then, you're the only Number Thirteen?"

"Don't I know it!" the Swamp Woman screeched, leaping to her feet. "Girlie, have you got any idea what it's like bein' the only substance of its kind in the world? It's like being God. Ain't nobody to talk to but y'self. Oh, ya should see my poetry—that'd show ya how lonely and blue I get sometimes."

"I'm sorry," Faith said.

"It don't matter." The Swamp Woman waved off the subject with a sweep of her hand, and returned to flapping Faith's dress in mists of steam rising from the cauldron. "Ya can't be happy and smart, too."

Still terrified, but at least past nausea now, Faith looked over her shoulder to a six-foot mirror trimmed in arabesques of gold. She realized she was naked, all flushed and protruding from her private places; she began to blush. The tinted blue glass reflected a thin girl whose hair mushroomed like a storm cloud behind her head. A few years ago she had developed, here and there, the appropriate bumps and contours, yet her figure remained soft and childlike. Smooth and the color of caramel. Inside Faith's head the Swamp Woman laughed, and the laugh was dreadful, a deep grating sound originating in the werewitch's round belly; by the time it reached Faith as telepathy, it scarcely sounded human.

"Now I know what ya come for," she tittered. "Ya wants bigger tits. *That's* why ya come, right? You young girls ought to know better'n to pester me for somethin' like that. I'm busy! The Lord knows if I couldn't steal somebody's life every now and then when I needed more time, I'd *never* get alla my work done."

Fists clenched at her sides, Faith faced the Swamp Woman, her eyes narrowing to watering slits to blur the werewitch's sickening smile.

"I only came to ask you a question—about what the good thing might be. . . ."

"The Good *Thing*?" the Swamp Woman cackled, her lips

bemused. "You sure you ain't committin' the Fallacy of Misplaced Concreteness, girlie?"

Faith shook her head. "My momma told me to find it. I know there has to be one. If there wasn't, I know Momma couldn't have thought of it."

"That's a good argument," the Swamp Woman said. "It's off base, but I like it anyway." The werewitch rested her head against the wall, coming as close as she could to smiling. "You're too sweet a girl to be worryin' about the Good Thing. Ya ought to be home afoalin' babies or somethin' practical." Her yellow eye closed completely, the green one stared. "I've thought a lot about the Good Thing," she said, counting off the possibilities on the twelve taloned fingers of her right hand, "and I figure it must be the right functionin' of an organism as it participates in a form, or the fulfillment of a teleological principle inherent in all matter, or gettin' in the right relationship with the Lord (or Lords, or y'self, dependin' upon your persuasion), or followin' the Hedonistic Calculus in all matters of equally appealing desires, or doin' unto others as you'd have 'em do unto you, or a leap o' faith, or abolishin' private property, or maybe avoidin' Bad Faith." The Swamp Woman giggled obscenely as though she'd told a joke. "Take your pick, sweetheart."

"But I want the *one* Good Thing," Faith said, still standing away from the werewitch. "I want the one thing all those things have in common."

Then Faith scrambled across the room—as far from the Swamp Woman as she could go. The old woman's body shook until its outline was hazy, her green and yellow eyes watered a viscous material that resembled molasses, and she beat her big feet upon and, finally, through the floorboards.

Faith stood breathless.

"Spirit World come through again," the Swamp Woman said when the seizure passed. "It's kinda like you've got a switchboard in your head and alla the switches are ringin' at once." With her right hand she smeared the thick fluid from her face, her long nails leaving tracks that soon grew red. "The word's out that it'll definitely be Blazetail in the fifth race."

"I'm not interested in that," Faith said.

"All right, *all right!*" The Swamp Woman jumped to her feet and

24

rummaged through several wire cages stacked in a corner of the room. From one she withdrew a chicken that fought desperately to free itself from her grip. The Swamp Woman strangled it and snapped off its head.

Shuddering, Faith looked away.

"Come over here," the Swamp Woman said.

Faith obeyed, but came no closer than four feet as the werewitch squeezed blood from the chicken's head onto one of her cluttered workbenches. She placed a monocle over her green eye and studied the puddle carefully, twisting her head from left to right, snorting, chuckling and following with her three left forefingers the contour of the puddle.

"What's it say?" Faith asked.

"It says that whatever is is either a substance or an attribute, mind or matter with the absolute certainty of the external world grounded in the self-evident fact that God could not be an Evil Deceiver and still be all-good."

"What does that mean?"

The Swamp Woman frowned. "I ain't sure. Let's look at the liver." Faith turned her head as the Swamp Woman dug inside the chicken and extracted the liver. She held it close to her yellow eye, like a gem-cutter inspecting a diamond, or an old philosopher studying an atomic proposition, and grimaced:

"The liver's in Latin! I can't read no goddamn Latin!"

Faith groaned, about to despair, but the Swamp Woman suddenly became animated, screeching, "I've got just the thing for you, sweetheart," and she lurched out the door. Faith rushed to the cauldron and felt her dress. It was dry, almost crisp to her touch, and she pulled it quickly over her head. From outside there came the squealing of a hog in distress. Faith took the opportunity to inspect her surroundings.

A museum: that was the only way to relate the host of marvelous, mystical contraptions scattered throughout the room. Nailed to one of the walls was a rotten ferryboat oar from the Styx. Wood there was from the cross at Calvary, strewn as kindling beneath a stove. A philosopher's stone held the door open, and speckled philosopher's eggs lay in weed-woven baskets on the workbenches. There were imaguncula—clay, wax, and wooden figures of lute-playing satyrs and mermen used for divination. Among them Faith also found the likenesses of many residents of Hatten County, including a figure of Reverend Brown with a needle stuck in his right side. There were magic drums stretched with reindeer hide, rings shaped like the sacred serpent οὐροβόρος and, toward the rear of the room, a small table with a free-swinging pendulum beneath it. The table's surface held metal plates bearing the numbers of the alphabet, and above it was a sign: COMMUNICOGRAPH—DO NOT TOUCH.

Faith touched it.

And the metal plates on the surface became illuminated with a sea-green glow, spelling first the word, "Listen," then, "Find yourself that good thing," and finally, "Momma."

Lights on the Communicograph flickered out and its plates went cold. Faith found herself drawn to a waist-high urn of water on one of the tables. She recalled hearing of magic bottles filled with electrified water that would, if a child asked it questions, respond with pictures for answers. The almost forgotten word whispered by conjure men rolled off her tongue, "Th . . . Thaumaturgic Mirror." That was it. All one need do was ask.

"What," Faith said, "will become of me?"

Water in the urn began to churn. Looking over its rim, she saw images forming, floating along the wet surface. There was first her own reflection; then she saw herself seated sleeping among many empty seats with a sign hung from her neck. Next: the bespeckled face of a wide-eyed man whose thin lips moved faster than the wings of frightened thrushes. Again, the water churned, offering this time phantasmagoric scenes of a stone-and-mortar building surrounded by dense smoke, of a wretched little room overlooking an alley where rats and worms sifted through garbage for scraps of food. Faces were yielded by the water—the image of an old man coughing and clutching a mysterious black book, another man—younger, high-yellow, and wearing a wig. She saw the back of a lean man who wore work clothing, and knew she would recognize him if he turned around. The man did not turn. His figure was replaced by a scene that caught Faith's breath: an infant girl ringed by rising tongues of fire.

Cloudy, the water offered no more. It returned to its clear consistency as the Swamp Woman tramped back into the room, both her hands filled with steaming hog entrails. These she dumped in the center of the floor. The werewitch wound the intestines around to form a crude pentagram, deposited the kidney, colon, spleen, stomach, and the rest in the middle, and wiped her red hands along the front of her gown. On her haunches, she sneered, "All right—give!"

Obediently, one end of the intestines wiggled into the air and bent toward the northwest. It wavered like a long finger for a few moments, turned black, and drifted to the floor as ashes.

"Go to Chicago," the Swamp Woman said wearily, sweeping the ashes under a table with her foot.

Faith beamed. "It's *there*?"

"I dunno. Why the hell you town folks think I know *every*thing? I'm not the Sphinx, y'know. You saw what happened the same as I did." The Swamp Woman scooped up the remaining entrails and dropped them into the cat's dish, still grumbling. "Sometimes hog guts is unreliable. Coyote or dingo innards is best, but there's a shortage on."

Taking Faith by her arm, chilling her with a touch that was at once moist and mushy despite the Swamp Woman's strong grip, the werewitch sat her again on the pallet, and positioned herself nearby. Absent-mindedly, she chewed on her talons.

"Honey," she said, "I seen ya comin' years ago, and I knew you'd be wantin' to ask about the Good Thing. I've got to be truthful with ya. I was readin' a horse's brain for old Widow Smith in town, and I seen yer face just as plain as day in the occipital lobe. . . ."

"You know if I'll find it, then?" Faith squealed. "You do, don't you?"

The Swamp Woman played with her nose, which must have had the consistency of putty, for she shaped it between her fingers first with flaring nostrils, then as flat. Finally, she chose to leave it as a long beak between her eyes, and said, "I never was too good on futures, levitation, or resurrections, but I sho 'nuff know how the Good Thing was lost."

Despite her dread, Faith leaned forward, entranced by the werewitch's rasping voice.

"Long, long ago, way before your time, the world was way different than it is now. Now, you can look at it, and sometimes it'll appear like a stately, ancient oak, a century's product of patience and time, broad and beautiful from its gnarled trunk to its treetops; then, at other times, it'll look rotten, child, hoary and as hollow as a politician's head, fulla maggots as big as yer fist.

"But it wasn't always that way. Uhh, *huhn*. Once, men knew their place and were loath to leave it: paradise. Do ya hear me? *Paradise.* They didn't live on the airy summits of Olympus, nor did they dwell along the straits of Ultima Thule. They had no nectar, no ambrosia; what they had, child, was the Good Thing—the one thing so good that no greater good can be conceived. Imagine, child, *imagine* awakening in the mild blue mist of morningtime to stand on the edge of another day filled from daybreak to dusk with the Good Thing; not just *your* Good Thing, but everybody's Good Thing as it manifests itself in an infinity of forms. Folks fancied that the gods put those forms of the Good Thing in the world. Now you can say men put them there—through dreaming, through some ancient need for order and certainty, and gave the gods credit, fooling themselves. But that way of putting it isn't pretty, and all good stories (and true ones too) have to be pretty, even the ugly ones. So I'm telling you that man's ethical life was quite in order ages ago. That is, until the day the restless one, Kujichagulia, was born.

"Folks said Kujichagulia should never have been born, because right from the start, only ten minutes out of the womb, he started screaming: 'Who *am* I? What can I *know*? Where am I *going*? Where have I *been*?' and worse, much worse, '*What* am I?' People were embarrassed by his questions; they had no answers. And soon, after Kujichagulia's cloudy infant eyes began to focus, he started criticizing the modes of the Good Thing. 'Shallow,' he called the thrice-daily worship of the forest gods; 'Quaint,' he said of the people's fireside dances, their ceremony of the harvest and fear of the night. Deliberately he absented himself during the rites of passage for the young men of the village; thus, he remained a child forever, with many, many questions. Not only did his questions disturb the village elders, but within time certain gods began to wax hot with rage. Faraway, over the hilltops and trees, you could see thick thunderclouds swirling like frightened fish around Mount Kilimanjaro, home of the gods; torrents of rain, drought and locust came, but still Kujichagulia questioned."

The Swamp Woman stopped and squinted at Faith. "You follow all this?"

"I guess," Faith said.

"Is it entertaining?"

"Uhh, huhn."

The Swamp Woman grinned. "All right. So Kujichagulia was spoiling everything. The gods—Amon-Ra, Isis, Osiris, and Shango—were checking out Kujichagulia all along, wondering if he would eventually set out after the source of the Good Thing, abandoning its modular reflections to seize the Good Thing itself. Some wagered that he would, but others, enraged by his restlessness, vowed to punish him and his tribe severely if he found it. For it was not only for Kujichagulia, but for everyone. On the night Kujichagulia finally realized the Good Thing could only be in the mountains where the gods were, all nature rose against him. Beneath his feet, as he traveled, the ground turned to mud under a terrible rain and the earth split from tremors that uprooted trees. But Kujichagulia pressed on. For sport, Amon-Ra sent many-limbed behemoths to stop Kujichagulia before he reached the mountains; these Kujichagulia avoided, being swift. From the depths of the sea, Osiris called forth slithering things with shining eyes to devour Kujichagulia. But the village boy scaled a tree and they died of thirst with upturned bellies beneath him on the ground. All these obstacles he overcame. Except one: at the base of the mountains he rested with an old tribe long respected for its magic and conjuring. His trials had weakened Kujichagulia; his tongue swelled in his mouth and he walked on burning, blistered feet. A girl named Imani wove her love magic around him; she took him to her dwelling, fed him, clothed him, and sat with Kujichagulia until he again was well. She loved him, girlie, and Kujichagulia returned her affections, soon forgetting his hunt for the Good Thing. For many years he stayed with Imani and filled her with children. Shango and Amon-Ra began to think they had won their wager, that the village boy had abandoned the Good Thing. But, as the years passed, Kujichagulia again became restless. Thoughts would burn his brain with longing; deep within he felt incomplete. At night he would stare from his hut at the clouded peaks of the mountains. Imani begged him to stay, to love

FAITH AND THE GOOD THING

and work and die in the way all did without question, but in the night, seven harvests before his seventieth birthday, Kujichagulia rose from their bed, tightened his loincloth, and began ascending the dark mountain. He climbed hand over hand for many days, bleeding from his feet and palms, thirsting now, hungering to glimpse just once before death the fabled Good Thing.

"Near the top Kujichagulia knew he was mad, driven so from his suffering. Through the peals of thunder and the strong cry of wind he could hear the gods swearing at him. Far below he saw the village —tiny mud huts scattered among rocks and trees. Yet still he climbed, still he questioned, "What can I *know*?" And there, in the cemetery stillness of the cool, gray mountains, Kujichagulia beheld the Good Thing. Like a light it bathed him, like fire it warmed him. Killed him. For he was old and could not bear the strain. The gods Osiris and Isis raged, girlie. So furious were they that Kujichagulia had seen the forbidden, they put their heads together and decided to torment all men with the curse of restlessness and questioning. They hid the Good Thing, child, and the world darkened like a room deprived of its only light. But even the gods could not destroy it. It is a wish, a possibility that can only be deferred; and so, even today, it remains hidden. . . ."

"Now," the Swamp Woman said, "just how's a li'l fox like you gonna find what ain't been seen since the beginnin' of our bondage?"

"I don't know," Faith said. "But I will." Somewhere in her chest she felt the warmth, the terror of dreams on the brink of fulfillment. "And when I do, everybody's bondage will end."

But was it real? Her heart said yes; her mind—no.

"Are you sure?" Faith asked. "Is that the way it *really* happened?"

The Swamp Woman scowled. "What difference does it make? I *could* have told you that the Good Thing escaped from Pandora's box, or that it lies waitin' for man in the middle of Eden. But none of that tickles me as much as what I just told you." She wiggled a crooked finger at Faith. "Before you ask if anythin's true, *first* ask y'self if it's good, and if it's beautiful! Was the story good?"

Faith nodded. "Yes. . . ."

"And was it beautiful?"

"Yes. Yes, it was."

"All right!" The werewitch snorted. She moved away from Faith to her strange machine in the corner. The Gila monster, exhausted, had fallen asleep with its legs dangling over the treadmill. The Swamp Woman yelled, "Haaa!" and the startled lizard began racing again. Lights flickered on the machine, and from a phonograph by its side there came music.

"Hear it?" the Swamp Woman cried. "That's the earth's music as it revolves. Ya hear it? It's singin' 'mi, fa, mi' 'cause life on the earth without the Good Thing is marked by famine and misery."

Closing her eyes, the Swamp Woman started patting her foot to the earth's mournful music. And while she was distracted, Faith inched backward toward the door, slipped out, and hurried across the bridge.

 isten.

Faith Cross, gambling on the legendary Good Thing, buried her mother and quit the South. Walking toward the quiet train station in town, her eyes on the overhead golden glow of the moon, she heard, like a refrain pounding in repeated rhythms through her brain, the inscription on her mother's tombstone:

LAVIDIA CROSS

She Was Given 400,000,000

Breaths and Took

Them All

Time and again, Faith recalled the eerie job of restitution Oscar Lee Jackson had performed on Lavidia's bloodless body. He obeyed the Laws—removed any reflective surfaces from the parlor (spirits, therein, are easily ensnared), positioned Lavidia on her left side as she slumbered when alive, and—most important—relieved Faith of the sundry purification rites by doing these himself. They can, for the bereaved, be a vexation. In her cherrywood casket at the rear of the funeral parlor, Lavidia had looked like a waxy, deflated balloon. Something had abandoned her, though what that was remained unclear: breath, perhaps. Shriveled she had been in her nineteen-year-old wedding gown, the Lord's unwilling bride. Dehydrated. In her lifetime she'd been a derisive, vindictive woman who criticized everything without distinction, yet looked for nothing better, which is sin—it breaks the Twelfth Commandment: *Thou Shalt Not Criticize before Questing*. She made, in her lifetime, few friends, thus none came to pay respects. Faith sat alone in the empty, echoing funeral home as an unperturbed Reverend Brown delivered his prepared speech on her mother's virtues. It was an old eulogy. He used it for every death in Hatten County, changing proper names, adverbial modifiers, and pronouns, yet always injecting a deep sorrow and promised glory into his words. Faith, therefore, didn't mind.

Her thoughts had been elsewhere. For hours she struggled with the desire to kiss her mother good-by. She did, finally, holding her breath and lightly brushing her lips along Lavidia's dry forehead. It tasted like wax. Nestled under Reverend Brown's arm for support, she followed the grim gravediggers back to the farm. The diggers—silent, muscular, and methodical men in faded overalls—opened the earth beside Todd Cross's headstone, situated just yards from the farmhouse. They shoveled clumps of loose sod over the casket, buried Lavidia's most prized possessions with her so she'd not return for them, and left with the minister like mute zombies in Brown's employ. Faith remained. What had she felt standing there in the sunburnt grass between the two square markers? Round wreaths lay across the front of each. Only five feet separated the headstones, but Faith sensed that if she thrust her hand between them she would be brought again into the turbulence, caught in the conflict between Lavidia's world and that of her father. She studied that space, watching it fill with remembrances fond, familiar, and sometimes frightening as her shadow swelled with the sun's passage toward afternoon. Lavidia would have been pleased with the inscription on her marker. The words capsulized her reaction to the truth as told by the man of science: the man called Lynch.

Time often distorted Faith's memory, but now it was clear. She remembered: a few months after Todd's death in the time of Dirty Mouth when children eat the new, golden grain, Lavidia took sick with a virus. Faith called for Dr. Leon Lynch, who practiced medicine in a cluttered, one-room office in town next to the mortuary and had, it was said, attended all the great schools. It rained that night, with thunder so violent portions of the roof buckled and dripped water to the floors. They say it was so dark that raindrops knocked on people's doors, begging for candles just to see how to strike the ground. Faith went frequently to the front window, smeared away swirls of steam on its glass, and watched for his coming. Betimes, the weather built to a thunderstorm. The outlines of water pumps and oaks in the front yard grew obscure. Dr. Lynch first appeared in the front yard as a distant shadow floating through the downpour, a plodding shape oblivious to the elements and electricity in the air. As he crept up the front porch, his shoulders hunched forward, and the brim of his hat ran water before his face. A shapeless hat, a down-turned, glowing Bull Moose pipe jutting from the drawn-up collar of his coat—these were all Faith could see until she unlatched and opened the door. Lynch wavered in the doorway, towering over her, so tall he could, at the same time, have gotten his hair cut in Heaven and his boots shined in Hell. He was *tall*, children. Before he entered, his tiny, alert eyes studied the dim interior of the front room, his gaze flitting from the cold fireplace, the old pine cupboard and sawbuck table, to the ladder-backed chair and candle stand by the door. Faith retreated to the bedroom, and he followed her, tracking soft mud through the front rooms and kitchen. In Lavidia's bedroom Lynch again scanned the walls, ceiling, furniture, and shadows nervously before dragging a bow-backed chair against the wall to her bedside. He peeled off his wet coat and spoke hurriedly, the pipe stem bobbing between his clenched teeth:

"Cold?"

"Yes," Lavidia said, shivering under several quilts.

"Temperature?" He looked at Faith. Who was too frightened to answer, but managed, though she couldn't find her tongue, to take his wet coat.

"Open your mouth," Lynch told Lavidia; then, as an afterthought, "please." Lavidia obeyed, and from his black bag Lynch removed a wooden tongue-depressor, a thermometer, and items Faith was unfamiliar with (Did he need all that for healing? Conjure doctors only used dove's blood, asses' milk, and fresh cabbage dew, and with them could cure everything from sores in a horse's eye to impotency). She was shocked that he had not asked her to leave the room before he pulled Lavidia's nightgown up. It was odd, upsetting, to see your mother's breasts, half-filled flaccid things lying across her like enormous leeches. Lynch ignored Faith's reaction completely, and she knew immediately that he was one of those people who thought all children were, if not sophisticated but curious animals, at least aberrations of nature.

Faith, seated behind him on a three-legged footstool, studied him carefully. He was revolting, hatchet-faced, and had a figure so scrawny it seemed to have been stretched on a rack; his long arms and legs were gaunt and angular in a blue serge suit shiny with age. Lynch's right leg must have been artificial, fashioned from plastic or wood, because whenever his pipe flickered out with a hiss from tar and saliva backed into its stem, he would bang the ashes free of its bowl by striking it against his right knee. The sound was that of wood striking wood. A golden watch chain swung from beneath his open suitcoat, and both his shoes seemed enormous—perhaps size thirteen, with inch-thick soles. The back of Lynch's neck was ruffled with obscene little folds, his face and hands looked sedimented with a grimy material that had permanently worked its way under his skin, beneath his broken fingernails and into his large pores. His head was pear-shaped and balding, his mouth was full of gum-line cavities when he smiled, and about him was the smell of rubbing alcohol and sulfur.

Understand, men like Lynch are rare in these parts. In truth, rare *any*where. They have in their hearts a homesickness that burns like an ulcer. Burns them up. Some find, in the end, their own hands turned against them. Like Beaumont Gaines, once said to be the smartest man in Hatten County. That he had to die like any other man got the best of Beaumont. "All men are mortal," he told himself, "Beaumont Gaines is a man; therefore—" But he refused to believe the major premise—decided, he did, to check it out. The hunters came across him while chasing a hart into the hollow. Armed with slide rules and medical instruments, he was tearing open graves in the hollow, which was where they found him; also, where they burned him.

Even though Lynch handled Lavidia roughly, she trusted him more than she did the root workers Todd brought to the farmhouse whenever she was sick. She believed in him and asked how she was, how she *really* was. What followed was a tale as strange as anything to come from the mouth of the Swamp Woman.

The doctor slowly replaced all his instruments after inspecting each by the light of the single oil lamp burning on Lavidia's night-stand. For a long time he said nothing. He filled the bowl of his pipe with a green, sweet-smelling tobacco, smoothed its surface even with his forefinger, and drew carefully, thoughtfully, with painfully controlled breaths, on the stem. Soon, clouds of smoke rose around his head.

"If I tell you," he said, "you'll have to promise not to interrupt me until I've finished." His voice had grown deeper, more strained and troubled. In tone it was a lecturer's voice, or that of a man talking to himself at some lonely hour. "I despise interruptions." His lips parted in a tigerish grin. Biting on his pipe stem forced his lips apart, baring brownish teeth. Uncertain how to respond, Lavidia smiled. The effort faded fast. . . .

"It's a terribly long story," Lynch whispered, "billions of years old. You must be patient."

She bobbed her head as the doctor glared at her. Only the right side of his face was lit by the lamp. His single visible eye did not blink, but its surface glistened with moisture.

He said, "Billions of years ago an explosion of tremendous magnitude occurred in space, and our universe was aflame with radiant energy until darkness fell." Lynch jerked his hands above his head to describe the event, and left them in the air, motionless. He described matter forming, gaseous clouds aflame throughout the cosmos, the impossibility and undesirability of infinite regress, and the Fallacy of the First Cause. "Around these rotating clouds matter condensed to form our earth, which was cold then, so cold that it froze water vapor, nitrogen, carbon oxides, ammonia and, of course, methane. On our earth, snow fell, and at a speed that could generate enough heat to melt this cosmic snow itself. A crust formed on the earth, and above it—oceans—"

Faith shouted at Lynch's back, "That's *wrong!* Daddy said the oceans were tears from the eyes of angels!"

One stare, one sophisticated snarl from Lynch were sufficient to silence her. Testy, he said: "*Entia nun sunt multiplicanda praeter necessitatum,*" and scowled like a whale.

"Faith," Lavidia said timidly, "please . . ."

Lynch fumbled through his vest with one hand and, with a deadly drumming, struck his leg with his pipe bowl. His knotty jaw muscles flexed in the darkness, his wide eyes set on Lavidia. He found dry matches in his coat pocket and, without looking at his hands, carefully relit the bowl.

"It was a long time, aeons ago," he said, turning to glower at Faith, "that the fissures split along the surface of the earth's crust, and liquid granite was vomited to the surface. The continents were formed in this way." Lynch leaned back in his chair, serene again, and fingered the stubble on his chin. Smoke streamed down in twin jets through his nostrils. He cracked his knuckles, leaned forward, and tapped Lavidia's arm. "The earth was barren. For uncountable centuries the only activity was that of the volcanoes hurtling up their contents until the earth froze and thawed, for several such cycles—until something living struggled into being. What was it, Mrs. Cross? Was it *man*? Will you submit that it, ha ha, was *Adam*?" Lynch's mouth smiled; *really* smiled. "It was *slime*! At the ground floor of life are primitive blue-green algae. Like all life, that life is composed of cells that come together, working in a harmony that destroys the strength each cell possessed as an independent entity. Do you see?" Lynch cried. "Life brings death."

He was on his feet, clutching the pipe in his right hand and limping across the room. He stared at his feet as though he'd heard a rumble, or a beast rising beneath the floorboards, cocked his head to the right like a curious rooter-dog, and waved his free hand through the air.

"Life itself is the condition of death—it's self-evident. *L'être amène le neant*! That was the strange secret that created religion and poetry, Mrs. Cross—this incredible contradiction. Life, on the level of the cell, can continue indefinitely—the cell regenerates itself *ad infinitum*. But," and he pointed his long pipe stem at Lavidia, "the cells come together to build a simple organism, to make algae and fish and . . ." he paused, his eyes like saucers, ". . . and *us*. But life cannot support itself. From rest, from the nonliving, it springs forth; to it, it must return. And why? *Why*, in reason's name, are we born only to die? The way of being of life itself, as supported by nonliving matter, ultimately requires the end of being, the weakening of the syncopated cells . . . the death of the organism."

Lynch hurried back to his seat and bent forward, blinking as though about to cry, his lips close to Lavidia's ear. He told her that the oceans shrank, that in the swamps plants appeared. "Can you witness this?" he asked. "Can you *see* it? Because, herewith, from dead matter to mollusks, from nothing to a plurality of life forms, man emerged through *accident*, madam! Life, as we know it, as we *worship* it, must come to know itself as an aberration—an accident in the universe—as God's greatest jest. Yes! As a ridiculous longing for itself!"

Faith closed her eyes. It had *not* happened that way. There were no accidents, no mistakes in creation. She remembered Big Todd's story of how black folks got to be that way: black. A gathering of souls in limbo were, after centuries of waiting, finally called to the Godhead for judgment. They all scrambled like evening commuters to get there, pushing and shoving until God, angered as only He can be, boomed, "Get back!" And all had thought He said, "Get *black*!" And they did exactly that. (Later, in the stillness of a summer eve, he told her the truth: from different colored clay were men made—and Faith believed him then).

She saw Lynch exhale a long column of green smoke, exhausted as though he'd staged the historical drama of creation himself (and he had, children). Lynch rearranged Lavidia's cotton gown around her shoulders and placed his fingers between her breasts.

"You take in close to twenty thousand breaths a day, at about twenty cubic inches of air per breath," he said. "The air carries oxygen, which the body warms and filters. It's moved to the bronchiae, on to the lungs, and finally to millions of cells that are air sacs surrounded by vessels and capillaries." Lynch located a thick blue vein on Lavidia's right breast and ran his ragged finger along its length. "Blood absorbs the oxygen through these cells and expels carbon dioxide. Fresh blood moves to the heart which pumps eight hundred gallons of blood each hour. . . .

"A machine," he said with slight disgust. "Do you hear the click-clicking of your delicate instruments developed over those billions of years from unliving matter?"

Faith remembered the empty stare in her mother's eyes. Lavidia, her pink lower lip drooping and her nostrils flaring like a colt's in winter, had not spoken immediately.

She blinked, and seemed to come out of a trance. "Yes. . . ."

"That's how you work," the doctor said, cramming loose tobacco from a cellophane bag into his pipe. He wet both lips with his tongue and cocked his head to the left. "That's what you *are*, no more than that complicated plexus of cells through which energy travels like an electrical current. You take in energy from your food, from the rays of the sun; you channel it through your body where it can move muscles, or be siphoned off into brain work. But regardless of what you do, you *must* move it. If you don't, your muscles will contract, your loins will ache with tension. Tension and release. Mrs. Cross, nothing—absolutely nothing beyond that can be called real."

Unbuttoning his collar, swinging his head from left to right, and his bemused eyes still straining at Lavidia, Lynch said, "The pitiful struggle of Jesus with his flesh—what was that but tension and release? Michelangelo's *Pietà*, van Gogh's *Starry Night*, Bach's *Sinfonia to Cantata No. 29*, or Dante's *Divine Comedy*? Nothing but novel ways to unload tension." Lynch laughed and leaped to his feet. "*That's* your meaning of life—bigger and better means to detumescence. Life is a constant, frenzied motion; death is when the circuit breaks. . . ."

Lynch grabbed his coat from Faith's lap, retrieved his bag from the bedside, and moved toward the door. "That explains everything."

Not quite.

Lavidia had been thoroughly upset by his explanation. "How do you live?" she asked, wringing her hands. "*Why* do you live?"

Lynch did not hesitate: "To function. To keep breathing when you know the breaths are numbered, and that the circuit will break to return you to stone." The doctor shoved his pipe stem back between his teeth and chewed on it. "You've caught me. The truth isn't beautiful, and it doesn't make me feel good. But I can't heal myself—the best I can do is keep living, unloading my day's energy, *élan vital*, essential juices, the best I can." He returned to her bedside and scooped Lavidia's dark hand into his own. "We live to die—only to die. But that's not *really* so terrible, is it?"

Lavidia's eyes turned from him to the shadow-swept eastern wall. An interval of silence passed.

"I'm going to keep you alive," Lynch whispered close to her ear. "Why? Because you know yourself you can't imagine any other way of being, can you? Of course not."

Faith had been witness to her mother's struggle with the doctor's story. Lavidia lay in bed, taciturn, frowning, and looking nauseous long after her virus ended, refusing food, pouting, and sleeping without rest. In the end, she transformed the story to destroy its content. What persisted in her mind was the reference to breathing: "I'm fifty-five today," she announced on her birthday to Faith, "and that means I've almost took four hundred million breaths; it's God's will. Everybody's got a certain number to draw 'fore they die. That's His way...."

And so it went until she drew her four hundred millionth. Standing there in the dry weeds before Lavidia's headstone, Faith had been unable to cry. Why cry? It—the struggle to complete life's monotonous movement—had ended for her mother. For her, as for Lynch, all that could matter were the absolutely perfect moments when one's breathing was the heaviest—great quantities of oxygen flooded the brain, gorged the cells. In battle, in ecstasy, in love, each *click, click, click* of the body's machinery came through with clarity. Discharge was what was good. Release. Life's meaning, if it had any meaning at all, was defined by death. Death alone.

But was that beautiful?

Parallel to but a world away from her mother's headstone was that of Big Todd. It read:

TODD CROSS

Carpe diem, quam minimum
credula postero

Faith, as a child, had often asked her mother the meaning of the words engraved beneath her father's name, but Lavidia avoided the question entirely: "Your father was a fool."

She had touched the headstone. That rubbing of the moist moss and the stone's cool surface against her fingertips were what the inscription meant. She was certain.

But also this:

The intimations ever on the tip of her tongue that never broke free into words; the sudden rush of rippling warmth through her skin whenever she stood on the highest hillslopes of Hatten County and peered across its smooth verdant fields and corrugated farmlands, whenever she stepped barefoot in darkness from her bed and peeped through the farmhouse window frosted white by winter to see timorous harts and ewes searching among moonflower vines in the yard for food. That was what it meant: all of it—the shivering animals and drifts of snow beneath a blue band of sky; all creation would have been sad if she missed its appearance, for the naked, twisting trees and bushes cared for her, responded to her admiration and—it was true—languished when she herself was sad. So sweet were the songs of the field birds in the time of Sweet Grain that she, if she could have located a dragon, would have tasted its blood and flesh, as the conjure doctors advise, to fathom their language. While Hatten County harbored no dragons that anyone knew of, it did have the old werewitch (though some saw her as a necessary evil like auto accidents and yearly locust), and stranger things still. Those words on the headstone were themselves strange; but strangeness was essential to what Big Todd preached.

Remembering:

Screeds of speech, shrapnel-like faces spinning again before her eyes like hail in the heart of a storm. She remembered Big Todd filling their kitchen table with fruits and sweetmeats and, for the dinner hour, encouraging discussions. Lavidia, given to silence as she shoveled sliced beets and potatoes into her mouth, rarely found the mealtime appropriate for talking. But Todd, pausing with his cheeks burgeoning like old luggage crammed with underwear, would grin and nod at Faith, his eyes half-lidded as he retold tales he'd heard in town from Crazy Lewis, the cobbler, or Paddlefoot Dean, who sat a daily vigil on the doorsteps of the town's only drugstore. Once, between his second and third helpings of beef gumbo, he decided to explain why men and women were different. Faith had raised the question after seeing, earlier that day, the unashamed mating of two Hampshire hogs in the mud. It thoroughly confused her, being somehow strange, rare, yet revealing as something kept secret from her for years. And Alpha told her that in town there lived a lonely widower, Needem Dewey, who longed for the affections of the flighty blacksmith's daughter, the most beautiful girl in town. He sought audience with the Swamp Woman, and received from her the formula for a love potion. Following her directions, Needem lifted dirt from his loved one's footprints, mixed it with his own clipped toenails and essence of pomegranate. And ate it. Immediately he knew of the Swamp Woman's trickery. It was a love potion, all right. But for the use of *women*. And for years thereafter young boys from the mill crowded like bogflies around poor Needem's door. Yes, love was strange. And Big Todd kept it mysterious.

Time was, he said, when all animals had no sex. Unsex, he called it, because they all had the same male and female equipment, and could mate perfectly well with themselves like tapeworms do today. That situation didn't last long. A god, some god, *any* god (or, maybe, Big Todd himself, who felt godlike when spinning metaphysical yarns) decided, as gods are wont to do, that things would be more interesting (and wasn't *that* what life was all about?) if he split all those animals in twain. Which he did. But not only that: he flung them around the world so none of the animals could find their proper halves, not without a lot of searching. It stood to reason that living half-lives like that wasn't pleasant at all. Everything on the earth—birds, beasts, grubworms, and especially men—were and still are incredibly lonesome, and suffer a lot until their lost halves are found. So, Todd concluded, leaning back in his seat and rubbing his stomach like a flesh-fed Druid, such was sex. That ever-so-often feeling that rolled across your brain like fog; it was nothing more than the call to hunt for your other half. Bad marriages, or ruined love affairs, were nothing but two wrong halves coming together. "Square pegs in round holes," he said. And he laughed.

Lavidia howled.

She lobbed an ear of corn across the table—it hit him on his forehead.

"Why you tellin' lies to this child?"

Todd was cool. With his napkin he wiped his face. "Ain't no harm—"

"No *harm*!" Lavidia wailed. "You're going to pump this child fulla lies, and the world's goin' to eat her alive! Faith," she said, "you'll learn about sex soon enough. Love is perfect till somebody pulls back the bedcovers on you—"

"Stop that!" Now Todd was furious. Faith had never seen him so angry, his monkey up, his mouth greasy with gumbo and twisted across his clenched teeth. His fork bent slowly in his fist. She sat between them, her head revolving from left to right as first her father, then Lavidia stood up shouting, like soon-to-battle stags. She was sorry she'd asked about sex, but knew they argued this way often. When she couldn't sleep, she'd tiptoe to their bedroom at the rear of the farmhouse, only to find her father all naked and hairless like a salamander, pleading with Lavidia, who pretended, and rather poorly, to be asleep or sick. Todd would finish the argument by storming from the house. His usual tactic. He would snatch his jacket from the rack at the front door, wearing it inside out so spirits would leave his person be, and disappear for long walks alone. Faith would steal out the back door, searching for him and, if she was lucky, she would see his outline against the road. For a long time he would say nothing while they walked. This was disturbing, for she was used to him telling her tales as she walked with him, and could egg him on with, "Tell me another mile." But after arguments with Lavidia he would be withdrawn and moody, unable to conjure even though she chattered nervously and sang his favorite work songs to him, songs he had heard on chain gangs, in cotton fields. Finally, he would smile, laugh as she imagined shamans did, and tell her something outrageous. Or he'd talk about haints, though this was dangerous and would attract them just as sure as liquor on your clothes brings them at your heels.

(Careful, this is sorcery. If you please, haints—a whole host of them—will be revealed to you, just as sure as hearing a moaning dove will give you a backache, if you look over your left shoulder, or through a needle's eye, through a mule's right ear, or into a mirror with another person, though the most certain technique is to break a rain-crow's egg in a saucer of pond water and wash your face with it twice. If all else fails, wipe off a rusty nail from a minister's coffin, insert it between your canine teeth, and spirits, like street beggars, will crowd around you. But if you wish to be rid of them forever, say, "What in the name of the Lord do you want with me?" thrice, and the spirit will (a) flee, or (b) carry you to some secluded spot where it'll bid you dig until you come to a pot of money. Read, if the haint returns, a Bible verse or a prayer backward, but *not* the Lord's Prayer, for this, assuredly, will conjure up the Devil and his lieutenants (it is the way of warlocks). Should all these methods fail and spirits still stalk like Jehovah's Witnesses at your front door, say, "Skit, scat, turn into a bat," and the apparition (also Jehovah's Witnesses) will go its tormented way.)

Sometimes, when sad, Todd spoke of himself.

Todd Cross never knew his birthdate, never really cared. In the attic of his memory he saw a huge woman in rags, so fat she'd need a shoehorn to get into a bathtub, so dark she needed a license to drink white milk. She was enormous—all over, even her arms, which were as big around as the flanks of a racehorse. In these she carried any number of babies often said to be his brothers and sisters. He remembered a house that rattled in the wind like old bones from an unearthed casket, but nothing more. Because he ran away from the woman. Never a day of education, he said proudly, never learned to read (but you knew he was lying because he listened carefully to the words of book-readers, and filed them away deep in his mind). He remembered vomiting in the hot sun while picking Alabama cotton, and the day he decided to leave that job and wander away his youth from one southern town to another, living off what he earned gambling or stealing. He remembered falling in with a traveling circus; that was in his twenties. He had really wanted to get to Mexico; to adventure just a bit more. But the circus job, watering animals and throwing up tents, appeared one spring in Tennessee. Mexico was forgotten each evening when he stood guard at the main tent, watching the fire-eater, monkeys riding bareback on ponies, acrobats and magicians in the center ring, and the trapeze artist swinging through the air as freely as a fish in the sea. He would never forget this: dry hay and horse manure tickling his nose, whitening his nostrils like those of a weary mule—the heavy musk of the animals, and the half sober but always captivating ringmaster who called these bizarre acts into being with a wave of his hand: freaks, dog-faced boys, and women in star-spangled leotards, who drank like fish late at night but could walk, with bright parasols in their hands, on wires thin enough to cut you in two. They were loud, these circus people, and coarse, but each was horribly uncommon. And though he could do none of their stunts himself, he, too, felt special—as though he *could* cleave waves and fell giants if he tried hard enough. The first woman he made love to was the Alligator Girl, who had extraordinary legs but had been disfigured by some skin disease in her childhood. She was the Fat Man's woman and Todd, to avoid his anger, hit the road again, wandering until he arrived bone-weary in Georgia. He met Lavidia, her mother, and her two sisters in a backwoods Baptist church. Why he was in that church he only vaguely recalled—it had something to do with shooting someone six times in a saloon the night before. Money had been involved. Also, the extra aces and kings he carried in his pants cuff. He remembered sitting at the back of the church with a painful, bandaged cut on his right side just beneath his ribs, hearing the minister shout, "Thank God we ain't what we were, are what we are, and can be what we *will*!" He heard Lavidia and her sisters singing like angels in the choir up front, all of them dressed in stiff white dresses, and their hair newly pressed and slicked down with butter. He saw clearly that if he didn't settle down, and quick, he'd be dead within a few years, belly-up on some barroom floor. Lavidia, more than any other woman he'd seen, looked exactly like his opposite: that was important. The woman you wed had to be everything you weren't—sober when you were drunk, calculating to check your impulsiveness, sane and with her feet on the ground, regenerating your strength and her own when something got in your blood like a disease and told you to move. Lavidia was all this, so much so that she ran from him when he approached her after service. Todd was persistent. He bought the best suit he could find, trimmed his sideburns, oiled his skin, and had a barber clip the long hairs hanging from his nose before he called on her. He told her he was a liniment salesman from Philadelphia, and would take her North in his limousine (presently in another town for repairs) to butlers and ballets. To wealth. After the wedding ceremony at her mother's home, Todd took her to a two-dollar-a-night hotel in town, and from there to the sharecropper's farm where they had lived ever since. Lavidia never, never forgave Todd for that. The truth of his situation killed her mother with a stroke; her two sisters never came to visit. Yet she couldn't leave him since Faith followed too soon on the heels of their wedding. So she suffered. Todd told Faith that he suffered, too, because he never wanted to go North in the first place, nor did he want to be a salesman, or own butlers, or do anything other than amble around his farmyard each afternoon and feel loose dirt and green grass between his bare brown toes. They would love each other, he thought; they would eat well, and live off the land, their stomachs full. Their hearts full too.

Faith, touching his headstone, felt too empty to cry. Todd was dead; that was that. Dead, slain by the hands of three men, each of whom probably unloaded a large quantity of his tension, his vital juices, in Todd's execution. Dead. Returned to stone or slime. And nothing could change that.

Night rose out of the ground and darkened the headstones. Faith returned to the farmhouse, where she began packing her few possessions. On her bed she heaped several dresses Lavidia had knitted for her during the winters when life was slower on the farm. She placed these in her laundry bag, drew the string, and carried it into the front room. On a large, square strip of cardboard she printed TO CHICAGO in red lipstick, and attached strings to its sides so she could wear it around her neck in case she got lost. Pausing, she noticed Lavidia's shoes—two big boats of leather as brown as shave grass in September—empty in a corner of the front room. They were creased where Lavidia's heels once had hung over their backs. But now they were eerie, empty as though Lavidia had been snatched from them at that very spot and transported by giggling demons out of the world. Too, the stillness of the front rooms was frightening. All familiarity had fled from the furniture, and every few moments she had to catch herself from dashing into the kitchen, where she heard a scraping noise. Mice, perhaps the wind: nothing more. She moved through the house from room to room, dousing out the wick-lighted oil lamps and closing doors, perhaps for forever. She shut the windows and, on impulse, snatched all the photographs scattered about the house and locked them in a closet. After counting her money— seventy-five dollars—and disposing of Lavidia's rings and a few hairbrushes, which could be used in conjuration and curses against her mother, she left, looking back down the misty, rain-soaked road occasionally, but glad to be again in the night air.

The trees along the road were monstrous—huge, ungainly, sprouting twisting limbs gnarled in one space, skimpy in another, swollen in a third; they seemed made of clay, half-formed and moist, grooved along their length with deep lines that hinted at the great hand of God, old and haggard, holding His sculptor's knife uncertainly, hesitating, then madly clawing at the clay of the trees in wrath or frustration or fearful divine woe. Terrible trees, these, washed by the light of an old moon, the star-sprinkled sky closest to its globe stained with a rich orange glow that emitted a stairway of rings and caught Faith's eye through the frail, claylike fingers of the tree branches above. Such a moon was said to be magical, an omen, or a mysterious occurrence to which one could cast a wish and have it realized. She believed it, and felt the moon was an old friend. Often, she'd stepped outside the farmhouse to watch the moon after Lavidia had gargled, dropped her teeth into a glass of water, and gone to bed. Its cycles triggered the odd changes in her own body: pain, tranquillity, pain again. Which were strange. Lavidia called them an ancient curse, and warned Faith to stay away from men, abstain from grinding corn, milking cows, and sewing with a needle on the first day of bleeding. If the moon could be so cruel, might it not be equally kind and grant her wish?

She made a wish: "Let me find it—the Good Thing."

And she repeated it several times on the train while watching the moon disappear behind the clouds. She relaxed, inviting the incubus, sleep filling up her stomach and mind, and drifted into a dream.

The Swamp Woman. She, Faith Cross, was the giggling old were-witch of the bogs, stirring with a divining rod a potion in her cauldron, a hellbroth that smelled like sewage and nine-day-dead alewives. Behind her the music of the spheres rang from the lizard-powered machine, each note as unsettling as a centaur's cry. The bug-eyed squirrels and dirty chickens made gibbering noises like elves from their cages; the elves, chained to her workbenches, screamed like changelings, and the changelings, lying with bloated bellies on her benches, howled like whales (a strange sound, indeed). Into the cauldron she peered, and her lips exploded outward: "*Hee hee!*" It was done. Her brew looked like cough syrup and now had the scent and consistency of cod-liver oil. She tipped her cauldron over; its contents oozed to the sloping floor and spread like something sentient out the crooked shanty door, filling the swamp, choking spiny catfish and snails. It mixed into the bogs, which were as mysterious as the Swamp Woman herself—heavily misted with the mephitic odor of decay, swarming with insects and fish forgotten by the sleep of death, and thus allowed to spawn in the stagnant waters eternally. Often, at sundown, the water was as red as the blood of a calf—rich, opaque; then, at dawn, almost transparent enough for the bones of ancient beasts to be seen on its bottom. It held birth, and death, and now the Swamp Woman's brew. Around the shanty, the swamp bubbled, overflowed the borders of the bog, and slid over the forests and hills of Hatten County. The brew ran endlessly from her cauldron, covering her knees as she waved her broken wand in wide arcs through the air and sang:

> "If you find what's Good,
>   You'd better knock on wood;
> You'd better hold it fast,
>   'Cause it might not last—
> You'd better squeeze it tight
>   And try to eat it all,
> 'Cause it'll soon take flight
>   Like a—pterodactyl! *Hee hee!*"

It covered the countryside, deluged the cities: it covered the world. Billions were covered with the brew. And when they managed to smear it all off, they looked like her: the Swamp Woman. Their limbs had become gnarled oak sprouting yellow boils, their flesh was as black as the ink of a squid. And all around the world people looked at each other, winked their clear yellow eyes evilly, and squealed in harmony:

"*Hee hee!*"

The dream dissolved, and Faith Cross slept the sleep of the dead.

eretofore sweet Faith slumbered; then, past midnight, after two days' tiring journey from Georgia to Chicago and a restless sleep in her train seat, Faith awoke to the wrenching of gears and a shrill whistle. Her car lurched backward, then was still, surrounded by the hissing of steam from engine valves. She rubbed her palms against her eyes, licked at a sour taste in her mouth, and smeared away moisture clouding her window. Outside, passengers with suitcases hurried through a semicircular terminal to a crowded exit. Brown men in dull black suits pushed carts piled higher than their heads with heavy luggage. The air rolled with steam. Faith pulled her bag from a gun-metal-gray rack overhead and hurried through the narrow aisle to the door. She stepped from the car, shivering in the midst of a fast-moving crowd that passed her on both sides, jostled her and, before she was in the clear, had brushed off her sign. She followed the other passengers down the broad strip to a bright waiting room. Men and women met, embraced, and left arm in arm. Others raced off alone, if no one met them, toward stairs at the rear of the room. Where was she to begin? Who in this room looked friendly enough to answer her questions? Their steps seemed to have a definite direction, their heels rang against the tiled floor with efficiency, with system and method. Faith stepped timidly in the shadow of a couple in matching trench coats and tams, following them at a safe distance up a slow escalator, down several narrow corridors plastered with political posters peeling with age, and into a hallway with parquet floors ending on the street level.

She felt panic when she reached the outside. The couple had already climbed into their car at the curb and driven off. Where, she had intended to ask, can I find a room? A meal? But they were gone. The street was silent save for the thudding of car tires on cobblestones and, from around the corner, the blast of horns. Standing still, her bag swinging at her side, she felt she'd entered a place desolate, despised by man, a canyon of jagged walls. The air was cold and heavy in her lungs. Her breath hovered before her face as blue wisps of steam. The sidewalk, too, was cold beneath her feet, its icy surface tearing at her soles as she hurried down the street to keep warm. A sign on the corner said Sixty-fourth. Which told her nothing. The storefronts were all covered with lengths of metal latticework. At the far end of the block she saw a man wearing sunglasses and a green Army jacket leave a telephone booth at the bus stop. Faith approached him.

"*Que es esto?*" the man said, almost shouting. He backed away from her as if she held a summons. Cried, "*Vayaaa!*"

"I'm just trying to find a room," she said, stepping closer. "I just now got off the train—"

He raised his glasses to his brow, squinted his black eyes at her, said, "*No comprendo,*" tersely, and backed away. He saw his bus turn the corner, and bolted into the street to meet it. From the rear window he frowned at her.

In the shiny glass of a Japanese curio shop she saw her reflection. You would have thought a witch had ridden her all night. (They do that, witches. The hags turn you over on your stomach when you're sleeping, shove a bit into your mouth, and ride you on all fours for hours. All night long. And in the morning you feel real blue and ache from head to toe.) Her dress, though skimpy and a riot of wrinkles, was still somewhat, though only barely, intact. Her hair was drawn up and matted in dark clumps; her skin had turned ashy and gray from the cold. Her mouth and nose—dry. Her stomach grumbled. It pinched with a hunger bordering on nausea. Looking away, she saw the city lights grow brighter, more numerous on the far side of the bridge that began just across the street. Faith started across, but stopped midway when a particularly vicious cramp knotted in her right side. She was used to gales, to soothing sirocco summers. The cold began to slow her movements, to seep beneath her skin. To burn. Faith's feet went numb, like weights cemented to her ankles. Her fingers stiffened. A small fire engine shot from around the corner, its bells ringing as it rumbled over the bridge and down a boulevard lined with bare leafless elms, and farther on, sirens blaring, to red flames twisting into the sky from a burning water tower. It was here, on this chilly South Side bridge, that Faith grew afraid, quailed and pined for home. She was alone, and in a strange city. Hadn't the Swamp Woman said she was a Number One and, therefore, needed direction to avoid disaster? Neither Todd nor Lavidia had prepared her to be alone. She wasn't equal to the occasion. But she couldn't say Todd didn't prepare her for fear:

During the riotous days of his wanderlust, Todd Cross had been a gambler and could take your money in a game of five-card stud faster than any man alive. This he did, and the others involved in that Saturday night game in the back room of the Bucket-o-Blood saloon reached for their pistols. Todd snatched the satchel of money off the wine-stained table, threw himself through the window, fell two flights, and landed on the sheriff's horse. Unfortunately, the sheriff was on it; that is, until Todd came hurtling down. The sheriff called a posse, the posse called the vigilantes, and *they* called the National Guard. Todd rode like the wind. But his horse petered out near the mountains, whinnied, "To hell with this," and Todd had to make it on foot, armed with but a single-shot derringer, his satchel, and a whole lot of heart. The hounds were at his heels the whole night long, vigilante bullets swarmed around his head like bees gone crazy. Todd kept stepping. He hid in a mountain cave. But they found him, children. His back pressed to the moist wall of the cave, he could hear the dogs outside, fighting one another to see who'd be first to chew the marrow from his bones. "Give up!" the vigilantes hooted. In a corner, just inches from his feet, Todd saw two gleaming eyes; he heard a grizzly growling. Above him was the bodacious beating of bat wings. Vampires. Todd fell to his knees, ankle-deep in a small stream that rippled through the cave. He prayed—he had to shout it, children, because those dogs and vigilantes and bats were loud! Todd fell on his side; he screamed when the bloodhounds came barreling in. Water touched his lips. He thrust out his tongue:

"Ahhh . . ."

But Faith felt in no way reassured. This wasn't home, this wasn't the South. Lost, directionless, any step she took would probably be wrong. Fatal. Faith leaned back against the bridge, trembling. . . . She felt something soft along her shoulders. Before she could turn a gloved hand with its cloth fingers worn away clamped over her mouth. Something snatched at her right arm, twisted it behind her back.

"Just be quiet," an excited voice said into her ear. "I don't want to hurt you. Just *don't* scream."

She should have bitten the salty-tasting fingers pressed against her teeth; she should have kicked back her heels toward his groin and screamed with all her strength. But the touch of his hand was electrifying—hard and rough. She was helpless, her eyes saw white, her knees dissolved.

"Just be silent," the voice stammered. "I'm a poor man—a desperate man, or I wouldn't be doing anything like this." There was silence and horribly heavy breathing. The air carried the rush of traffic faraway. Then a rasping intake of air. "I was a professor at Princeton. Once—I was a scholar, you see? I've published, lectured, created courses unheard of before my coming. But my ideas cost me my job. No, you wouldn't understand, of course, but what I wanted to teach was the truth, not, not—" His voice trailed off in a whisper, then came back booming in her ear. "Pray that the poets were right —that someday, *some*day the rich will find themselves governed in a hell ruled by philosopher-kings. But until then, child . . . give me your bag!"

Herewith, the hands released her. Faith pivoted, nearly falling, and glimpsed a squat, red-eyed, wolfish man in a mauve-colored coat. He wrenched the bag from her hand, shoved her aside, and sprinted across the bridge, shouting, "Forgive me! The victim and victor are One!"

As he ran, rifling Faith's laundry bag, the thief collided at the end of the bridge with a silhouetted figure. He recoiled and shouted, "Mercy!" She saw him fling the bag aside and, through a series of jerky feints, elude the figure. Who picked up her bag. He hurried up the bridge, its lights bringing into clarity his dark waistcoat, then a hat pulled over his eyes. He was sweating profusely. From his face there drifted steam.

"Your bag's empty," he said breathlessly. "There wasn't money in it, was there?"

Faith collapsed against the bridge. She held her head. "Just a few dollars—call someone—" She looked up, startled by his silence. He was shaking his head. What struck her immediately was his glasses— silver wire-rims hooked over winglike ears and holding lenses so thick his eyes seemed to float behind them like dark blowfish. Between those lenses was a thin bridge dropping to a bulbous nose and wide nostrils. And below that—tight lips surrounded by a scraggly goatee. All over he had the hue of coffee colored with skim milk: a hesitant brown. His feet were tiny and delicate, poorly supporting his wide girth and watery, womanly hips. This was he who saved her. Also he who said, "I hate to sound like a pessimist, but there's no point in calling the police. Your money's gone. I can take you home if you like." Again, he licked his thin lips. Faith found him frightening, not because he was intimidating or because he seemed aggressive, but because he appeared ready to fly apart— nervous, put together with phlegm, gristle, and paste. She looked away, shuddering, her teeth rattling as the wind stole like a lecher up her legs.

"Where can I take you?" he asked. He glanced over his shoulder (which he did often), then produced from his coat pocket a hand-kerchief so neatly folded it seemed the product of obsession. "Where are you staying?" He cocked his head. "What's your name?" Finally, he raised his voice. "Can you speak?"

"My name is Faith Cross and I don't have a place to stay." The region around her mouth felt brittle, her chattering teeth clipped at the edge of her tongue. "I don't have a place to go—"

He started to speak, but held his breath, picking his teeth with his tongue. At the bridge's end two officers appeared with clubs swing-ing like pendulums at their sides. He grabbed Faith's arm and tugged at her slightly. "There's a nice spot just around the corner," he said. His voice was as thin as his lips. "You look like you could use a drink."

Tugging Faith along the bridge, he directed her into the close foyer of an all-night tavern, then through a glass door to a semidark room. He found a booth at the rear, and sat poker-faced toward the door. In the dim light cast by the glowing blue screen of a television set above the bar, Faith could see soft kernels of sleep in the corners of his bloodshot eyes, could smell, when he leaned close to her across the table, his milk-sour breath.

"What do you drink?" he asked.

"Drink?" She hesitated, feeling crowded in the closeness of the booth, congested both in her throat and in her thoughts with the unfamiliar sounds and sensations in the room: those in the room around her were either looking for or trying to forget something, though she knew not what; but a portion of it was lost in the blue strata of cigarette smoke screening her vision of the peaked and anxious faces of drinkers at the bar who, as they tipped their glasses, regained it, only for others to have it lost again when a woman's shrill cackling rose above their threshold of insularity. It was happiness they sought, or so Faith imagined; and it was sorrow they sought to escape. In and out, from those seated along the wood-paneled wall to those at the bar, something both light and dark moved, brightening a face here, causing a mouth to droop there, but continually moved silently from one nightlifer to another. Despite her original dread, Faith no longer felt afraid. Her host seemed to move through the smoke and pulse beat of this crowd easily. He had returned her bag, he seemed genuinely interested in her. Perhaps he could be, if given the chance, not a friend in utility (for these are flighty), or a friend in common traits and interests (far too superficial), but a friend, truly, in faith.

"You look like a Bloody Mary to me," he said, smiling.

Faith's left hand touched her face. "I do?"

He grinned, left her, and slipped through the noisy crowd to the bar. During the interval of his absence she again felt unprotected. It reminded her of the way she felt when she stood on the platform at the train station in town watching Alpha Omega Holmes leave home. It had been a terrible day. By chance she had encountered Alpha's mother at the feed store in town and learned that Alpha, in just an hour, would be leaving Hatten County to look for work up North. She had not seen him for months, he working and all. After delivering the box of dry goods to Lavidia, she raced back to town. And missed him. She could see his sad profile in the train window—sad because of the necessity of his flight. She shouted his name, but the train whistle smothered her cry. The train pulled off, bathing her in white steam as she ran behind it, tossing pebbles at his window. She had been there; it was important that he know that, that he should carry her memory with him always. Probably, he never knew. She remembered her feeling of isolation as being unbearable. He, like all those in the bar, had been only inches from her in physical distance, but beyond touch. It lay heavy on Faith's chest. She started talking the instant her host returned to slide a frosty glass toward her.

"You haven't told me your name—"

He pursed his lips, and pulled at the tip of his nose. "Arnold T. Tippis."

"Well, Mr. Tippis," she said, "I can't thank you enough for all you've—"

"Forget it." He yanked his nose again, then adjusted his glasses. "You don't owe me anything yet." For a second he looked embarrassed, perhaps by his eyes, which wandered in sweeping motions across her face, stopping momentarily to study the asymmetry of her eyes, then her mouth, and moved on to her shoulders and suggestion of breasts. Men judging livestock, or women inspecting fresh eggs at the fair have such eyes. "You're nice-looking," he said flatly, ". . . cute."

It was a purely objective statement; nothing, she convinced herself, lurked behind such a simple statement of fact. This she told herself at least twice, believing it until Tippis, after clearing his throat, reached across the table and folded his hand over her own.

"I'm looking for something!" Faith blurted.

With his free hand Tippis alternately chain-smoked, blowing smoke from the side of his mouth, rather than in her face, and nibbled at rye saltines from a bowl. "That's bad," he muttered.

Her feelings were drained into the immediacy of the warmth between his hand and her own. She looked away from him again, but left her hand still, aware that her palm was growing moist and her fingers trembling. Not in erotic response; it was more like fear. This was not, in *any* circumstance, a safe man to be with, not because of what he might do to her but because of some strange thing he'd done to himself. Suddenly, her hand went dry, and she was all thought, pure intellect, and concentrating on the way his lips curled back like proud flesh around a half-healed wound.

"I'm looking for the *really* Good Thing." She sipped at her drink, discovered she had never tasted tomato juice prepared in quite this way, and accepted, when the barmaid noticed her empty glass, a second drink. To be truthful, it made her a bit braver.

"Stop looking," Tippis said. He arched his eyebrows sleepily. "Everybody's looking for what's Good and True and Beautiful. It's damned foolish, really. Be content. Self-analysis will put you at peace with your problems—really."

After the third drink Faith's stomach felt even emptier than before, like a warm pit, or the inside of an old, old cave unvisited by beast or fowl for centuries. Her head felt the same way. As a muffled muttering, his words came to her:

"Me," he said, "I can live with my problems. They make me unique, so they're okay. You don't mind listening to this, do you? I mean, you girls have to hear a lot of this sort of thing, right?"

Dizzy, Faith said, "Right," her brain besotted. She bugged her eyes at him. It was getting hard to see. She looked away briefly and was shocked by her condition, knowing that the swelling and detachment of her thoughts, like subdividing amoeba, had changed the room in a peculiar way: the bar looked glutted with bodies—fat ones squeezed into loud, pastel shirts, lean and tall ones rising from the floor like reeds; and their outlines formed an odd unity similar to geometric shapes, flowing together, implicating each other in a terribly necessary way, jelling into a colorless whole. This was not rhythm, only chaos. She felt outside them, or locked within herself with all of them beyond her. Overhead, a star-shaped chandelier cast the entire room in inundating bolts of ocean-blue. Watching it made her nauseous. She attended to Tippis, who lowered his eyes to the table and scratched his forefinger at cracker crumbs on the checkered cloth.

"My analyst told me to scream when I get frustrated, but that's not really as crazy as it sounds, not at all, because all my life there've been things I've wanted to scream at, to strike out of my path, or trample under my heel. But I kept silent. I tried to be cunning, thinking that—like the young sapling that bends in the wind—I could eventually conquer the world through endurance. Things started to churn and bubble inside me until I thought I'd explode. Passivity wasn't working. It was like there was a grenade in my guts. That make any sense?"

Faith concluded hastily, unclearly, that her host was possessed. It happened all the time. Someone was, perhaps, working evil mojo on him. Leechcraft was what he needed, or a talisman, but she had neither, or anything to protect herself, or even anything to keep her heavy head from nodding like an old drunken hedonist gorged with grapes. Faith jerked herself upright. Her teeth felt soft and her bones rubbery; and every few minutes she felt herself sliding down her seat, prevented from going under the table only by Tippis's hand gripping her wrist.

"So I went to an analyst downtown when things started going wrong on my job. I practiced dentistry on the West Side—made good money, too, and had a good name. But one day my nerves started going, hands started to shake, and I kept getting headaches and hearing voices, y'know?"

She nodded. Yes, she knew. The living dead, when bored, often communicated with their relatives, their friends. The point was to listen to them.

"So I started seeing a psychiatrist. He said I should have come to him maybe ten years ago. He said it was fifty per cent in my head and fifty per cent in the world. Everybody's got an ego that arises from the id when they have to satisfy their instinctual needs—" As he talked Tippis's face twisted as though he tasted bile; he reared back his shoulders, squared them, and squeezed Faith's dry hand. It didn't matter. Her hand felt numb. She accepted another drink and nibbled ravenously with her free hand at the stale crackers.

Tippis continued, a muscle beating in his jaw as he looked at but did not quite see her, "He convinced me to do my own research into the psyche." What he told her made Faith giggle—that is, until she realized he was serious about infantile sexuality, and all those other things neither he nor she could see. Lavidia, she remembered, had derided Todd for believing in things he couldn't see. But that was different: Lavidia simply hadn't looked hard and long enough. Tippis said, "It's so damned obvious! Everything you want is an object for the satisfaction of drives developed in childhood, and you, in society, are an object for others, hardly ever for yourself. But society, through the family and peer group, suppresses these drives so civilization doesn't evaporate in a collective lust involving billions. Tell me," he said, pulling at the tip of his dark goatee, "what is it you want most from life?"

It shot from her lips: "The Good Thing."

Tippis stared, then chuckled, lighting a fresh cigarette, his tenth. "There is no such object. Surely you mean some specific thing that makes you feel good—like scratching, sneezing, or the pleasurable feeling when the valve to your full bladder opens—"

"No, I mean—" She stopped, her eyes wide with incredulity. She stared past him to the wall. What *did* she mean?

"You're in serious trouble if you have a drive for which there's no object. *That's* what the world is really all about—subject-object antagonism. Objectifying a thing, making it no more than an object so it can be grasped, manipulated, and ruled is, obviously, dehumanizing, even cruel, I suppose, if done to another person. But too many of your drives can only be satisfied, and only then temporarily, in this way. There *is* no other way unless you kill off your feelings like a musty old monk or Indian Bodhisattva. So find an object. The world provides several, and they're useful and approved besides. Set an accepted goal for yourself—comfortable living, that's a good one, or fashion, collecting antique bottles or comic books from World War II. Sublimate, child." He looked at her over the rims of his glasses and smiled. "Do you like cuisine?"

"I don't know," Faith said. "Isn't that what they clean in the Army?"

"That's latrine," Tippis snorted. He waved his hand dramatically, then lowered it, stroking her wrist. "You can't escape history, or the needs and neuroses you've picked up like layers and layers of tartar on your teeth (Pardon me, I couldn't resist that, dentistry and all)." He laughed deeply, "Mhah ha ha ha," amusing himself. "Your every past action and thought have made you what you are. Am I right or wrong?"

His words troubled Faith. The past, remote and distorted by the mercy of waning memories, had the terrible power to be present at all times in its effects: this was true. It was some kind of law. Didn't sorcerers control their victims by possessing an old truss they'd worn, old cigarette butts that once touched their lips? And Dr. Lynch—

wasn't what he meant—that what was, was only the form of what had been, even if what was past had been accidental? In their corner of the bar, Faith tried to make her peace with the problems of change, permanence, and the free-will-destroying tyranny of history. Everything, including the Good Thing, seemed to hinge on it. But you couldn't have it both ways—change and no change, freedom and the comfort of the past. Either you were brand new at each instant, innocent and undetermined and, therefore, free, or you were a bent-back drudge hauling all of world history on your shoulders across the landscape of your life, limited in all your possibilities, enclosed within the small cage of what had passed before. Each event would weigh you down, alter you, send you through endless changes. You were in bondage. And the other way?—*could* you be brand new each instant, remade by the power of either your own hand or magical thoughts? She turned it over and over: the Good Thing, if it could be at all, if it was indeed the truly unique *good* thing, had to be in the second way, above and beyond the wastepaper basket of the past; but didn't that imply that it, being so aloft, so absolute, was not really in the world—that the slim line between perfection and impossibility was no distinction at all? It was all so confusing. Her thoughts became sluggish and lost their connections. Tippis's voice drifted back again, breaking the mood. . . .

". . . am I right or wrong?"

"That's so grim . . ." she wanted to say, but her tongue, heavy as lead, would not move.

"It's the same for everybody," Tippis sighed through his teeth. "Civilized life is based on suffering, on the enslavement of the instincts and the self-alienation implicit in never being an object for your own needs. Look at this." He released her hand and unfolded a paper napkin upon which he made a hasty sketch:

$$W \longrightarrow \quad \longleftarrow D$$

"That's what should happen," Tippis said. "The instinctual drive is directed from the pleasure to the reality principles by a secondary process that points it head-on at the world. But it meets an anti-cathexis, and gets displaced this way:

$$W \longrightarrow \quad \longleftarrow\!\!\!\overset{\frown}{\longrightarrow} D$$

". . . so the libidinal energy of the instinct itself feeds the neurosis."
Tippis stared at his sketch and groaned, "That's me, Arnold Tyler
Tippis! All I ever wanted was to be a musician, but that little arrow
there got bent all to hell!"

"Tha's . . . turrble," Faith said. "You wanted to be a moosician?"

Pain sprang across Tippis's face. His eyes seemed to swell like
blowfish behind his lenses, and he shook his head violently. "I'm
over that now. It doesn't bother me any more. I can even laugh about
it. . . ."

Faith did not hear him laugh.

"My parents were killed in a highway accident when I was a child,
so I grew up in a little Midwestern town with my aunt and uncle. I
called him Uncle Bud, and he played a banjo like nobody's business
—he taught me chords and transitions, the whole works. Naturally,
I wanted to be a traveling musician, he being my ego-ideal and all.
But my aunt wouldn't hear of it." Tippis's eyes moistened with
remembrance. "She used to beat my fingers with a poker whenever
she caught me playing Uncle Bud's banjo after he died." Tippis
placed his cigarette in the ash tray to his left. Faith realized that his
right index and forefinger remained outstretched and rigid though
his hand was empty. Tippis held his right hand up, staring at his
fingers with ill-suppressed horror:

"She broke those two once. They never did come back exactly
right. But she had my best interests at heart—I know that now. So,"
he sighed, "I couldn't fret Uncle Bud's banjo any more. About the
only thing I could do after that was read. I graduated from college
when I was nineteen. . . ."

"And the fingers didn't heal?" Faith asked.

"Nope." Tippis glanced over his shoulder, then shoved his right
hand into his pocket. "Like I said, it *used* to bother me. I couldn't
date girls or anything like that for a long time. I felt too self-conscious." He peeked at her over his lenses again. "You *do* understand,
don't you?"

"I'm sorry," Faith said.

"But that's okay, just as long as clever girls like you can stay on
the streets the object I need is provided. You ready to go?"

Though she knew not where and could hardly stand, Faith said,
"Yes," feeling inside and out all toasted, tight-chested, and trusting.

He, this somehow sad and pitiable man dirty with the dust of his memories, supported her on his right arm, led her back onto the cold, empty street, and hailed a taxi. At Stony Island he took her to an old building bearing a sign out front—HOTEL SINCLAIR—a place so small its cockroaches had to walk single-file through the hallways. A stocky woman at the desk startled awake when they entered and studied Faith apprehensively before shoving Tippis the ledger and asking, "How old is she?" Tippis grunted, "Twenty-six," and the woman handed him the key, grumbling, "No drinking—I run a decent place here, Mr. and Mrs. Taylor," the last part of that being malevolent and as dry as witches' ashes on a Puritan's pyre. "Mrs. Taylor?" Faith said. Tippis ignored that and led her up a narrow, creaking flight of stairs to a dingy room at the end of the fourth floor. He closed the door and, in the darkness, dropped Faith across a mattress moist at its center. He stepped farther back into the shadows.

Lying there on the bed she could hear no sound but the rush of Tippis's birdlike breathing. Her eyes could not adjust to the darkness of the stuffy room—it was like fog, or the oval heart of a hippogriff, laced through and through with an inky material that absorbed any light from under the door. A feeling of vertigo crawled from her stomach to her throat. Fingers caught at her wrists.

To the darkness Faith said, "Arnold—?"

He gave no sign. But upon her fell his entire weight, driving her back along the bedspread on which she felt the raised pattern of flowers. She guessed—peonies. And gasped. A long, agonized breath smelling of tobacco and sour cream blew against her face, slipping down her throat as she struggled to take in air. She wanted to scream.

Tippis did things to her there in the lightless room at the end of the hall that should, if possible, be exorcised from memory. She lay perfectly rigid, tight-lipped like a corpse with rusty pennies on its eyes—praying. No one, apparently, heard. For Tippis continued, his lips humming, and in his mouth was a gurgling sound. Faith twisted her head and vomited over the side of the bed, no longer praying now, but thinking, "To me . . . not to *me* is this happening." Not to that well-protected portion of herself that came spinning forth whenever she said, "I . . . me . . . myself," not to her, but to some part other than herself, some weak and vulnerable part that could so easily be made an object, that was incapable of escaping circumstance and chance. To herself she whispered, "This is *bad*, Faith. Bad . . . Faith." The darkness helped. She couldn't see him, or what he was doing, and it was easy to dam her ears to his breathing by shouting deep within her mind again and again:

"I am Faith Cross . . .

"I am Faith . . .

"I *am* . . .

"I . . . ?"

Outside, through the thin walls, she heard from afar the racing of an automobile engine, rubber squeal against pavement and the sound fade away, then—in her ears, louder now—Tippis's short breaths hungrily sucked in through his nostrils, and a whistle hiss through his teeth. He showered her with sweat and raked at her with his nails. She was his. There was pain and the salty smell of blood, but, oddly enough, no longer was there terror. For this was not happening to her, only to another, to a shadow of herself. To a thing apart, *out there*, like the odd-shaped bottles and brooms in Lavidia's kitchen, like the people in the bar.

After what seemed like hours Tippis was done. He clicked on the ceiling light, and Faith saw the wretchedness of her room: a water-ringed door, big yellow flowers on gray wallpaper, cracked sink sticking from the garishly papered wall like a goiter; a broken writing table beside the sagging bed, sticky, damp corners behind an enormous radiator, and bare, warped floors. And on the spring-mattress bed—enough blood to account for a knifing, and whiter stains where Tippis, somehow thinking of her at the last instant, had withdrawn. After dressing he placed a twenty-dollar bill on the bed. His face was pained, it lacked all pleasure. He looked like one possessed, though momentarily freed, but only briefly, only for a heartbeat. At the door, he tried to smile, and broke into song:

> "Here's to fucking that makes a man a fool;
>   Opens up his pores, wears away his tool—
> He gets on a woman but hasn't long to stay,
>   His head's fulla nonsense, his ass's fulla play;
> He gets on like a lion, and slips off like a lamb,
>   Tries to look passionate, but he isn't worth a damn."

Tippis left.

On the bed, breathing in the heavy blood-and-semen smell filling the room, Faith lay spread-eagled, her eyelids closing and her limbs as motionless as those of a wind-up doll now run down and lying like dirt, or defecation, or yesterday's newspaper, wet and blurred, in the middle of the road. Through the wall behind her she heard radio music playing in the next room, but this she grew unaware of, for her mind—clear and as smooth as a sea stone beaten by waves and elements for a millennium—registered no sensation, held, in its broken glass frame, no reflections. It was, momentarily, dead. No thoughts came to her, not for a while; then, gradually, her breathing grew as rhythmic as the music next door, rising, falling. Falling. She thought, but did not stir. She started to inch slowly, her eyes shut tight and fists clenched, along the interior of her memories—some immediate, some older, some perhaps written into her blood, or cells, or synapses before she was born—timidly feeling the impressions etched there, like ancient friezes or the faded images of brown bison in moist mountain caves. From cavern to cavern she moved, like a child lost in the anfractuous corridors of an art museum with high walls, until she saw, for reasons obscure to her, the first time her father had taken her into town, on a Saturday morning, and for the purpose of buying meal. The summer sun had baked the road to hot, dry dust, had heated the inside of his old Edsel so its torn cushions burned her skin at the touch; the air itself was thick with steam, hot in her lungs, and raised water from the pores on her chest and arms. Todd stopped at a one-pump filling station two miles outside of town, put in a dollar's worth of Ethyl, and Faith—quite young then and naïve to the ways of the world—had asked to use the washroom. She was refused. The man responsible was really a boy, an ugly one at that, with ash-white hair tumbling into his eyes. He had bony arms knotty at his elbows, and his smooth belly pushed through an opening in his plaid shirt, overrode his cowboy belt. He was snaggle-toothed, and bent forward slightly when he took Todd's dollar, careful not to let Todd's darker hand touch his own. Todd raged—no. No. It had *not* happened that way. Not at all. Clearly now she saw her father grinning sheepishly, lowering his eyes to the boy's muddy boots, and asking in a slow, clumsy voice where—if it was permissible and would not upset the delicate, divinely established order of things, of spiders and sinners and martyred saints whose hierarchy led to a too, too remote Deity—Faith could relieve herself. "In the bushes," the boy said, "behind the station." And Todd, taking her by her hand, and trembling across his six feet— though now he looked less than five—led her past the open door of the clean women's room and set her down in the bushes. He said nothing the remainder of the hot ride into town, nothing as he shopped, and nothing on the way back home. Nothing. And this, she knew, was how he reacted *always*: never defiant, never confident save when he was alone, or walking behind his farmhouse, or seated late at night like a peaceful wizard before his own fireplace; never indignant or righteous until that spring day three hitchhikers from the next county stopped him on the road, first asking directions, then asking if—through accident or design—he had ever had a white woman, and finally demanding that he remove his trousers to satisfy their curiosity. It was all so clear: the way he stepped quickly aside, or into the street, regardless of mud or traffic, when men smaller than he, perhaps in soul as well as body, came abreast; the begrudging yet servile and obsequious way he used the rear entrances of stores in town, bought clothes without first trying them on, without letting them touch his flesh as the management demanded—the look of futility in his eyes at the end of each summer when he released, without a word of objection, half the produce from their sharecropper's yield. And especially the way he acted when men, roaring by in cars on weekends, would hoot and jeer at Lavidia while she worked in the fields: Todd turned his head. So Lavidia hated him, perhaps because she knew that pitiable side of Todd that lay within the confines of history, or perhaps because she knew his subservience was necessary to put food on their table, that he ceased to be human simply . . . to be, to taste, to hear and smell and see the infinity of worldly sensations, even though he enjoyed them through the odd, invisible bars of his imprisonment. So it came to this: his world of pots and pans with proper names was not created by an act of freedom, but by necessity—an escape it was. A valve. On the day of his death alone had he been forced too far; they ignored his forced, jocular, and polite replies to their pointed questions concerning his promiscuity. He had laughed even when they demanded of him what he could not do; and then he turned on them, screaming as though his mind had snapped when they forced it upon him. And so Todd died. But the situation was worse than she'd imagined. She saw, plummeting deeper, that the past was final, irreversible. Each act added to her ongoing essence, was whipped in like batter, or dissolved like sugar in water—invisible, but there nonetheless. Worse, not only your acts but those of others, those who made you an object, were mixed in as well. And these you could *not* control. What to do, what to do? Tippis had taken her, and paid for his taking; she was placed, placed, and burned deep into her was the label: whore. It was true. A part of her was no longer her own, not for her now, but for another. Had it not always been so? Deeper, farther down the descent, she saw the extent of her own otherness. How much there was in her make-up that was beyond her control, her freedom and reason and magical thinking could only be guessed at, for she could not have witnessed all history. She could not have seen every human deed done, kneaded, whipped into her essential self, her factualness. But she saw its broad curves, its crucial contours. . . . She saw them coming, leaving the great amphitheater of hills at Havana Harbor in a three-hundred-ton slave ship called *The Trinity*, a sleek ship with an arrowy hull cutting through the storms of the Atlantic, coming with bearded freebooters and buccaneers, coming with cotton bales hollowed at their center, watered-down kegs of Irish whisky and kegs of gunpowder stacked in rows in the hold. Coming for trade along the Gold Coast. Armed with firelocks and cutlasses, they lower their skiff against the water and move to the slave factory at Bangaland, miles from the interior where, the month before, Mandingoes and Fussah were herded in leg irons, whipped, brought to heel—all of them, the debtors, the thieves, the dark prisoners of war and religious heretics. They pick, these restless seamen, no women over twenty-five, or sickly youths, or the ones with tribal incisions and spiraling tattoos on their faces. But they pick the young princess, the chieftain's favorite daughter: they pick Faith. She is easily worth two bars, a musket, and a case of gin; the others—the men—they, too, are picked, but only for a lifetime of labor on Alabama plantations and Argentina *estancias*. Faith they pick as the captain's concubine: it has always been so. In her eyes is defeat and —yes, even submission (though the legend-makers will lie of this to save face), for she has seen the gutting of her village with flame and sword, seen the smashing of her centuries-old temples and, thus, the death of her gods. She struggles with her leg iron and is brought by the action of the boatswain's whip to her knees. Her head is shaved, her ornaments, anklets, and skin kilts decorated with bright brass beads are stripped away, her body is bathed in oil, and her buttocks branded with a bent wire dipped in fire. Around her, in the difficult Soosoo dialect, her own tribesmen shout for mercy. But their gods are dead. They are separated, husband from wife, father from son, and tossed into the belly of *The Trinity* with tribesmen of a different tongue. Faith crosses the Atlantic in darkness, sitting chained on another's lap, or lying, not on her left side where the pressure will be against her heart, but on her right for the entire voyage, surrounded by the sick, the dying: dropsy, pleurisy, flux, malaria, and scurvy—the worst cases are jettisoned overboard, but not at a loss, for in Liverpool, Boston, and Madrid, *The Trinity*'s shareholders expect only sixty slaves, the ship's capacity. On this voyage, as on all others, *The Trinity* holds one hundred. Naked, weakened, and frightened, she arrives, is taken to the auction block after a bath and hasty meal, and sold. Twenty dollars. But that is not the beginning, not at all. Beneath her thoughts are more impressions, older ones of an ancient, eolithic world—a continent in the lush, tropical zone now sunken into the Indian Ocean, but upon which a highly developed race of bearded anthropoid apes traveled in bands through the trees. Some drop to the ground. It is she among them, a woman-thing with pointed ears and razor-sharp teeth; yet she is as strong as all the others, perhaps stronger, because within her loins is the mystery of being. And there, on the not yet firm soil rolling with monstrous vegetation, covered with white volcanic ash and crawling with fierce, many-fanged accidents of nature, she—an accident, too—discovered that her forearms, once used for clasping limbs and scaling trees, were free when she took to the ground. They were free to snatch fruit and stones, spears and clubs. And in that habit of clasping, the hands themselves changed; the bones grew differently over the ages, altered to perform more delicate operations such as seizing red, raw meat from fires sprung by lightning, such as planting seeds and planning harvests from observation of the moon and stars and seasons, while the brain itself and larynx and her body as a whole rushed to pace the development of the hand—to create man, society, and history; to build swift clippers and slave ships and manacles to make men, and especially women, the objects of desire; to weave the thick rope that stretched the strong neck of Todd Cross that hot spring day.

All right.

Rising to a sitting position slowly, as if someone had replaced her spine with a two-by-four or ridden her on all fours, Faith saw the twenty-dollar bill on the bed. She reached for it, then drew back her hand, aware of a sharp ache all through her body, particularly her legs, thighs, and sore abdomen. She swung her legs over the side of the bed and hobbled to the sink, where she washed herself, then smoothed down her dress. She rested against the sink, her head bent into its bowl. With the twenty dollars she could attempt to return home. What awaited her there?—an empty farmhouse, the self-satisfied smirk of Reverend Brown?

No.

She raised her head and peered into the cracked glass of the mirror above the sink. "Nice-looking," she whispered to her reflection, ". . . cute." She had twenty dollars. She knew, without further thought, how to get more.

hildren, Fate put a terrible hurt on this sweet sister. So hungry was she before her first big break, in the form of the man called Barrett, that her backbone could have shaken hands with her stomach. Yeah. The soles of her shoes were so thin she could step on a dime, then tell you if it was heads or tails. She was so poor—you ready?—she couldn't even pay attention.

Faith grew weak, and so thin her eyes looked as hungry and haggard as those in a kraken's skull; her figure, once the rich color of *café-au-lait*, became ashen and harried from drugs, lots of gin, and the endless parade of people who appeared at her room in Hotel Sinclair. Before Barrett came she even tried religion and, failing in that, tarried there restlessly during the long rimy months of winter, her days not like days at all but akin, she fancied, to sausage links, each flat and bland and tasteless, arching away from her, and filled the day long with the interminable disquietude of her mind's revolutions. At dawn Faith damned the day, and called on night; at dusk, she rued the night, and pined for day. "Perhaps," she told herself at forenoon in her tiny room, "we can be what we think we are," but by eveningtime she knew; "We are nothing, nothing at all." There was no truth, no certainty save the fact of her life's fall into bondage, no reality but that of the endless procession of unhappy humanity that arrived, by and by, at her door. How they came to know of her condition and exploit it, she knew not. They did. They knew. They saw—in her eyes, in the slow, uncertain way she gestured and spoke, that in her ethical pother they could, if they tried, place her at their behest. She walked the city's winding streets, smoking reefers, thinking, and, before long, encountered on a lightless street corner, or in a tavern or club, soft raptorial eyes with swelling irises upon her. The struggle began. She saw a face, a human form, perhaps a smirk, and knew that he who watched her was, in some strange, inexplicable yet natural way, taking hold of her life. Looking away, back to her table or at a menu, she felt she was Faith Cross with such-and-such possibilities; but when those eyes fell upon her, imagining her reclining on the back seat of a car parked in the woods, or sprawled on the covers of a bed in some musty two-dollar-a-night hotel, she *became* that and was nothing more. What that other mind thought of her she was: you could not deny it—you railed, fought it, but those eyes saw you, in part, as what you were or might be. Faith fought back, denying this transformation, and—as always—lost.

It happened often. Every day before Barrett tried to set her straight. She was wholly herself only when alone, locked in her room, or traveling the quiet city streets. As soon as another appeared the struggle began anew: to Mrs. Octavia Beasley she was monthly rent, to Arnold Tippis, a huge ear to hear his woe. Faith fancied that these folks found this pleasing; in a world wracked by the incessant war of billions of wills, it satisfied some ancient need to have completely, if only for an hour or an evening, a life in one's power—the other's, if not one's own: to be no longer in bondage, the object of an alien will, and forever manipulated and ruled, but to be—if only in illusion—completely effective, to rule with suzerainty over their soft, compassionate, coffee-and-cream-colored Faith.

She laughed; *really* laughed. Because she'd learned, through many reversals and indignities, what she took to be a lesser secret of life. It was in no way profound, and certainly neither universal nor necessary—she had, in fact, heard it before: *You are nothing*. Yet what she had to be for others changed that for them. In her presence their worlds snapped somehow into perfect focus, it shaped itself around them, and they stood free and independent at its center, commanding, deigning, and having their wills obediently done. She accepted her bondage and bolstered herself the day long with denial: "I am *not* what I am," for there was a fear, a nagging suspicion, if not a certainty, that what she did, through her own will or coercion, would not bring her a momentary descent into shame but make for her a destiny. Should she die tomorrow of a heart attack, or beneath the wheels of a car, people wouldn't say, "Faith Cross, daughter of Todd and Lavidia, the quester for the Good Thing, has died." No, they would smirk and say, "Death sneezed the whore." She had suffered more beatings, near evictions, insults, and threats in four months than she cared to recall; but the worst, the most denigrating service her situation demanded she render was simply listening. Listening to the secret thoughts only one such as she could be called upon to bear. It gave her headaches so violent they seemed to sunder her mind into two equal, warring halves: one heavy with the amaranthine, inviolable awareness of her autonomy and unsullied faith; the other a consciousness caught within the mad swirl of a personal history over which she had no control. Others wrote it. It was etched in by each cramp of hunger in her stomach and, thence, sent her back onto the wintry city streets to eke out survival. There was no surcease to the struggle of feeding herself and fighting what others thought her to be. To survive, she sold them, not only herself, but her father's stories of the South.

On Saturdays, a Mr. Jonathan Crowell, always punctual, appeared at her room. Faith, on his last appearance, opened the door and stood staring into Crowell's sea-colored eyes, struggling to combat the wave of control overcoming her. Crowell, square-jawed and chubby with thin sienna hair, would smile—it overwhelmed her, as certain smiles are wont to do. Her will began to fold; Crowell entered and, after flipping back his blue coattails, lowered his weight onto her bed. He, she could tell, was like all the others: certain of their power over her, yet blind to the bonds that such power brought. He withdrew a billfold from his pocket, a dollar from the billfold, and laid it on her wrinkled pillow, thinking, as he pulled off his shoes and unbuttoned his shirt, that he was in control.

"Give me some sugah." He pursed his pale lips.

Faith closed her eyes and kissed Crowell, contemptuous of him as he leaned forward, lowering his head to say, "Tell me . . . something nice. . . ." He always asked that; like the rest, he could not get his fill of her tales. Thus, her power in bondage. Though Faith hated selling her favorite stories so cheaply, she came up with one Big Todd told her when she was only three and always fighting with other children, always contesting her will against theirs, then wailing when, due to her frailty, the others won. "If you think there's ever a winner or a loser," he said ,"you're dead wrong." No, Faith thought, this tale is too dear to sell. But, looking at Crowell and seeing his self-confidence, it was evident he needed this. She began . . .

It was Sunday morning. Everyone was in church, or still in bed in that tiny Kentucky town where Big Todd Cross found himself meditating over a game of solitaire and rum in an empty saloon. He drank, feeling miserable for having wounded a young boy too full of piss and vinegar the night before. But his reputation was always getting him in trouble; besides, the boy had been caught cheating at cards. All around Todd this morning were chairs turned upside down on round wooden tables. A balding old Negro in coveralls drifted around the room with a wet mop and pail, scrubbing at the blood stains near the bar. He stopped, leaned on the bar, and said to Todd, "That was Jim Slaughter's boy you shot—he'll be coming after you 'fore long." He shook his head soberly, said, "Slaughter's mean; he'll drive you like a flash o' lightning through a gooseberry bush." Before Todd could reply, the door behind him burst open: Slaughter stormed in. Todd tried to remain cool, tensing himself as still as a cigar-store Indian. He watched Slaughter from the corner of his eyes. Children, Jim Slaughter was a huge, barrel-chested man, with a beard hanging to his belt. He had a shotgun; he shoved it straight into Todd's back.

"Cross," he shouted, "I'm going to send you straight to West Hell!"

"Damn," Todd whispered, "why you want to come in here and make me look bad?" And Todd took another drink.

Click.

Todd began to sweat.

Slaughter, too, poured sweat. Really, he didn't want to do this, but some vague sense of honor was at stake. "You're a player, eh? A *gambler*?" he snarled. "Well, I wanna see you play fo' your life, I wanna see you win it back from this gunbarrel!" He motioned with a nod of his head to the terrified janitor to sit across from Todd. Said, "Willis, you're gonna play this sonuvabitch and beat him, or I'll blow *your* brains out!"

"Suh?" Willis stammered.

"And you," Slaughter growled at Todd, "I'll kill you if you lose."

He cut the cards with his free hand and returned behind Todd with the gun. "Play!" he shouted.

The plastic cards kept slipping from Big Todd's trembling hands. Sweat blinded his eyes. But, by and by, he realized he was winning the game. He looked across the table at Willis. Todd's heart sank. Poor Willis was pale; he clutched at his heart, and Todd could hear the old man whimpering and sobbing like a child. An emptiness filled Todd, a space so wide he felt himself fall therein and the gulf between himself and the old janitor evaporate like smoke. Todd misplayed his hand.

"What're you doing?" Slaughter cried over Todd's left shoulder. "Ya had that hand—ya had him beat!" Slaughter shuffled the cards again, and dealt another hand.

Todd sighed. He blew that one, too.

"Stop that!" Slaughter screamed.

Todd kept losing. Then he started to laugh, and big, clear tears dropped from Willis's eyes.

"You're crazy," Slaughter said.

"Yeh."

"I got the right—the duty to kill ya now!"

"Sho."

But he didn't. Dazed, Slaughter lowered his gun to his side and stumbled, scratching his head, from the saloon. Todd and Willis, as soon as Slaughter was gone, broke into the whisky barrels in the basement and drank themselves blind.

Crowell smiled at Faith and said, "I guess that was okay," and gave her an extra five dollars. He slept with her until morning, but before drifting off, he flung his arm around her waist, whispering, "It's a shame the world isn't really like that, isn't it?"

She could not sleep that night and hated him for saying that, for calling into question that which she longed to believe. This disquietude—it followed her day and night like a stray dog, a curse, or damnation. It bothered her so that Faith could not eat the following day, or rest, and, finally, withdrew in desperation from her purse a circular she'd found on a bus the week before:

Why is there suffering? Is there a possibility of rebirth and hope in this life? Are you tired of living apart from the Truth?

Are you tired of asking questions like this? Let us answer them for you. Come to The Church of Continual Light, 64th and Stony Island.

She went, giving herself completely to the urge to again be, if not free, at least saved. Though married in her childhood to God, she'd been a bad wife, had taken another lover: the Good Thing. But Faith, as she rode the bus south, consoled herself with the cleanliness that penitence possibly could bring. She found the Church of Continual Light wedged between a crumbling old brownstone and a bakery. Outside, she stood in the snow, shivering and listening as the singsong chants within merged in a single, dreamy hum; she closed her eyes until the lights from inside lulled her with images and cloudy shapes forced along her eyelids. Reverend Brown had spoken of that shadowy, senseless, Cimmerian world where groping things collided like blind, hungry moles: she was there. Suffocating in it. Lost.

"Hallelujah!"

The cry rang inside, again and again, driven by a belief, a security she longed to have. Faith cracked open the door; she timidly peeked in. The storefront church must at one time have been a delicatessen; it smelled of raw salmon and catfish. It was packed. Toward the rear where she stood, snow dripping from her coat, were old, old men in green and gray workclothes and, farther up, fat, chubby women who clapped their hands and stomped their heavy, rectangular feet. They stopped, even as the wet-eyed women on the wooden moaning bench went still when a lean-fleshed man in black pounded his podium at the front of the room. In his right hand he held a Bible, in his left—a big fistful of thunder:

"I gave my heart to know wisdom, to know madness and folly," he said, "and I've seen all the wonders under the sun and—*behold*—all is vanity. . . ."

Silently Faith stepped to the last row of chairs. The minister's voice thrilled her; she felt safe again, at ease and acquainted with the anxious, sweating faces around the room.

Up front, the minister folded his hands. Intoned, "I know what's in your hearts, brothers—I know, because I've *been* there, I've seen it myself. The whole world's been there, because every one of us has to cross that deep sea of questionin' by himself. You think you're the center of the whole world at first, you think it whorls around you like the planets around the sun—don't you?"

"Yes, Lord!" a woman shouted.

"But one day, you come across someone else who thinks just the very same thing. You've got to fight then, to do battle over who's gonna be supreme, you or that other fellah, 'cause that's the way we men are—strugglin' against each other with our wills, our dreams. . . ." The minister's mouth opened. Faith caught her breath. His mouth was bright red inside, the color of fresh blood. "And you both lose!" he boomed. "You both see neither one of you have *any-thin'* to do with what pushes the world along. What, then?" he said. "Where do you turn, *then*, brothers—sisters, what do you seek?"

Pensively Faith pushed forward in her seat. She bit her fingernails.

"You look beyond—both you and that other fellah, and see that the world's moved by somethin' bigger than either one of you—somethin' more than you'll ever be, but somethin' you *must* know, *must* be like if you're ever to be free—"

"Yes," Faith whispered. Her nerves and brain hummed; she gave herself to the enchantment. "Yes—"

"And," he said, "you go on lookin' for it. You look all over the earth! You look to the South, to the East, some of you even came up North to find it, but you never do see it, *do you*?"

Faith wanted to stand up, raise her hand, and cast a question. Instead, she waited, certain he was talking to her.

"So, because God was so remote, so inaccessible, He sent his only Son, as flesh, blood, gristle, and bone, to show us how to get closer to Him—to seize the root of this thing greater than any of us can be." He slammed his Bible on the podium. Raised his voice. "And even *that* wasn't enough! It was still *too far away*. Can you imagine that gulf between man and his greatest goal? Can you see how *horrible* it is to be separated by all the universe from the thing we need most? Only one step remained: to look inside ourselves—to put it so close we don't have to search all over the world no more!" The minister tapped his chest, then smacked it hard. "It's in here! That's the only place it is, or could ever be—in your hearts!"

In *here*. Faith laid her right hand along her left breast. She held her breath and closed her eyes, searching for this truth but finding only a memory there. A bad one, at that. She remembered the spring evening eight years after her father's death when Reverend Brown came visiting. No—he came to confess. She'd always wondered to whom troubled men of the cloth carried their cares when the Lord did not or could not answer their call. Brown took his to Lavidia. Why he did she could only conjecture: because Lavidia had known and transcended grief, because she realized in her flesh, in her blood, at the floor of a hot tent that summer night long ago, all Brown could know only in theory. And theory alone. He came. They saw his car roaring up the road before a cloud of crimson dust.

Brown parked it in the brown shade of an oak in the front yard, and slowly removed his bent straw hat. Said, "Evenin', Sister Cross." His voice cracked. Faith knew something was wrong; she could feel it in her throat. Especially when Brown looked irritably at her, winced, then turned to Lavidia. "Can I talk with you alone?"

Without waiting for her mother's response, Faith fled into the farmhouse, creeping barefoot across the quiet front room to the window where, behind a drawn curtain, she heard Reverend Brown's agonized voice.

"What's troublin' you, reverend?"—Lavidia.

Faith, her hand on the dry curtain, expected them to conceive yet another plan for her wayward soul's salvation—some nocturnal trip to the river of another county where she would be baptized, or another riotous prayer meeting in a close tent on a sweltering summer eve.

"Jennie Scott just died," Brown said.

"Lord have mercy," Lavidia cried. Faith heard the scraping of her mother's nails on her brow. "Reverend, she wasn't but sixteen! It was that sickness she had, wasn't it? Loo, looo—"

"Leukemia," Brown sighed.

Through a crack in the curtain Faith could see Brown leaning as lifeless as a scarecrow against the porch railing.

"I prayed night and day for that gal," he said. "Damn if I didn't almost go down to the bogs to call on that crazy woman for her!" With his thumb and forefinger he squeezed his nose, so hard Faith felt the bridge of her own nose ache. "I told her parents—when there didn't seem to be no hope—that sufferin' was a teacher, that there was some lesson in it that we just couldn't see . . . but *what*? Livvie, that child never hurt *no*body!"

"I know, I know," Lavidia moaned. "There ain't no answer, I guess. It sure wasn't your fault, reverend."

"Wasn't it?" Brown cried. His fingers tightened on the railing; his knuckles were white. Brown turned his back to Lavidia and hung his head out toward the yard. "It must have been me!" Then he turned around, open-mouthed. Sweating. "Have you ever doubted the purity of your faith, Livvie—I mean, *that's* a good reason for the Lord never answerin' when you call, don't you think?"

"No." Lavidia's voice trembled. "I don't never doubt it—"

You could hear the floor of the porch cry under Brown's heels. Faith imagined him breathing with irregularity, like an overworked horse, the sweat steaming at the curly roots of his sparse gray hair. "Haven't you ever . . . doubted that what you were doing was right?"

"I do what the Lord wants," Lavidia said.

The porch buckled again; the floorboards creaked as Brown moved closer to Lavidia's rocker. "Some people—like you, 'way back when you got the spirit and heard Him talkin' to you: you *knew* then, didn't you? I mean, He touched you, rolled you around that tent floor with His big, black toe. I saw it happen to you, Livvie! And you knew clearer than I'll ever know what He wants." The reverend's voice went sharp, splintering like dry kindling split by an ax. "It never come to me that way. It don't happen like that to most people. I've got faith and religion, but not like I seen it come to some people like you. It didn't happen to me like that. I . . . decided to follow the Cross, 'cause what it stood for seemed to be everything I wanted to be like." Brown looked away from her, as though he'd said too much. "I pray for understanding, Livvie. I look for some kind of sign. . . ."

Lavidia's breathing was as loud as that of a cow.

"Nothin' comes," Brown groaned. "How do you *really* know what you're doin' and believin' is right? Don't mistake me now! I don't doubt for a minute that He's *out there*, but, from day to day, how do you *really* know?"

Faith suffered a long, long silence as Lavidia waited, puffing her best briar pipe. "You feel it, I guess," she said. "You ought to know 'bout that better'n me—"

"Feelin's ain't *certain*!" Brown slammed something, perhaps his fist, against the wooden railing. It shook the house. "I *feel* Jennie oughta be alive!"

It seemed suddenly to Faith that the porch was empty. She heard the mindless prattle of chickens in the barnyard, the wind crackling, like the rustling of crumbling cellophane, in the trees. She peered from behind the curtain and saw Reverend Brown resting silently on his knees beside Lavidia, searching her face for a sign.

"Feelings belong to the flesh," he said. "I can *feel* the wind comin' up, I can *feel* it gettin' cooler, 'cause the sun's goin' down." He pointed a finger at his temple. "But my mind ain't at ease with that. It wants to be absolutely sure!" Brown pressed the heels of his hands against his wet forehead. "Sometimes I ain't even certain if Father Divine or Prophet Cherry knew what was right all the time!" He touched Lavidia's bony wrist. "When it happened to you—what was it like, Livvie?"

For reasons she could not describe, Faith felt a wave of uneasiness. It was like he'd asked for a description of the way Lavidia and Todd made love.

"It was kinda soft, like the way you're touchin' me now," Lavidia said. "But it wasn't like the touch of *no* livin' man. It was like He put His hand across my breasts, and they exploded, and shot out into the tent, and carried somethin' inside me through the air, clear up to some dizzy spot above the world. I was kinda dead, but alive, too, because I couldn't stop shakin' on the ground. I saw myself shakin'— it was like I was lookin' at myself from far, far away, right beside Him, or maybe all alone in some dark place like a cave. And I was watchin' what was left of me the way you look at the wigglin' of a chicken with its head wrung off. It didn't matter none. That thing on the ground wasn't me. I knew that, reverend. It was like a box I'd been kept in all these years—"

Reverend Brown nodded. Water fell from his eyes. "And you *knew* the soul was immortal; you knew it brought you 'cross that wide sea between man and God. That was the sign he gave you. . . ."

"I reckon," Lavidia said. "I try not to think 'bout it too much. It's like you said at the last meetin': the best thing in the world is inside us."

"I said that?" Brown looked at her quizzically, then snapped his fingers. "Yes!" he shouted. "I *did* say that!" He jumped to his feet, stood still for a moment, then spun on his heels. "That *is* what I said, isn't it?" A smile split his mouth; he slammed his palms together and laughed. "I wasn't thinkin' right! That child, Jennie, *is* in a better world—she's saved. She's thrown off that box she was trapped in, and there ain't nothin' separatin' her from the most real thing of all!" Brown straightened his coat, regaining himself, happy now. He smiled at Lavidia, and touched her arm. "That space between Him and us ain't so flamin' wide after all, is it?" He said, "Thank you, Sister Cross," and took his leave. As for Faith,

She jumped, stupefied, to her feet. Shouted, "There's nothing there!" They were looking at her now; she'd shattered the mood of sanctity and peace in the Church of Continual Light. She didn't care. Her thoughts rose as a veil before her vision, recalling her times spent walking across the city at the blackest pitch of night before the break of dawn, at that time so like a sick man's momentary slumber. State Street, parallel to the lakefront and glistening with melted snow, was silent. There she would walk, then along the misty, moonlit beaches, thinking, inuring herself to this life in the depths of the cave, but always certain that something about her remained vernal, clean, and beyond it all. It was a transparent time, akin to the great space between a gremlin's hourly heartbeats, or between a zombie's outstretched arms. Inner and outer worlds flowed back and forth beneath the integument of her skin like water in a pipe. She remembered sitting on the hard Civic Center benches beneath Picasso's wraithlike statue, feeling that flow and sensing for the first time that what was outside—in the world, on its streets, and behind its façade of buildings—stole within her at times, and was balanced by her own soul's emanation, altering that world with compassion, her father's legacy of mythopoesis and love. But in this church,

She leaned against the empty wooden seat in front of her, and made a witness to the truth: it was a one-way street. Warmth did not burst outward from her, filling the world with dreams, but the city, strangely like a burial place at that odd, half-remembered hour, had invaded her, made her, shaped her wholly, because there was nothing in *here* as the minister up front and Reverend Brown maintained. All was *out there.* Faith looked at the minister. He awaited an explanation for her outburst. She saw through him to the wall behind. He, too, was nothing—life was a play of shadows and mist on the marmoreal wall of a cave. . . .

"What is your name?" he said sharply.

"Name?" Faith wondered—should a thing as transitory as a human life have a name? It was a stupid convention, but she decided to play the game. "It's Faith Cross."

"And what will you tell us, child?"

Because it hurt so bad Faith set it free. "I came to Chicago looking for the one true Good Thing, the one thing that would end everyone's bondage, and would bring us all out of the dark!" Tears dropped from her eyes and made her cheeks shine, and she felt herself hovering again between the wish and its impossibility. "I believed in it—I was devoted to it, just like you said. I looked for it, because I knew it *had* to be! Don't you see? Wasn't it possible that there were all kinds of things around us that we never knew about until we looked for them? Wasn't there a purpose just *waiting* to show itself to someone who looked?"

The minister's brow knitted with deep lines and furrows as thick as a well-plowed field. "It's within you, child—"

"I looked there, too!" Faith cried. She sensed the weight, saw the horror of her realization. "That's too easy. . . . You all stopped looking in the world because it was too hard. You tricked yourselves!" Something solid and stiff seemed to flip over in her stomach, fell to the floor of her stomach, and lie there like a log. "There's nothing inside, and there's nothing outside—"

A curl stiffened the minister's lower lip. He screwed his mouth to the right side of his dark face, the edges of his white teeth visible as he frowned. "When people see things the way you do, we say they've got the Evil Eye. It's a false way of seeing life—it's like wearing dark glasses that blind you to the truth of things. You've got it, child—a belief that's an argument for the Pit." He scratched his cheek nervously and glared at her. "And if thine eye offends thee—"

"What?" Faith said coolly. Her composure returned, creeping in beneath her fatigue. "Should I change my glasses, or tear out my eyes, or pretend the Good Thing was always inside me, or—" She stopped, looking around the room at the drawn, startled faces. They were drained and almost the color of unleavened bread. Faith stepped into the aisle, drew her coat close around her, and turned to the minister. "Or should I use this darkness and suffering to get what I need?" It didn't matter that he failed to understand. Faith saw him step down from the podium and start after her when she reached the door.

"Sit down on the moaning bench," he called. "Fawn, if you confess—"

"It's Faith," she said. Her thoughts were sharp and clear. "My name is Faith Cross."

"Fawn or Faith," he said, his arms open to her, "does it matter?"

"Yes." She pulled shut the door, returned to the bus stop, and rode to State Street and Washington where she walked for a while. Thinking: *this* is home—a strangely ordered city seething beneath its veneer of rigidity and regulation with growing pockets of anarchy, theft, murder, a death every day, and crimes which the authorities suppressed quickly, like a finger dousing a candle's flame. All night the city's lamps were lit, all night the borders of order buckled and receded and were reinstated before day. A losing battle. The truth would steal into this and every city like a Mongol horde, turning dreams into nightmares, incrusting even the most brilliant, self-certain careers with the dust and decay of time. Walking through the garment industry, along the obscure, reeking canal, then in and out of the weaving maze of curio shops, wax museums, and opium dens that was Old Town, Faith considered the possibility of release. There could be nothing good, or true, or beautiful when inner and outer worlds were as empty as she divined. There could only be small comforts, the solace of bittersweet illusion that her customers seemed to enjoy. She walked on, stopping to sit on the rocks near the frozen lake, and feeling, as she remembered the window displays in the Loop, anger strong enough to slay a troll in its tracks. One had to be independent of fortune, to be comfortable in the cave. To wear those fine furs she saw draped over manikins in store windows and on the slim shoulders of the haughty women who paraded down the streets: this is what she wanted, what she swore to achieve. She looked toward the apartment buildings rising above Chicago's skyline, imagining how those women, less nice-looking, less cute than she, lived—in the sky, warm, well fed, as free as one could be in the endless, mad flux of things. "The Good Thing," she said. All bitterness. The sound of it made her sick. The minister had, in a small sense, been right: you had to bring your goals closer. Call them by another name. It was too hard to look, to suffer frustration, and keep searching in the face of probable defeat. It was true: you had to settle on *some*thing, to make your peace with your dreams and take, when the chance came, what you could get. Peace of mind. What else mattered? Inside her, the waves resounded. She looked at the sand beneath her feet, at the small impressions the thin soles of her shoes had made. Before dawn the wind would have erased them. None would know she'd sat there; in time, she would slip out of the world like a shadow. It reinforced her conviction, giving her strength to start back to the hotel, planning, vowing that, if nothing else, she would trample if need be the heads of thousands, and their ridiculous theories as well to get what she needed. She would number her days, but only to squeeze from each whatever comfort could be secured.

Faith hurried, star-shaped snowflakes melting in her hair, trying to beat a snowstorm already clouding the morning, obscuring it with just the slightest tinge of mystery. She entered the lobby of Hotel Sinclair and found a folded note, scrawled in the large, nearly arthritic script of Mrs. Beasley, in her mailbox: *You have a visitor.*

aith crumpled the note in her right hand. It could only be Tippis, coming to have his mind set at ease. She set her jaw, cursed him under her breath, and started climbing the stairs to the fourth floor, prepared to settle the issue as the Swamp Woman had for the Widow Thomas ten years ago. As it was told, the Widow Thomas's husband died of drink, leaving her penniless and with enough unpaid bills to wallpaper her privy house. She traveled to the Swamp Woman's shanty and offered the werewitch all her possessions—cheap jewelry, a spinning loom, small change, and two emaciated he-cats too sick to bristle if you yanked their tails—all in exchange for peace of mind.

"Gimme your mind," the Swamp Woman said. They say she was sitting outside the shanty, mending the bridge over the bogs with nails made from human bones.

The Widow Thomas was startled. "How?"

The Swamp Woman drove in a nail with her bare, black fist, laughed, and said, "Hand it over, and I'll do what I kin for it." She cackled as evilly as a fiend in a cloud. "If ya can't find it, then there ain't no problem, *is* there? Hee hee!"

But Tippis, Faith knew, was not so easily set at ease. She was certain he would lose his mind. Originally, he had told her he was a dentist, and this she believed. But thereafter he appeared at her door in a burgundy porter's uniform, and the following week in a double-breasted suit, a brief case filled with insurance forms at his side. After that he came peddling medical dictionaries. Of course, he explained: his license to practice dentistry was revoked for malpractice—taking advantage of an etherized girl spread out in his leather chair; his next job was as a porter, but he lost it for repeated insubordination. Yet still he tried, straining to situate himself in a world that resisted him at every turn. She remembered his coming to her with an armful of evening newspapers all opened to the want ads; he would cringe at every ad for a musician to play in a local band, throw up his hands finally, and groan, "Nobody wants me—they want accountants, salesmen, movie ushers, and male nurses, but not *me*!" His confessions were unbearable, and Faith told him on numerous occasions to show more strength, to resist the changes outside himself. She'd pleaded with him, told him every fine and noble tale she knew, because his problem, in part, was undeniably her own. That she was new and different each day was indisputable. It would be fitting to reintroduce herself to herself each morning when she stood before her mirror, saying, "Who am I today?" But Tippis's changes were never from within, only catalyzed from without. Seeing him suffer so saddened her, because there was no end to his transformations, to his plastic personality first servile and groveling as a porter's, then jocular and rapacious as a salesman's. Who was he forced to be this time? Suppose he'd become a mortician's assistant?

By the time Faith reached room 4-D she had worked up enough anger to shoot him. Mercy killing. She imagined buying a Saturday night special, raising it instantly at his head without aim, shooting— crack! crack!—and Tippis would be released. It was not morbidity that brought this on but the weariness she felt, acute now after her scaling of three flights of steps. Her joints felt as stiff as steel. She threw open the door to her room and stifled a scream. Sitting cross-legged on her bed, paring his ragged toenails with a tiny penknife and reading from a book, was a little man in a mauve-colored overcoat. Red-eyes. He, startled too, scrambled to his feet and dropped the knife.

"Get out of here!"—Faith. She bolted back into the dark hallway, confused. Thinking: Surely it was too late to recover her money. He'd probably spent every penny, and in a single night at that, on liquor. But she could awaken everyone, call the police, file a charge. . . .

"I've found you!" Red-eyes roared. He shuffled clumsily in his single shoe toward the door, sweating like a horse, and leaned in the doorjamb. He cried in a reedy voice, "I've looked and looked and—"

Spinning around, Faith pulled at the doorknob. She caught his right thumb between door and jamb. Red-eyes screamed. She pulled. "*Mercy!*"

She pulled.

His bulbous thumb grew red. She heard something cracking like soft bone, or brittle wood, and pulled harder. Inside the room Red-eyes moaned.

"I hate you!" Faith shouted through the door. And, children, she *meant* it. Watching that twisted thumb swell was almost as satisfying as the sight of slavemasters burning in the inner circles of West Hell. She remembered vividly its rough and salty taste running along her gums—the texture of his skin, like coffee grounds; she thought of her miseries incurred since that first night in the city. And pulled.

Behind the door his broken voice warbled in choking, plaintive, pitiful cries. "*Mercy*, child . . . !" Blood spurted from beneath his fingernail. He moaned like an old woman at a wake. "You must hear me—ou-*open the door!*"

"Bullshit!" Faith shouted. She liked the sound of it; it made her feel evil, rebellious, because Big Todd had allowed no swearing in his house. It was a delicious word, and she sang it above his cries for "*Mercy!*" canceling them, because in all her months in Chicago she had seen no mercy, no love, no peace, no possibility of release. "Bull*shit!*" It made her feel good.

"*Please!*"

Shivers ran along Faith's skin. The moment of Justice was sour, stinking in her nose now with the loud smell of blood, of empty rebellion. Her stomach clenched, her head spun, and she could only hold the door shut by leaning backward on her heels. She heard choking behind it, which chilled her. It was like some hidden, supernatural agony on the other side of the world—unseen behind this wooden barrier, and hence not wholly real. The grief of ghosts. Only the bright, distended thumb disclosed his unseen suffering. Revenge was not worth this. Faith, sickened, released the door and stepped aside. Slowly it swung open, framing a frightened little man rocking back and forth on his knees. He held his thumb vertically, squeezing it, his nearly toothless mouth open. She guessed he was in shock of some sort, staring black-eyed and simpering in a long, low wail. Like wind outside a cabin window, his breath whistled through his teeth.

"Listen—" he broke off suddenly, hunkered on his haunches for a while, leaped to his feet, and flounced around the room, his watery eyes pinched together, his mouth hanging open like a stove lid. Faith forgot her thoughts of vengeance. She hurried to the sink, ran cold water to its brim, and said testily, "Stick your finger in here."

Red eyes—turbid eyes anxious to communicate—opened. They seemed to bless her, to say the thousand silent things expressed by dogs and cats and cows when you treat them nicely. He plunged his hand into the water, winced—"Ah-*ahhhh!*"—and watched the water suffuse with blood as bright as the Red Sea.

Begrudgingly, Faith said, "I'm sorry," and stood quietly beside him, at least two heads taller than he, and studying his reflection in the mirror: a wasted, pock-marked face laced with day-old dirt and holes like craters in the moon; a flask-shaped body, obconical nose, and, on his right cheek, a rectangular red patch that must have been a birthmark or a burn. It appeared that he still wore the same mephitic clothes she remembered from their first encounter. He smelled as if this were indeed the case. He was, in no small measure, dissipated, probably dying from internal disorders of a terminal kind that wracked his withered form the day long. He was, in truth, so apparently beaten that he was beautiful. Like the grizzled, gimped old men she remembered in Georgia: bent of back, ill beyond succor, their dun-colored clothing shiny with dirt, their ashen eyes discolored and incapable of the visions of youth. They were not so much revolting as revelatory, not so much broken as bending, in a kind of grace, to the fate of all flesh. . . .

"I've looked for you," he cried, sucking in his breath, "looked and looked and looked—"

Faith took his wrist and lifted his right hand from the red water. No bones seemed broken. She glanced at the door, saw splintered shards of wood, and, for some reason, was relieved. Only his black thumbnail was shattered, and hung obliquely from his thumb. There was much blood, but no irremediable damage that she could see. She tore a strip from her bedsheet, wrapped it tightly around his thumb, and pointed with finality toward the door. "Now, get out." She knew she was too tired to struggle with him, and hoped he would leave.

Red-eyes shivered, sneezed, then coughed up clear phlegm with such violence that Faith grabbed his shoulders so he would not fall. She felt his forehead. It was burning. His arms—livid. She led him to her bed where she sat him down—spiteful that he occupied the space she needed there. He tugged his ragged shirttail from his trousers. Blew his nose. Hoo-*oonk!* And dried his eyes.

Faith put her hands on her hips and arched her back, trying to stretch the stiffness out of her spine. "Are you all right?" she said.

"I am not such a fool as I look," he said. He peered around her room and curled back his tawny lips. "Much like van Gogh's wretched little room, isn't it?" She didn't appreciate that. It was true that the room was too much like a prison to be comfortable. She didn't want to think about it and, instead, half closed her eyes, squeezing the sore muscles of her right arm. Red-eyes sighed. "But here we are—Comte's Woman and Priest." He looked at his swollen thumb curiously, as though it were affixed to a stranger's hand, then hid it in his lap. With his free hand he reached into the large pockets of his coat, prattling, "I suppose I should say something about Universal Religion, but I'm not up to it." He began producing from his pocket, one by one, articles which he laid on her bed.

"This is yours"—a wad of bills wound with a dirty string.

"Ugh! Not *this!*"—lint.

"But—yes!—this"—a cigarette lighter.

"And this"—a silver key.

He stood up, retrieved his book from the floor, and handed it to her. "And this. The little key will open it."

Faith weighed the book in her hands. A small leather strap stretched across its dog-eared edges. It was lightweight, covered with black binding, and bore a name in cerise letters on the cover: Dr. Richard M. Barrett.

"That," Barrett said beside her as he removed the bandage and sucked at his swollen thumb, "is all I own. You're in need, so it's yours. I can tell these things—it's a nimbus around you, child. I'd give you more—ah! life itself if I could—but my *Doomsday Book* is the best of my possessions."

"What?" Faith gripped the book. She fumbled at its rusty lock with her key. Barrett placed his piebald hand over it and shook his head. "Don't open it just yet. The Tree of Knowledge is not, I'm afraid, the Tree of Life." He smiled broadly, and blew his nose into his hand: Whee-*oonk!* Then wiped his hand on the front of his shirt and said, "It's the final vintage of a life devoted to incessant inquiry, the sum total of every truth I have come to know and believe. Haven't you always wanted to see such a book?"

"Yes," Faith said. And though she knew her curiosity dated only from the time of Big Todd's death, she said, "All my life."

"Well, that's precisely why I wrote it—supply and demand; but there's only one copy," Barrett said, scratching his upper lip thoughtfully, "so be careful." His pupils struggled behind cream-colored cataracts to focus on Faith. "What is your name, child?"

"Faith."

Barrett smiled; his cheeks were round and puffy. "*Und Wunderbarist der Glaubens liebstes Kind, eh?*"

"Huhn?"

"Never mind." From a pocket inside his coat Barrett withdrew a half-finished fifth of Scotch and two very used and wrinkled paper cups. He filled both, and thrust one at Faith. As she drank, he soaked, in his Scotch, his sanguine thumb.

"Why are you doing all this for me?" Faith asked. "If you think I'm going to forgive you, you're wrong!" Her anger and outrage were building again. "I wouldn't be in this mess if it wasn't for you!"

Barrett wet his cracked lips, fingered a wide fold under his chin, and said in a thin voice, "You'll have to explain. My memory—it fades, you see. . . ."

For once Faith felt like confessing, like opening herself completely and unraveling her entire odyssey on the bed beside Barrett. She was almost out of stories, and it seemed that truth and beauty and the Good Thing were only there—in fabulous fictions and austral tales told in a mystery-freighted voice. Is that why people told stories? Was it because beauty and order could exist only in the fairy tale, in a painting, or sometimes in well-told lies? She remembered Big Todd telling lies so often it became unclear what was and was not true. She thought of the one about Lucille, Hatten County's only street-walker. Old, inured to being always for others, she had, according to Todd, been untouched by her condition. Example: one evening Lucille opened the door to her room above the town saloon and found, wrapped in a beige tablecloth, an abandoned baby girl. "Right," Lucille said, and without another thought she took the child in, clothed and fed her, and reared her for an entire year. The child's mother finally appeared, guilty and bereaved, and demanded her daughter. "Right," Lucille said; and in the same tone she said "Right" when drought ruined the county's cane and cotton crops, "Right" when the weather was good, "Right" to everything; for somehow, Todd said, Lucille knew the secret. She was the secret, and the secret, he said, had everything to do with ease—with the way water effortlessly wore away boulders, temples, and thrones. Like the way Big Todd boasted he could beat any man in Georgia, in the world, with what he called his perfect defense. Faith and everyone else thought he was lying. But when Ed Riley, the black-smith, put Todd to the test, he made good his claim. Riley climbed to the top of the courthouse—the tallest building in town, three stories high—and told Todd to block, if he dared, the anvil he dragged to the roof with him. Big Todd stood bare-chested on the ground below, fingering his mustache. The crowd took bets that his head would be crushed as flat as a dime. Lavidia, sitting in their wagon with a blue umbrella to shield her from the sun, squawked, "Go 'head, kill y'self, ya damned fool! Go 'head, make me a widow," and then began to cry. The odds were one hundred to one against Todd's walking away from there alive. And only Faith had come to believe he could block that anvil. Riley, his black muscles bulging, dropped the anvil from the roof. Faith saw it hang momentarily, a black bolt in the beryline sky, then plummet like a dead bird. Todd stood still. Its shadow fell across him. The crowd cried, "*Eeeeee!*" and Lavidia hid her eyes.

Big Todd stepped aside.

It had everything to do with ease. Faith started. Barrett, with his forefinger, was wiping a tear from her cheek.

"Tell me," he said.

"People fail when they start looking for the Good Thing," she said.

Barrett nodded and clucked his tongue. "*Es irrt der Mensch, solang er strebt.*"

Faith paid him no mind. Once started, it bubbled from her, became a deluge. "There isn't any Good Thing! There never was! It's all an evil lie to keep us happy! There's nothing!" She shook her head and felt very old. "*Nothing!*"

Barrett, before she could finish, was on his feet, his hands behind his back and pacing to and fro with heavy footfalls from wall to wall. His progress reminded her of the way he-bears move, swaying with their arms swinging at their sides, their feet shuffling. Uncertainly, to and fro. By the open door he stopped, looked out to see if they were being overheard, then whispered, "'Herein you have, my daughter, raised the grand problem of man's existence, which is'—Comte to the contrary—whether everything that is actual must, like the sound of the tree that falls in an uninhabited forest, be perceived or thought to be!"

Faith's mouth hung open so wide a bird could have flown down her throat. Barrett noticed this. "Let me put it another way. What is the relation between thought and being? Does what you think direct what *is*, or is it that what *is* controls what you *think*?" He tugged at his lower lip, looking at his sore thumb all the while, and wheezed. "If you chose the first way, you become a magician—like Nostradamus; if the second way—a metal ball on an inclined plane. An *automaton*!"

Tippis's face flashed before Faith's eyes. She blinked to dismiss it, raised her cup, and grimaced. It was empty. She grabbed her coat, a cheap article of wet-look leather she'd purchased in a thrift shop, and said, "I'm thirsty. Let's go out."

"The book," Barrett mumbled. "Where is it?"

Faith stuck it beneath her arm and started out into the hallway, Barrett at her heels. His voice echoed in the lobby and out into the street.

"Let me tell you a story," he said. His hands were thrust deep into his pockets, his head was pulled in, and he peeked over his turned-up collar, his eyes darting from her face to the shattered cement of the sidewalk. "When I was a boy, long before your time, in

Pennsylvania, there was no doubt in my mind that there had to be a greater good than any man could conceive. Why? Because that greatest good would *have* to be because part of being good is being actual, right?"

"I guess," Faith said, but she wasn't sure.

"And I nurtured that tenuous belief all my life, child. Everything paled beside it. I could be enjoying myself immensely—I could be drunk—literally—with joy, or in the middle of sex, but suddenly I'd become conscious of myself. I'd sober up immediately, or lose my erection, and something in my head would say, 'Is this *really* the greatest good?' And once you've asked *that*, you've ruined it. You've destroyed that particular joy with questioning." Barrett stopped to look at his thumb; he frowned and shoved it back into his pocket. "Years later, after I'd experimented with everything under the sun, settled down, married, and began teaching at Princeton, the questions still persisted: is *this* it? And always it was—No. My colleagues pooh-poohed the entire idea. They were good fellows, I suppose, but like my parents, schoolmates—even my wife and children—they were unable to understand my desire, my need for this thing. One even asked me, 'Dick, suppose I imagine the most beautiful, the most perfect woman in the world—does that mean she has to be?'" Barrett snorted and rubbed his nose. "*Petitio principii!* They didn't understand. . . ."

Faith discovered she was growing fond of him. The man beside her and the one who stole her money seemed entirely different. In fact, he seemed different from most people, like the Swamp Woman, like Big Todd. "What did you do?" she said.

Barrett blinked and rubbed his eyes as he and Faith stood under a streetlight. His hesitations bothered her for an instant—they were either from failing memory, or the respite needed to think up some good lie. "I investigated the problem," he said. "I wrote books and articles about it until that approach ran dry. That is, until the quality of my research became suspect. Which was a sham! They simply wanted to get rid of me." He glared at Faith as though she had been responsible. "Any imbecile knows that all scholarship begins, like science, in passion, in the lust for certainty, virtue, what have you. Anyway, I tried a last-ditch effort; I tried to build a following among my students. It didn't work—I was fired." His eyes lit up with anger, then watered. "Can you imagine what happened? A logical positivist took my place!" Faith could see that the affront hurt him still. He gazed far away, beyond her, in grief. "My wife left me, of course, when my salary was gone—ah, but I pressed on, Faith. Yes, and I press on still. . . ."

"Yes?" Faith said excitedly. "And—"

"And," Barrett said sadly, turning to her, "here I am today—old, sick (these aren't spare tires bulging my midriff, child: they're tumors), yet not quite as foolish, I remind you, as I look."

Faith, disappointed, started across the empty street toward the entrance of a tavern. "So the story isn't over?"

"Is it ever over?" Barrett sighed. "People are somewhat like novels (don't make *too* much of that simile)—we operate on beginnings, middles, and ends; subjective aims deposited in ongoing history to be prehended by other subjective aims. When you reach the end of one road, say, as a professor, you begin another." Barrett smiled to himself as they entered the dark tavern. "I fancy myself to be a didactic poem now, and you, Faith?"

"Pornography," she said. "I'll buy you a drink."

Barrett's mouth, as they waited on their drinks, sagged in silence, as if pins in his jaws had been removed. After two sips of his drink he was again animated. "We're co-workers, child—I knew that from the moment I saw you tonight. You and I are after, I sense, the same thing. Yet my age gives me the upper hand. I've been through more and, perhaps, can spare you a few unnecessary and unfortunate pitfalls."

Faith tried to concentrate on what he said, but found herself nodding from lack of sleep. Her mind couldn't seem to get hold of what he meant.

"We all need a guiding principle—we *must* have one, or our world falls apart. But the catch is that when we start seeking that principle it must first, in every instance, be wholly removed from us and exist in some absolute, unsullied, perfect form. Yes, I *know* the principle originates in us—*yes!*—but it's better to say it's realized through us. But to be what we desire, that principle must seem completely other, greater than we are—something tangible, a thing of some sort like wood from the Cross at Calvary, or the grail, or a shred of the Saviour's robe." Barrett sipped at his drink, dipped his thumb therein, and sighed. "I'm trying to say something important—"

"You left off with the Saviour's robe," Faith said, surprised at her own attentiveness.

"Ah—yes!" Barrett wagged his head, getting back into the swing of it all. "But that has problems. *If* it's a thing we're after, and *if* that thing is absolute goodness and perfection, then we'll never have it. It'll escape us at every turn—that is, until we bring it a little closer to us. . . ."

Something went tight in Faith's stomach. She cautiously said, "How?"

Barrett gestured, dribbling alcohol down his pointed chin. "Historically, men could turn to good works to find the realization of that principle; in your case that might be difficult, but I suspect that even as constricted by circumstances as you are, you can do a little good in this world."

Faith tuned Barrett out, studying him from the great distance of objectivity, the way one reads a novel about philosophical ideas, with haste and indifference. She decided he was dead wrong. She knew what she needed and could see it in the possible, pleasing image of a younger man, someone who would wait on her as she now waited on others, a man who would save her from the sick, tossed thing she saw each day in the mirror above her sink: Faith Cross. "Let's go," she said, weary of words. Her patience was at its end, and her mind made up. One had to survive; only that was certain.

"This Good Thing of yours," Barrett muttered as he slouched along beside her, "it *is* a reality like so many things on the horizon of faith *and* reason, but it's certainly not a . . . *thing*."

"Then what is it?" she said dreamily as they strolled downtown. But she knew the answer, could see it: a comfortable home, clothes, a car, and a big-hearted husband to do her bidding.

"Ha!" Barrett laughed. He spread his arms. "This is precisely what you and I will discover, Faith. It's *the* human adventure, this quest for the Good Thing. But you must believe; it'll never appear otherwise." Barrett broke off, noticing, not two blocks away, a park bench beside Soldier's Field. He led Faith to it, coughing horribly, sat her at one end, and stretched out, his hands behind his head.

"As co-workers," he said, "we're questers for that which in all ages was the one thing denied man: absolute certainty." He leaned back his head, looking upside down at her, smiling, then taking in the dark stretch of blue sky above. "That makes us fools. My wife, Amelia, always called me that, because this thing possessed me so, but I'd always come back with, 'Yes, dear heart, but a Great Fool.'" Barrett sighed deeply, scratching his neck. "There's a big difference. Amelia never understood that. She was a beautiful woman, such *haecceitas* you've never seen, but she was never tortured by beauty— she never looked at a rose and, by dint of reason, went beyond it to yearn for roseness. You see, the entire world was allegory for me— ah, I *was* a strange child! It always pointed beyond, or perhaps below, itself to something more good, more real and glorious than what I could see. Uncovering this meaning—*that* to me was philosophy. Not only philosophy, Faith, but life's work itself—exegesis of the rose, of the world." Barrett coughed; he nearly strangled, then looked at the thin light of dawn, smiling mysteriously. "My son is an electrical engineer in Vermont. Bright boy, Jimmy. My daughter, Lillian, is a fashion model in New York City. Can you imagine a father's woe at having children who rebelled against my vision, who thought I was senile and, in cahoots with Amelia, tried to have me committed to a home? *Faugh!* I ran away. That was eight years ago, on my sixtieth birthday, and I've been growing younger ever since. . . ."

Faith, alert now and rapt, rested on the hard bench beside Barrett, surfeited with the stillness of a morning so blue that sky and water on the lake were merged without the slightest suture. The sky-scrapers were the color of deep-sea pearls, as were the clouds, an armada passing overhead. She longed to look upon them forever, to fix them in her mind, to hold on to *some*thing, because she lacked so much. Lacked the rose, let alone roseness. She looked at Barrett as he clutched his *Doomsday Book* to his chest, and saw him as a projection of what she would be if she continued to search: moral wreckage. But he was sweet. To search with him—would it be so bad?

"Co-workers," she whispered to herself. Faith laid her hand on Barrett's head, felt movement on his scaly scalp, and lifted—with her fingertips—a flea from his hair. He was unkempt, oblivious to the external world that seemed to wreak such woe on her and Tippis. He was unsightly, had breath like that of a dying dragon, and probably needed to be in a cancer ward. Yet what he said deeply impressed her.

"Will you look with me?" she asked. She heard Barrett's stomach rumble. It sounded like a sewer.

He coughed in a terrible way and said, *"Und zwar von Herzen . . ."*

"Does that mean yes?"

Barrett seemed sleepy; he closed his eyes and smiled from ear to ear. Faith understood—Jimmy and Lillian Barrett had hurt him sorely; she would replace them. Faith removed her coat and spread it across his shoulders. Then she slipped the book from beneath his hands and opened it with the key. She was not surprised. In the thin, irenic rays of morning, as she listened to Barrett's throat rattling under the chirping of pigeons in the trees above, Faith saw that each of the hundred pages of the black-bound, dog-eared *Doomsday Book* was, from top to bottom, blank, as empty as she imagined the world to be, and by virtue of this a sort of screen onto which her thoughts spread out like an oil slick on the surface of the sea. She smiled to herself and stared at the pages as though they actually held words, images. They did, but only as long as she conjured them there. On the first page she saw her father crossing the dung-brown fields behind his farmhouse, fields splattered with rivulets and pools by late summer rain—weather vanes, silos, hound dogs lying on their sides in the shade of a tree, tiny hay bins and barns filled with ensilage were in the distance against a sky that looked like water— broad, blue, its clouds rolling like great, feathery waves. Then, because she willed it, she saw Lavidia splitting thick logs from the woodpile by the toolshed, singing some old, warm hymn and making up new verses while blackbirds flew as tiny specks in formation above her head with a sound like clothes flapping on a line, then came to rest on the ground nearby, searching the woodpile and yard for scraps of bread and meat. She saw Alpha Omega Holmes waving to her from a wind-ruffled cane field, walking in a drying wind through its golden, swaying stalks to sweet-gum trees where she, still a child dressed in blue, waited. As long as she looked and flipped the stiff pages of the book, she could see the farmhouse with

clouds of gray smoke curling from its chimney in the dead of win-
tertime, then the lilting sewing bees and barnyard suppers in the
spring, goats nibbling turnips, the picnics in Indian summer by the
quiet ponds near the woods—the particular magic and music of a
world to which she might never return, but loved all the more
because it was unattainable.

Faith closed the book. She touched Barrett's arm, for he had given
her this. And this: a thought she almost believed—that beauty, truth,
and goodness could be born in shipwrecked lives, that flowers might
yet bloom on a dead man's grave. Once livid, his arm was cool.
Cooler than the blue morning itself. She knew this sleep well, had
seen it take Big Todd, then Lavidia from her as it had now taken
Barrett, releasing him as if the green hand of death were stayed only
until that moment when a life devastated by suffering had produced
its *Doomsday Book* and given it to another, until it had scaled
Mount Kilimanjaro or fallen exhausted, clutching the elusive Good
Thing.

Faith quickly lifted her coat from him and walked to a telephone
booth at the corner. She counted the money Barrett had given her.
Two hundred dollars. Then she searched her pockets for a dime, and
called the police.

Trying to control her voice was hard, but she managed when
someone on the other end answered in a gruff voice, "Yes?"

"I'm at Soldier's Field," she said. "A man just died on the park
bench—"

"Dead!" the voice roared.

"Yes," Faith said, her hand moving to replace the phone on its
hook. "But he's not such a fool as he seems. . . ."

he grave released Richard Barrett.

Children, the crypt couldn't contain his spirit any more than death could end his concern for Sweet Faith Cross. Dutifully, he returned as a wraith, companion, and troubled conscience that would not let her rest. Without fail each Friday and always at midnight he came to her hotel, the stench of Hell's outer circle heavy in his train. Such resurrections happen nearly every day. Esau Holmes, covered with mold and maggots, scrambled out of the cemetery back in '26 to attend his daughter's wedding, and everybody's heard of how old Annie Bell Finch reared up in her casket when her husband Fred arrived at her wake with that fast young gal from Georgia. Listen, if you die before achieving some long-cherished goal, or before seeing some sight long nurtured in your dreams; if you die before seeing the sun rise red as Satan's eye over the sea, or before hearing the cry of swallows break the stillness of dawn, or before feeling dew from some enameled expanse of country between your toes, then nature in you, too, will not be stilled at death.

Barrett came back.

The first Friday it happened, Faith had just finished with her final customer, and sat at her table for a spell, mulling over her life's meaning as she twisted her hair into tight braids, smeared on facial packs the color of thick bottom land clay, and rubbed the ash off her ankles and legs with mineral oil. Her fingers wound her hair mechanically around into tiny curls while she thought, first of Barrett, then of his *Doomsday Book*, which sat beneath a Gideon Bible on her desk. Then she clicked off the ceiling light, her head burning with the tight braids, and went to bed. By and by she smelled the scent of brimstone, of old clothes scented with moisture and earth.

Then: the feathery tickle of ashes in the air. She sneezed, panic bubbling in her chest. Off in the room's northeast corner she saw a snow-white cat sidle slowly from one wall to the next. It said, "I can't do *any*thing a'tall until Richard comes," and passed through her locked door like a spirit.

A much larger cat, the size of a suckling calf, appeared at the same wall, walked the same way, and said, "I can't do *any*thing a'tall until Richard comes."

Beads of sweat burst upon Faith's brow. Faraway she heard, or thought she heard, the rustling of graveclothes and the scraping of bare feet along the floor above the hammering of her heart. Faith lay still as a board.

In the same corner a third cat, this one the size of a pony, appeared; it swayed slowly across the room, looking at her through large, luminous, laughing eyes.

"I can't do *any*thing a'tall until Richard comes." But before disappearing, it said, "But I think he's here now."

She felt it. Her stomach clenched like a fist around his name. On the other side of her bed, Faith became aware of a form creeping in beside her—she heard the bedsprings groan, felt them settle under a great weight.

"Oh, God—" Her voice shook. She prayed, then glanced to the pillow beside her. It held the indentation of a head. But no head was there, none at all. Floating free in the air were Barrett's features, just inches above the pillow: turbid, hazel eyes, a toothless smile and crooked nose. She was across the room—uncertain how she'd moved so fast—her braids unraveling in the sweat from her scalp, and her limbs shaking like a leaf. How had it happened? Spirits could not return unless their hosts had committed suicide, or were conjured at their gravesites by wereworkers who, in the new of the ☽ , and in the hours of the ♃ and ☉ , said to one of the inhabiter signs of the ♋ , ♐ , or ♓ , the following:

> I conjure thee [deceased's name] by the bloud that ranne from
> our Lord Jesus Christ crucified, and by the cleaving of heaven,
> and by the renting of the temple's veil, and by the darkness of
> the sunne in the time of his death, and by the rising up of the

dead in the time of his resurrection, and by the virgine Marie mother of our Lord Jesus Christ, and by the mysterious name of God: Tetragrammaton. I conjure thee and charge thee my will be fulfilled, upon paine of everlasting condemnation: Fiat, fiat, fiat: Amen.

(All of which must be uttered in utmost piety, none of which sweet Faith remembered). But somehow she recollected the way to exorcise haints:

"What," she cried, "in the name of the Lord, do you want with me?"

The ghastly grin widened but did not disappear.

"*Please* . . . !"

That mouth, that disembodied, grisly grimace in the dark—spoke. "I . . . *still* think . . . therefore . . . I am. . . ."

Faith clicked on the light. He was gone. But four days passed before she stopped shaking or took food. She avoided the hotel on Fridays, wandering instead through the crowded city streets until Saturday morning. But Barrett was always close by—a will-o'-the-wisp glimpsed furtively or felt intuitively in the alarm at the base of her neck before he disappeared. She changed addresses, hoping to escape him. Faith gave Mrs. Beasley twenty-four hours' notice on Wednesday, and was out of the hotel with six hours to spare. With the money Barrett had given her she moved into the low-rent Eden Green apartments on One Hundred Thirtieth Street.

Children, there's nothing worse than being haunted by a philosopher's spirit—waking up in the middle of the night with your heart heaving heavy strokes to hear, next to your ear, something muttering, "You may well be free of Barrett, but not Barrett*eity*," or worse, "Riddle me this, if you're so smart: Will an arrow ever strike its intended target if, before it can cross that distance, one-half of that distance must be crossed first, and one-half of *that*, and one-half of *that*, and one-half of *that*—"

Faith feared for her sanity. For months this went on, even after she'd settled in Eden Green, cut back her streetwalking to supply only what she needed to balance her budget, and enrolled in secretarial school. Even this day Barrett shadowed her as she sat across a breakfast table from a clean-shaven, fresh-smelling young man named Isaac Maxwell, her eyes searching the room for the wise man's haint.

"Everybody wants power," Maxwell said in a brassy voice trained, he told her, in a six-week course in public speaking. In his left hand he held the op-ed page of a morning paper, *his* paper, *The Sentry*, above his plate of cooling ham, eggs, and hash browns. "But few people understand what real power is," he said, softer now, waving his fork and watching her closely. "It's directly connected with ethics, with what's good, y'know. And what's good is what makes a man feel more powerful." He was chuckling, his eyes crafty and his shoulders hunched. Some folks might say that Isaac Maxwell looked a bit queer, as though, at birth, he'd been unable to make up his mind about what he wanted to be. There was a little goat in his long head, the look of a cow in his moist eyes and, in his slight figure, you could see the outline of, perhaps, an upright wolf. His chin was weak and peppered with shaving scars, slightly blue at the edges. He lingered over his breakfast, scratching sleep from his eyes, the wings of his nose widening whenever he spoke. The color of his skin, it seemed to Faith, was yellow and had the same chroma as the yolk of his eggs—like urine from enflamed kidneys. Though he was only twenty-four he was balding, which explained his wig and why he tugged at its corners whenever it slipped back on his head, loose like a yarmulka. When this happened Faith looked away. This time she lowered her eyes to concentrate on his editorial, "The Contest of Wills."

"All that garbage about black and white and gay power misses the mark," Maxwell said. He paused, his attention remaining on his reflection just behind Faith in the broad glass of the restaurant window. There he saw his bright orange suitcoat and blue butterfly bowtie, and carefully lifted flecks of lint off his shoulders. "Faith," he said, still looking over her shoulder, "everybody's out for Number One—*Nu-u-u-mero Uno*, and anybody who tells you different is a goddamn liar. It makes sense, doesn't it? Society's composed of individuals, and every one of 'em's got an individual will. Society *thrives* on the clash of those wills." Faith listened from the back of her head, her chin on the heel of her right hand and a cigarette between her fingers. Maxwell's eyes flashed for an instant. "Please," he said sharply, "my asthma . . ." She doused the cigarette, hid it in her purse, apologized, and tried to concentrate on his editorial. Which wasn't easy. The elastic in her underwear cut into her abdomen. She was eating better these days at Maxwell's expense and it was showing. She shifted forward in her seat, tugged at the fold of her slip, and attended to him. He said, "Power"—still studying his profile in the glass—"is what it's all about." He wagged his fork at her. "But *every*body won't get it." She looked up as if to say, no? "Some people are naturally weak and, to tell it like it is, deserve to be flunkies, others—like myself—are strong," he tapped his chest with the stem of his fork, "way down deep, I mean. The weak ones go out to demonstrate, march, boycott, strike and picket—they try to change the world, you understand? The point is to use it." He shook his head, his free hand pressed to his forehead to hold down his wig. "Those people will never know what *real* power is. You know what it is? You know what's really good?"

Faith bent forward a bit farther, pushing her tight slip lower down her back; that helped, but the movement gave Maxwell the impression she was straining to hear what he said.

"It's cash," he announced, "cash money." Then he slapped the checkered tablecloth with his palm. "Why, you can be as ugly as a witch, you can be evil and selfish and wicked, but cash money can make you beautiful, right?" He saw her face freeze up and softened his voice. "If you haven't got talent, you can buy folks who do— whatever you want, whatever your Will points to is yours. That's what I said in there," and he tapped the back of the newspaper in her hand.

Faith said, "I see," but she didn't. She had changed in many ways, but not so much that she was comfortable with his ideas. In fact, she wouldn't have recognized herself if she'd seen herself months ago in the glowing waters of the Swamp Woman's Thaumaturgic Mirror. She would have seen, not a girl married to God in her childhood, or the terrified ethical adventurer who tarried an evening in the Hatten County bogs, but a woman with long artificial eyelashes, light rose lipstick, and crescent-shaped earrings; she would have seen pink nail polish on her long fingers, a turtled sleeveless bodice, navy shirt and jacket, and brown pumps. You wouldn't know her. Maybe it was her make-up, her mascara, flesh-toned powders, perfumes that recalled the essence of exotic flowers, and waist-long falls that fooled you. You might have seen her legs, or noticed the brevity of her tailormade dresses and coats, as Maxwell had a month ago when he saw her in this restaurant on Washington Street and invited himself over to her table. At that time he was new on his job as an assistant editor for *The Sentry*, and new to Chicago, hailing as he did from Columbus, Ohio. He found his new job of editing, rewriting, and sitting through morning news conferences quite a cross to bear. He needed someone to complain to. And like magic there appeared Faith. Once a week he'd find her at the same restaurant, at the same table by the window, looking woebegone as she sipped orange juice and studied her secretarial manual. But seeing her once weekly was not enough. She'd listen to *any*thing you said (he was amazed), she very rarely contradicted you (he found the sense of power unbearable), and she even agreed with you, but not before you'd finished what you were saying. It was too much. He took her to dinner thereafter on Sundays and now, since she didn't have a job, paid her rent at Eden Green. Strange to say, whenever he left her it was hard to remember anything about their conversations but the sound of his own brassy voice.

Faith finished the editorial, handed Maxwell his newspaper, and stuck a Viceroy in her cigarette holder. This time he didn't complain, only said, "Smoking testifies to the weakness of your will," and lit it for her. She would have agreed with him immediately but saw, floating over the heads of the other diners at the rear of the room, a whiff of blue smoke. Tensing, she turned to Maxwell, who had seen her reaction.

"Did I say something wrong?"

"No," she said quickly. "Go on. I think you're right about all those things."

Maxwell broke into a broad grin. "You do?" And he blushed up to his ears. When he spoke again there was confidence in his voice. "Take the death of that professor a while back. The man just lay down on a park bench and gave up the ghost—no Will, no taste for conflict. You remember, don't you?"

Faith cringed—recovered, and smiled. "No."

Maxwell broke the delicate film over his sunny-side-up eggs with his fork before filling his mouth. He chewed largely with his eyes narrowed and mouth open. Her focus drew in from the room that framed his pear-shaped head to his face and concentrated on his cheeks, which fascinated her. Pack rats had cheeks like these, as big as overstuffed luggage when full. Maxwell shoveled in eggs and neatly cut squares of ham, slices of toast, and hash browns mechanically like an engine taking in fuel; then he began to bite and chew with a certain rhythm, the distended sides of his face decreasing in size like balloons releasing air. At the end of each mouthful he wiped his lips (yellow egg yolk still caked in his mustache and that area of the anatomy just beneath the nose, which Lavidia always called a man's "snot-cup") and gulped so loudly it hurt Faith's esophagus. She wondered how he managed to taste anything he ate since he ate so fast. . . . But her focus slipped back out again, fixing on the background behind Maxwell and the blue wisp of smoke across the room. It drifted toward them, ghostly, like mist over the fields each morning in Georgia, or gas, and she thought: Damn! Could only she see it? It figured.

"He deserved to die," Maxwell said between mouthfuls. "I wrote the story on the old man, dug up the information on him and all that. He had everything going for him at one time, you know?— good job as a professor, published some books, but he just left all that behind. For two years nobody saw hide nor hair of that man." He snorted. "That kind of foolishness makes me mad—I mean, somebody who's on top of things and just throws it all away! Maybe," Maxwell chuckled, "he lost his mind."

Faith laughed politely. All pretense. She'd learned some time ago that if she laughed heartily with her eyes shut tight and her mouth open in a toothy grin for precisely seven seconds, not an instant more or less, she could easily slip away from the attempts at humor forced upon her usually humorless state of mind. It took a lot of training to perfect that smile, it took hours of standing in front of a mirror, timing herself, then testing the reaction on all the customers that she knew at the hotel. And it paid off. People warmed to Faith's laughter immediately. For a second she thought about Alpha Omega Holmes. Had his smile been deceit? It was tricky but she thought it through: there was what you saw—appearance, and there was what was truly real—the Good Thing; but you couldn't have the latter. So you learned to control appearances, to construct elaborate, well-timed pretenses and lies to get what you needed to survive. Faith clicked off the seconds to the beat of her pulse and looked up at Maxwell.

"I figure I can make fifty thousand a year if my Will Power's strong enough," Maxwell said. "I mean, the publisher of *The Sentry* doesn't have anything *I* don't have, except that he's white. I watch him a lot, y'know? He comes in that front door every morning and slams it behind him. Wakes everybody up, y'know? When he slams that door the noise says 'Here I am!' and everybody snaps up straight at their desks. That's how you get respect—by slamming doors like Ragsdale does, or by letting everybody know who's in control around there." Maxwell reached for Faith's cigarettes and took one. He took one puff and watched himself exhale in the window's reflection. Then he abandoned the smoldering cigarette in the ash tray to Faith's right. "Someday I'm gonna run that newspaper. You watch. Just as soon as I get myself together." For the span of several seconds he looked at the manicured nails on his right hand and played with two silver rings on his left. "When that happens, Faith, I'm going to be rich." He winked, foxy. "But I'll still be my same sweet self!"

Faith smiled. Seven seconds later she excused herself. The mist had maneuvered itself above Maxwell's head like a storm cloud. Her slip was again pinching her waist, and she hurried across the room to the women's lounge and, once inside, began struggling with her underclothes. Satisfied, she moved to the mirror and fastidiously reapplied her lipstick. She stared at herself in the glass, wondering if Maxwell would propose tonight after they attended the concert at the Auditorium Theater. She had worked hard toward that end, had pulled every trick from her memory, even ones she only faintly believed in and had had to forage pet shops to complete. Like carrying tufts of his wig in her pocketbook, and the Frog Charm (somewhat complicated, but effective: Kill a frog or toad, dry him out completely in the sun—or bury him in an ant's bed until his flesh is gone. Among his bones will be one that resembles a fishhook, and another that looks like a fish scale. To win your intended lover, hook the fish bone into his/her clothing; to expel him/her, throw the fish-scale bone in that person's direction). She was never sure, though, if it was the charms, *her* charm of listening, or Maxwell's own fatuity that brought him under her control. He was incredibly slow, but could be cajoled into anything she willed through an elaborate process of innuendo and suggestion that left her fatigued and frustrated, but always victorious. Indeed, he seemed dull to her, as simple as a three-headed, treasure-guarding troll, but, she told herself, intrinsically good (unlike trolls—they'll drink a Christian man's blood), and harmless in a cowlike way. She bent forward, powdering her cheeks, certain that Dr. Lynch had been so right: everything was stimulus and response. Machinery. She remembered the occasion when Maxwell, set in motion by her elaborate act of submissiveness, made his first advances toward her. He'd been nervous that night, wheezing with asthma, staining his tie with brown steak sauce and spilling black coffee onto his crotch. He'd lowered his eyes self-consciously and slipped his trembling hands under the table.

He'd said, "You've got class," then fumbled in his sports jacket, produced a plastic respirator, and sucked on it while awaiting Faith's reaction. She didn't quite know what to say. The air in his apartment was stuffy. She opened a window, but that didn't help Maxwell's breathing. His eyes watered; he coughed, closed his eyes, threw back his head, and gripped the edge of the table with his free hand.

Faith stepped behind him and placed her hands on his shoulders. "Can I do anything?"

"Yes." He took a deep breath, and threw back his head again. "Let me be seen in public with you—"

It was an odd way to put it, but she bit. "You want . . . ?" She watched her timing, controlled the tone, the timbre in her voice. "Why?"

He had seemed to be in some kind of agony, with pain so quick it lifted him from his seat like a puppet. He circled the table, slightly bent, his face pale and sunken with his need for air. She had become afraid then, imagining what it was like to feel one's chest narrow, tighten, and admit only a thin tunnel of oxygen. Maxwell's face was blue; he held himself erect by holding the back of a chair.

"You're . . . b-beautiful," he said, coughing violently again and falling back, frightened and weak, fluids bubbling in his stomach like liquid in a shaken jug.

"Please!" Faith cried. "Don't waste breaths trying to talk."

He waved her away feebly, forcing out the words. "Can you imagine what it'll be like if I'm seen with you? People—they'll turn around and stare with admiration when we walk down the street. That's important—what people think, I mean. It's the world of business, and you can help me get ahead if—" His wheezing had become horrible, so deep it frightened even Maxwell. He sank into the chair at the table and lowered his head into his folded arms. "I'm just an average guy . . . I'm nobody—I'm a *cripple*! I know you know lots of guys, healthy guys. You don't need me. I can understand that. I'd just like to be seen with you sometimes. That's all—"

Standing there, watching him gag and spray the acidic contents of the respirator between his lips, had both embarrassed and exhilarated her. She had power. With one word she could crush him. And, to tell the truth, it did make her feel good. She remembered sitting up with him all night, he lying propped up in his bed with pillows behind his back as she refilled his spray and brought him water. She'd given him what he wanted, smiling when—as he'd predicted—pedestrians turned around to glance at her when they walked down the street. She overlooked his stammering, smiled at his jokes, and approved of his garish ties and gauche sports coats. He, as predictable as a physical law, beamed from ear to ear, fed her, loaned her his car, and swore these ideas occurred to him of his own accord. Yet he was good to her, and though his predictability could sometimes make her scream, she did not want to lose him. Faith looked at her image in the mirror and was pleased. Tonight, if all went well, she would induce Maxwell to propose, pretending to be taken aback, honored, tearful, and left speechless by his proposition.

Then she broke into a sweat. On the surface of the glass of the mirror and superimposed over her own image were two sad, hazel eyes and a knitted brow that scowled gravely at her undertaking. She grabbed her purse and returned quickly to her table.

Maxwell was already at the counter near the door, paying the tab and counting and recounting his change. He took her arm, and they stepped out into a soft and flabby mid-spring morning. But Chicago no longer seemed dismal, not quite as lifeless or ominous. The Good Thing, after all, was here—it weighed about one hundred and fifty pounds, received paychecks twice a month, and would do anything she asked. She was so excited she almost squeezed Maxwell's arm with genuine affection. Almost.

"You're wonderful," she said.

He rubbed his nose until it was shiny, grinned proudly, and perked up when two young men passed them by and whistled at Faith. Maxwell drew her close. "You're just *saying* that."

True, she thought. But she said, "I mean—you're always in control of things. I feel so . . . safe when I'm with you." She could almost hear the *click, click, click* of reaction as his chest swelled. She decided to say no more. Once, as they drove home from a movie, she'd overdone it, had overloaded the machinery and brought on an asthma attack that had nearly lifted him out of his skin.

"I've got to run," Maxwell said at the corner. "There's another conference this morning." Then he rolled his eyes at her. "Most of them are pointless—just meeting with the circulation department or the ad boys, but something important might come of this one."

"Mmmm?" She hadn't heard a word. The warmth of the morning was reaching into her and she suddenly wanted to be free of him.

"We're starting a series on the prison in Joliet. It's not *my* idea, you understand. Those characters belong right where they are. But it occurred to me when the idea came up that this just might be my big break. The editors want to feature a column on day-to-day life in prison, but they'll need someone to organize it." He swiveled his head toward her, smiling, twirling the edge of his mustache. "Whoever gets that assignment may be moved up a couple of notches."

Faith was about to speak when she started at a fingertip touching her arm. She turned, stepping back and seeing an old man behind her, his right palm outstretched. In a croaking voice he said, "Can you give a little something, lady?" Cocked over his right eye was a shapeless hat; his shirt was wrinkled as though he had slept in it, and his trousers were loose and baggy and hid his shoes. If he had a face, she couldn't tell. His nose rested between his yellow eyes as shapeless as a kneecap, his hair was dusty and drawn up into tight little balls like gnats and May flies caught on flypaper. Two clear streams ran from his nostrils into his mouth. He licked at his lips and presented the pink surface of his palm to her again, his hand trembling. "It's been four days since I et, lady. . . ."

"Leave us alone," Maxwell said almost under his breath. He stepped closer to intimidate him, realized he was a full head shorter than the man, then stepped back, making a great show of reaching into his pocket as if to find a gun.

The old man ignored Maxwell, turning to Faith, his hat off now. He twisted the brim around in circles and looked at her feet. "I just need a dollar to put something in my stomach for a little while." He sniffled, looked at Maxwell out of the corners of his eyes, and chaffed his face with his slimy coat sleeve. "I can't lie to you—I got a habit. Do you know what it's like to be sick and—"

"You make me sick!" Maxwell snorted. He stepped behind Faith, said, "Get going before I call a cop," and then he went silent and clenched his fists when Faith withdrew a ten-dollar bill from her purse and handed it to the old man. He took it without a word of thanks and turned away, never looking back, and walked a few paces down the street into a bar.

Maxwell's mouth hung open. "Why didn't you let me handle that?"

Faith played with the tight elastic band beneath her dress. She felt a headache beginning on the left side of her brow. "I felt sorry for him."

"I don't mean that!" Maxwell shoved his hands in his pockets, his nose wrinkled like a puppy's as he glared at the sidewalk. "You always do that to me—override me when *I'm* the man." He glanced up at her, then looked away when their eyes met. "I don't like it! I don't like it at all—it's not natural. You did it at that party last week when I was telling a joke and you said I got it wrong." He thought about it, colored, and stomped his foot on the ground. "I hate that, Faith. It makes me feel small when you or *any*body else does that. I was mad enough to hit you upside your head for embarrassing me in front of all those people." For a moment he was silent. Then: "And I would have been right if I'd hit you. Women have less Will than men—*that's* a fact of nature; they're less rational and more emotional, and they need to keep quiet until spoken to and let men take the lead." And, as if to demonstrate this general principle, he walked faster so Faith remained two steps behind him.

She didn't want to hear it. The sunlight broke between two sky-scrapers overhead and seemed to focus on that part of her brow burning with pain. The elastic in her underwear felt as tight as a corset and (she was certain) was ruining her digestion. Holding her head, she said, "I'm sorry, Isaac. I suppose I stepped out of line." Something inside her laughed but she kept her face straight. "You're right."

"Sorry don't help." He scowled, trying to breathe as slowly as possible. His throat rattled. "Don't feel sorry for anybody from now on, especially for lushes like that one. He gave you a line, honey! People like that'll use you!" He chewed the corner of his mouth, watching the streetlight on the opposite block turn green. "You're just lucky you've got me around to watch out for you." Then he kissed her for the benefit of anyone who might see by holding her shoulders, pushing his face against her and tipping her slightly over backward. That done, he wiped his lips and crossed the street with a slight swagger, forcing other pedestrians to step out of his way.

. . . five, six, *seven*. Faith let the smile fall from her face. He was across the street, strutting like a rooster toward the bus stop. As she stood there on the crowded street, people parting and passing her on either side, she wondered, and not without a sinking feeling in her stomach, Who *was* Isaac Maxwell? What, after all those evenings sacrificed in snaring him, after all the times she'd tasted the interior of his mouth made bitter by his asthma spray, did she really know about him? Perhaps it wasn't important. Perhaps it was only important that he was pliable, like soft clay, and at least thought that he loved her. Her own feelings were more nebulous. She remembered that it took three days of looking in department stores before she found the Valentine card she wanted to send him. Not that she wanted to send it, but he considered such things as greeting cards and ties at Christmas to be important. Most of them had said something wholly unacceptable like "I love you." The thought of it made her shiver. Another had a cartoon figure of a girl with a caption that read, "Thinking of you." Which was a lie. In the end she had made him a card, cutting it out herself and writing her own noncommittal message. "You couldn't afford to buy me one?" he asked, holding it away from him as if it were a bit unclean. "*That's* what you think of me?"

What she *did* think of him, she could never say to his face. If she loved him—and she had by no means made up her mind—it was the way a Confederate and Union soldier had to love each other, as adversaries who unwillingly draw closer in conflict. The scene of battle was his bedroom (a horrible affair in her mind; there were *Ebony* pin-up girls pasted over the head of his double bed and patterns describing a hundred and one positions for sexual congress on the bedspread). It was touch and go, a chess game. The first night she had allowed him to kiss her, there on the battlefield, he felt somewhat victorious. Then he turned sour and stepped across the room from her. "Who the hell taught you to kiss like that?" His face was pinched and sad, like a child's ready to cry but not wanting to. "*I* didn't teach you to do that," and he demanded to know who did. And so it went each weekend, he trying to possess more and more of her, and she trying to squeeze a proposal from him. He was her object, pure and simple, and she was his, and between them this twirling exchange for supremacy of wills, as he called it, built a tension or bond that she was willing to call, for want of a better word, love. You took what you could get. Somehow it was all right. It worked out even fine (the bills were paid and the worst part of her bondage had passed), even though, late at night when she stood before her apartment's picture window, barefoot on the thick carpet Maxwell had nailed down himself, and looked at the stillness of her neighborhood, she thought she heard Barrett's voice just above the wind, telling her all this was horribly wrong. And she would feel grief build in her chest, and for no apparent reason at all, except that she felt filled with some oceanic, painful-pleasurable awareness of her own self-betrayal in contrast to her life's half-forgotten promise. Laughing, she'd wipe away these tears, calling them foolish and feeling astonished by her own weakness of will, which Maxwell so deplored. Weakness, sympathy, faith, love—all these were stupid, surely. She knew she was in bondage (the image of a frog caught in the mouth of a snake came to her, only one of its green legs visible and wiggling in the air), knew herself to be encrusted with the filth of a past beyond her control. The filth of the present beyond her control was understandable then. But at those hollow, lonely hours her thoughts would return to Barrett, then to Reverend Brown, and the terror and closeness she had felt and felt still in the depths of the cave. She would purse her lips, her eyes shut tight to close out even the light of the moon, and whisper, as in days of yore, "Thank

You. . . ." Chills crawled along her spine and a sense of dread or fear stuck in her throat like a cotton hook. Even for this, Thank You, for this confusion and pain because, through pain, I know I can still feel; for this chance to persist, even if in deceit as Todd had done. . . . Thank You—for this clownish, pitifully genuine, but cow-like lover, this good thing of mine. . . .

Tired, though she had only been up a few hours, Faith went home to sleep, certain Maxwell would propose and bring the battle to an end. She could feel it in her throat.

After a time she awoke in her bedroom, stretched out, and checked the electric clock on her nightstand. Six-thirty. She'd slept late, as much as eight hours, but felt she deserved it. She could have passed the morning in reading her shorthand book from the Mueller Vocational College on the North Side, but why study when she might soon be able to avoid work altogether? Maxwell believed that men were the providers and women should stay at home. Fine, she thought, glad he was so foolish. The idea of work, she remembered, had affected Big Todd in this way, too. Long ago, on one of their walks, he'd told her about the time he worked in a cotton mill. The work wore at his spirit. In a week he'd lost nearly seven pounds from the heat alone. They expected Todd to work five days a week, but he came only three, Monday through Wednesday. This went on for five weeks straight until Todd's foreman could stand it no longer.

When Todd appeared Monday morning, the foreman cornered him in the locker room. Said, "Cross, what the hell *is* this? For a month you've been comin' in three days a week! You got an explanation?"

Todd leaned close to him, picking his teeth with a straw. "Listen, I come in three whole days of the week because I really need the money. . . ."

It was that simple. But Maxwell already earned enough for him and Faith to live on, and that was what it—life—was all about, to hear him tell it. Getting by. No sooner had she thought this than she heard a whisper in her bedroom: "Consider, child . . . your Good Thing. . . ." Rattled, she rose to her feet, pulled on her bathrobe, and went to her mirror, angry and refusing to acknowledge the suggestion of Barrett's sad eyes staining a corner of the glass. "I don't need advice!" she said to herself. "And I certainly don't need the Good Thing any more." She brushed her hair for one hundred slowly counted strokes, showered, rubbed cold cream on her ashy ankles and legs, and dressed in the living room. At exactly eight she heard her door chimes and, since Maxwell had a key, he let himself in. He staggered into the room, his toes pointed outward as he took long strides to the sectional sofa where he dropped his trench coat.

Something was wrong. Faith waited, playing with a button on her dress.

Maxwell threw his arms around her waist and said, "They went for it!" His eyes were glazed and dilated, two tiny dots in a head swollen, she realized, with alcohol. Also, he had an erection, which he attempted to hide by sticking his right hand in his pocket.

Faith looked him dead in the face, frowning. "You've been drinking." When he exhaled she smelled a good amount of gin on his breath. "What happened?" Then, because she was afraid of the situation, she sat down on the sofa. "Isaac, I said you're *drunk*!"

He spoke quickly, clipping off the ends of his words and sliding articles into nouns as though he were speaking French. "Guess who's going to handle that column *and* at a raise in pay *and* starting next month!"

Her eyes were on his ridiculous attempt to keep his profile turned from her. It slowly dawned on her that he wanted her to share his enthusiasm. All right. She stood up, still playing with her button, turning over phrases. Before she could decide on one Maxwell said, "Ragsdale—he's the publisher, he went for it in a big way." He was breathing heavily and paced the room, waving his arms and oblivious to the bulge in his trousers. "I didn't think he would, not with the hell they've been giving me for weeks. Hey, I didn't even think he liked me, you know?" He remembered his condition and turned to give Faith a three-quarter view of himself. "He's shelved every idea I came up with since I got there. *Great* ideas! Like switching from their nine-column format to magazine style. *Nobody* uses nine columns any more!" Maxwell crossed the room, placed his hand in his pocket, and managed to shove his erection down his right pants leg where it was less noticeable. Then he hurried back toward Faith. "The whole day started off wrong, what with that drunk this morning. And I missed the bus and had to walk the rest of the way to work. Jesus, I must have looked terrible, I mean, *un*professional! There were these big sweat rings under my arms and I was breathing hard and there was dirt under my nails. . . ."

Faith sat silent, watching him pace like Socrates before the Court. She tried to listen, but there was a pain in her right foot, which had fallen asleep. She'd crossed her right leg over her left; the blood rushing back made her foot feel leaden. She lowered it to the floor and wiggled her toes until feeling returned.

"So they're all waiting for me, right. When I came in they were looking over my proposal in the conference room—Ragsdale, Cummings, the evening editor, and Lowell, he's copy editor. Faith, lemme tell you—I was scared enough to pee in my pants. A chance to get over comes, maybe, only once in a man's lifetime! And if you're black, it may never come at all!" Maxwell gave a short, knowing laugh. "I mean black folks have been down so long, on the bottom, that our Will's been weakened. We don't know how to think big like other people. You know what I'm saying: poverty is a state of mind," he pointed at his temple, "and I just wasn't born to be poor, you know?"

Faith wiggled the right toes on her foot cautiously. "Yes, I know." But she wondered about that, about what she really knew of Maxwell. Her information was scanty. Sometimes, when she looked at him, he didn't seem to be there at all. She saw a somewhat poorly polished gesture, but never anything she might call Maxwell. Not even when he was naked—even then he seemed heavily clothed with layers and layers of popular culture grafted on but never reaching to that level she could call Maxwell himself. Maybe he was like a suit of armor, empty inside. Regardless, it was easier to pretend he had no past—that they, like two slaves promenading on Sunday in their owner's old clothes, had just met in the French Quarter in New Orleans, that they needed to know nothing other than that she was a woman and he was a man who would take care of her if they ran away from bondage. A suit of armor, after all, would shield her from the cold. Still, she remembered the salient elements of his life: attending one poorly equipped ghetto school after another, soaking up all the literature, books, and movies that presented an image of a more affluent life, and writing to purge himself of frustration. Unexpectedly, he won a scholarship to a junior college, and, just as unexpectedly, he graduated at the head of his class and gave a commencement-day speech on—you guessed it—"The Power of Will." Faith closed her eyes. It was easier to pretend he had no past. "I know, Isaac," she said.

"It was crazy, Faith! Ragsdale looked up from my proposal and said, 'It looks good.'" Maxwell stopped in the center of the floor, his face wooden and his shoulders hunched forward, a queer hitch in his voice. "I wish my father was around right now. It would have meant a lot to him, you know? He never really got off the bottom." Maxwell pulled at his nose, sober, staring at Faith. "He was a janitor *all* his life and *glad* to be one. Sometimes I'd be at home, writing in a corner of the room, and he'd drag in from the plant with dust in his hair and eyes, and ask me what I was doing. And when I told him, he'd say, 'There ain't no place for a black boy who does that.' You understand? He was whipped, Faith—somebody snuffed out the Will in him like you do a candle." Perhaps Maxwell tasted something bad: he curled back his lips as if he did. "He pandered me! I couldn't stand it. He thought I was weak and asthmatic and couldn't do anything else—I mean, do hard work with my back like he did. But he was wrong, you see, because Lowell nodded his head and said they wanted to start the column in about a month, and Cummings told me to pick the prisoner I want to author it." Maxwell smiled, a warm feeling in his chest. "I'll get an extra day off—Monday, and about a hundred dollars a week more. . . ."

Faith's eyebrows raised. "A hundred?"

"You can't get rich in media, honey," Maxwell laughed, "not unless you own the paper. *That's* freedom of the press—the publisher's free to print anything he wants. The point is that they're finally giving me some responsibility—I can branch out, put some money away and, maybe, in a few years start my own magazine." He looked straight into her eyes for the first time that evening. "They *trust* me."

"*Faugh!*"

"What was that?"—Maxwell.

"Nothing, maybe someone in the hallway." Faith felt at a loss. She understood in a cerebral sort of way, not with her heart, his need for this thing. She even wanted him to have it. "I'm glad," she said. It sounded false; she shot her voice up an octave: "I'm *glad!*"

He seemed to believe her. "Anyway, I *will* branch out soon. It takes time, you know? If I show them I can handle this, maybe they'll let me do a signed column next—on race or something. I've got some strong opinions on *that.* I've got time to move up and I've got potential. Ragsdale said so, those were his words. You know *I* wouldn't toot my own horn." For a second he was silent, visibly exhausted and a little bit high from so much speech; his shoulders slouched, his arms hung like slabs of beef on meathooks at his side. "What do you think?"

"I think it's wonderful," Faith said. "I hope it turns out all right for you."

"For *us!*" Maxwell shouted. "I'm doing all this for both of us!" Then he smiled, wily, and laughed as he took her hands and lifted her off the sofa. "But you'll have to act right, stay in a woman's place, I mean."

Faith said, "Right," and he released her, stepping in front of her living-room mirror to adjust his wig and smooth back his mustache with spittle. "We can talk about what I have in mind later. If we hurry," he glanced at his wristwatch, "we can make it to the theater in time for the show. I can't stand being late."

For the occasion, Faith dressed in a cream-colored, box-pleated skirt, argyle cardigan, and brown pumps, deciding, when she was inside Maxwell's Buick, that the prospects for a life with him were propitious. She could push him; it wouldn't be hard. They would work out a comfortable agreement, an unwritten contract involving, on his side, food, furniture, comfort, and security somewhere in the surrounding crime-free suburbs; and on her side, the provision of children, but not at first, cooking until they found someone to cover this inconvenience, and, of course, the obligatory sacrifice of sex Lavidia had found so abhorrent. She looked at his profile as he drove down Michigan Avenue, quieter now with couples strolling along the sidewalks, into restaurants, and toward the lakefront. Would he, at some unforeseen time, expect more than duty from her? She closed her eyes, experiencing first the play of light and patterns along her eyelids, then a vision that was brief but terrifying: suppose after thirty or forty years or so, after a lifetime of duty and coping and ceaseless arguments repeated so often they could start each one up anew at any point, at the beginning, middle, or end; suppose after fifty years they found themselves sitting across from each other in a semidark kitchen overlooking a quiet back yard of peonies, petunias and sweet-smelling ferns, the sink filled with greasy dishes behind them, the walls lined with shelves of teapots that jingled "Tea for Two," milk-glass statues, and placards engraved with kitchen prayers like:

Bless my little kitchen, Lord,
I love its every nook,
And bless me as I do my work,
Wash pots and pans and cook ...

suppose they stared across that table, looking up from their untouched bowls of salad, glaring at the outlines of the kitchen, at the stark figures of the electric wall clock, the gigantic ornamental spoon and fork made of wood, the calendar they'd forgotten to change, the bulletin board covered with phone numbers with which they could associate no names, no faces; suppose in all that they peered at each other across the gulf between their lives like two duelers facing one another on some misty moor, wondering, in that brittle, graying age, *Who is this? And, I—?* Would he be openly hostile then? His hairline would stretch back behind his head, ending in gray fuzz. Hard old age would be upon him. He would wear blue-and-red suspenders that strained over an obscenely rotund belly. His toothless mouth would look like a fresh wound, and he would accuse her of his failures, his humiliations so sure to come. Faith smiled to herself, leaned over, and kissed Maxwell's cheek. She would be just a wrinkle then—old, evil like Lavidia. But she remembered the statistics: 13,500 black men stricken dead as stone from hypertension, one out of every seven, the newspapers had said. They had twice the chance of collapsing from stroke as whites. Maxwell's life expectancy would, if he was lucky, be no more than 64.1 years. She would outlive him; she could wait. He would begin wheezing and clutching his wrinkled throat at the table; his head would pitch forward into his salad bowl. She saw herself rising from the table, starting to dial the police or the fire department, then stopping, turning around, and descending the rubber-matted back stairs to the yard. She would bend down to the white peonies growing beside the sidewalk, bury her nose in one, and withdraw it filled with a fragrance as sweet as wine. Dew from the petals would be moist against her lips. She would smile, thinking of the insurance. . . .

"I'm almost too worked-up to enjoy the show," Maxwell said. "I *should* be at home working on the column, you know? Turning over all the possibilities so—ha ha—nothing can slip through my fingers." He glanced at her sheepishly, sly. "I never did tell you my whole theory of Will Power, did I?"

"No," Faith said, but she remembered the curious collection of books stacked along the floor of his bedroom. Some belonged to *The Power Book Library* and were long out of print. She had flipped through a few when he left to buy her a pack of cigarettes. The titles were peculiar: *Power of Will, Will for Success*, a few books by Horatio Alger, Colin Wilson, Norman Vincent Peale, and a slim one about a sea gull. She hadn't been able to make sense of any of them. "You never told me," she said.

Maxwell chuckled and began beating rhythms on the steering wheel with his palm. "It came to me when I was watching a Rose Bowl game—sort of like a revelation. All those men in conflict and one of them carrying the ball across the field through dint of pure Will. Beautiful!" He looked at her, all seriousness. "That's life in a nutshell. Tennyson said it better than me—*O living Will, thou shalt endure, When all that seems shall suffer shock*. Will Power can overcome anything, you see? I know it for a fact, because whenever I feel an asthma attack coming on, I can just will it right away."

"You can?" Faith looked at him hard. "How?"

"Pure strength of Will," Maxwell snapped. He sucked at foreign matter in his teeth and shifted the car into fourth. "Will Power's a self-preservative principle of evolution. I figured it all out. It's superior to matter and stronger than mind, and *that's* why man's been able to survive on this miserable planet for so long. If nature threatened him, he could conquer it." Maxwell's right hand left the steering wheel; he held it out above the dashboard, drawing his fingers together in a tight fist. "A man can accomplish *any*thing if his Will Power's strong enough, Faith." He seemed to remember something

116

and lowered his hand, glancing sideways at her. "But you have to direct the Will toward what's right and good, of course."

Faith slid up in her seat. "What *is* right?"

"Security and comfort," Maxwell laughed, still sucking at his teeth. "Being on top of things, having nice things, respect, a little authority—feeling like a man. Things like that."

She left that alone. It hung heavy in the close space of the car, like gas from a sick person's bowels, until she, to clear the air, said, "I guess." It didn't matter what he thought, or if he thought at all, which was still questionable, as long as he was sweet. Sometimes. "That's your theory?" she asked finally. "That's *all*?"

Maxwell reddened a little. "I know it needs some work. I'm not writing it up for *Mind* or the *Philosophical Review,* you know! All the implications aren't worked out—I know that—but it's how I feel about things and it helps me stay in the race." He shoved out his lower lip and changed the subject. "You got our tickets?"

She said, "Yes," and produced them after Maxwell left his Buick in an underground parking lot and led her to the door of the theater. He guided her into an immense lobby embellished with Oriental decorations, then up four flights of red-carpeted stairs. From that height, the proscenium was minuscule, adrift at sea before hundreds of people seated below. Maxwell looked curiously at their tickets, then for their seats.

"Those people," he said finally, pointing to an old couple, "they've got our seats."

The couple looked nonchalantly at them. They were both nondescript, just an average, portly, moon-faced man and wife dressed in Sunday-service clothing, waiting for the show. Maxwell bent toward the man and tried to explain that those seats, paid for in advance, were his. The man said nothing. His face was like the cement in an old cellar, rough irregular lines lying thick and lumpy along a hard, white surface. He remained rooted in place like an oak. Maxwell perspired, fingered his respirator nervously, and returned angrily to Faith.

"I'm going to get an usher," he said. "I *know* those are our seats." And he was gone, squeezing back out into the crowded, smoke-filled hallway. She waited, irritated by her full bladder, and afraid she'd miss Maxwell if she went searching for the women's room. The billowing curtains before the stage below parted, and applause thundered around, below, and above her ears. A pianist appeared on stage, animated, his long fingers stroking the keys, his feet pumping the pedals, dark sunglasses flashing with floodlights directed his way and his head nodding with the melody now filling the auditorium. Faith exhaled nervously and pressed her thighs together. It would only take an instant to find the bathroom; she could be back before Maxwell returned with the usher. But she stayed, licking her dry lips and wringing her hands. She crossed her arms, then began to lose her fight with this sudden sense of dread that had no location, no cause; it broke free, not as she stood there pinching all her abdominal muscles together, but when she turned around and saw Maxwell returning with the usher, a six-foot, bespectacled man wearing a blue uniform. He licked sleepily at his lips. She wanted to hide. It was Arnold Tippis.

"We'll get this thing straightened out right now," Maxwell said. He turned to the usher, but Tippis stopped cold in the aisle, tearing off his glasses and gawking at Faith.

"Where've you been hiding, girl?" Tippis cried. "You've got no idea what I've been going through trying to find you!"

She was going to wet her pants. She knew it. Faith glanced at Maxwell, already halfway down the aisle, then at Tippis, who was sliding toward her. People seated around them began to stare, scowl, and hiss like broken ventilators. She started to back away, but felt herself losing control.

Tippis placed his hand on her right arm and thrust his face near hers, saying, *sotto voce,* "I need somebody to talk to. You'll listen, won't you, Faith? I looked for you at the hotel, but Mrs. Beasley said you'd moved out a long time ago." In the darkness of the theater she could hardly see his face.

"Please," Faith said, "take your hand off." Its pressure was upsetting her delicate equilibrium of tightened muscles, squeezing from her what she knew would be a very embarrassing deluge of . . . "Please . . . ."

"Things haven't been right with me since I last saw you," Tippis said. "There's nobody to hear me out like you used to. Where are you staying? Faith, I've got to talk with you—"

Maxwell bounded back up the aisle and stopped, swaying at

Faith's side. "What're you talking about?" He stared at Faith, his face blue, his chest heaving. "You don't know him, do you?"

"Tell him, honey." From Tippis. He put on his glasses and stared at Maxwell.

"No," Faith whispered. She inhaled deeply, imagining her bladder to be as gravid, as swollen and distended as a womb. It was swelling up inside her like a tumor, was about to explode—*boom!*—and drown them all.

"*No?*" Tippis roared. He slipped his glasses on again. She could see the pain spring across his face, tightening his jaws and the muscles around his eyes and lips. Why couldn't he go away before she had an accident? "Faith," Tippis said, stumbling over his words, "you remember what we used to talk about—about how happiness and peace isn't possible in society." His face opened like a trap door. "But I was *wrong!* God, it is possible. When I was with you and when you heard me out I felt something like genuine tranquillity. . . ." Tippis bobbed his head and his voice shot up. "I see that now! You *do* need other people to be whole, to discover who you are—"

All the while she said nothing, only held her stomach and groaned.

Tippis cried aloud, "Faith, this is *Arnold!*" and stepped back, slipping off his glasses again as if they concealed his face. "Look at me, please," he said, touching his cheek. "You act like you don't know me!"

Faith turned her head. Maxwell cocked his. Said: "What *is* this, anyway?"

"You weren't this cold before," Tippis said. His voice had an edge on it. "Maybe you don't need the money, or me, or *any*body like you used to, but will you at least *speak* to me?"

Maxwell had had enough. He squeezed between them, his back to Faith, and his chin lifted. "She said she doesn't know you, fellah," poking his finger in Tippis's chest.

"But she does!" Tippis laughed, short and uneasy, pulled at his blue collar, and squinted at Maxwell. "Girls don't forget men that once made a difference in their lives, especially when—"

Then it began, the transformation of Isaac Maxwell. Before Tippis could complete his thought Maxwell slapped him—the sound like a shot, the force of it turning Tippis completely around. Maxwell looked at his stinging palm as though in a trance; he held it up to his face, fascinated, then stepped forward, smiling curiously, his legs stiff, and slapped Tippis again, exploring his sudden hatred, discovering himself through Tippis's destruction.

"Isaac!" Faith shouted. But she could not move.

And Tippis took it passively, wind rushing out of him like a bellows when Maxwell drove his knee sharply into Tippis's crotch—testing himself, moving from one insight to another. Faith screamed like a wild bird. She raked at Maxwell's back, pulling away only pieces of yellow cloth as he showered the other with oaths and punches and pulled at his hair until a patch of bloody scalp came free in his hands. He turned, looked at Faith, and the valve to her bladder sprang open. Anger, children, had opened hallways in him, unlocked secret chests, and allowed him to chart in himself dark labyrinths that only the deep key of anger could disclose. So it was, children. So it often is. His eyes frightened her: wild, irascible, drunk, their vision inverted from the world to dark new dimensions Maxwell saw in himself. And enjoyed. The fight had been exhilarating; he'd heard every *click*, *click*, *click* of his confused life with clocklike deadliness during the fight, and felt—it was so obvious—truly whole for the first time, all the threads of his life converging and crystallizing at his moment of anger. But Tippis—his face was meat and blood. Below them, people looked up, and the musician stopped playing to stare.

Faith shouted again, "Isaac!"

The spell of this new side of himself—Maxwell the Berserker—held him fast. Physically lighter, his head clear and humming with a sudden sense of the efficacy of his Will, he did not hear her. Not even Faith might enter into and break the mood of that moment. She dragged him by his arm back down the stairs, the front of her dress and hosiery and underclothes soaking and clinging to her like skin. Once on the street, she stopped to support herself against a waste can, amazed that the air outside was quiet and still, that people passed them by without a single look, ignorant that her world had fallen into shambles.

She hurried Maxwell to the parking lot, and there he found his voice: "Did you see that sonuvabitch's face? Did you see what I *did* to it?"

"I saw," Faith said wearily.

She stopped to catch her breath beside his Buick, then slid behind the wheel, not trusting Maxwell, who shook and seemed too dazed to control the car. She was thankful he had taught her how to drive by letting her cruise around *The Sentry* parking lot occasionally. But she didn't have a license. And she wasn't about to give that a second thought. Faith took the keys in his outstretched hand, and minutes later they were tooling south down the Eisenhower Expressway.

"I'm sorry," she said. "I haven't the faintest idea who he was, really. Isaac . . ." She looked at him shyly. Did he suspect? No, or at least it did not seem that way. His eyes were still narrowed, and he held his head in his hands, still swinging deep inside, still reliving that brief but perfect moment in the theater aisle.

Fog had descended on the city like a curse, a gray-green gloom that stuck to the sides of the car. Fog filled up the spaces between trees and bushes on the boulevard; fog bloated the alleys and lay in great formless clouds that blotted out the sky and street; fog hung above the road like an alien intelligence. Down the street a car emerged with glaring headlights from the gloom, blinding Faith, who gripped the wheel tighter and slowed down until she and Maxwell coasted into a small pocket of clarity much like the clear spaces in a dream.

"Are you all right?"—Faith.

Maxwell was staring at his bloody right knuckles. "Did you see what I did to his eye?"

Faith said, "Yes," and turned her attention to her own problem. Not only were her stockings wet, but her shoes were now slowly filling up, too. She started to cry.

"I'm sorry, honey," Maxwell said as he came to himself again. "The evening's ruined. If there's anything I can do to make this up to you—"

After parking in front of his apartment, Faith slid across the seat and rested her head on Maxwell's overly padded shoulder. She slid her hand into his open sports coat, and let it rest, rising, falling. Falling on his chest.

"I'm so glad you were there, Isaac." That didn't sound soft enough. She adjusted her tone. "That man, whoever he was—he frightened me."

"That sonuvabitch!"

Maxwell lifted her chin with his right forefinger. He stared blankly for a long while into her eyes, and Faith was thankful that nothing in them could be seen, inferred, or guessed about her feelings. He opened the driver's door and helped her out, then guided her along the sidewalk and into his apartment building. Once inside, he left the living-room lights out and, directed only by the small bulb over his kitchen bar, fixed them drinks, calling to her in a quavering voice, "He acted like he knew you! Can you *imagine?* The lines these characters come up with. The nerve! I wish I'd had a gun—"

Her wet clothes were unbearable. In the darkness of the front room, she slipped off her shoes, stockings, and the rest. They were a ruin. She dropped them behind the sofa and sat down. Maxwell returned to the front room and stopped a few feet in front of her, a glass in each hand, his shoulders trembling as he looked her over. His breathing was louder than the whir of the air conditioner, the humming of the electric clock in the kitchen. Slowly he sat down, handed her a drink, and began pumping his respirator between his lips. "It's a g-good thing I was around. . . ."

Now.

"Isaac, I really *do* need you. That's clear now."

"What?" *Click, click*—whir . . .

"I simply can't . . . make it by myself." As she said it, her right fist closed, as if squeezing some object, then opened, as if she were releasing dust. "I need someone who can control a situation—like you do."

"You *do?* Faith!" He grabbed at his throat, and she thought he was about to faint. "No," he said in a strangled voice, "it's not that. I never dreamed . . . You *do* care, don't you?"

Click.

"It's true," Faith said. She looked away, out the picture window behind them to the shadowy suggestion of trees beyond, to a squirrel peering at them from one of the lower limbs. She remembered having a squirrel once, and that it was so friendly she could feed it peanuts, bread crumbs, and candy right out of her hand. In the mornings it would follow her into the farmhouse kitchen, then eat with her at the table like an honored guest. By and by it came to think everyone was as kind as Faith, and wandered up to Eula May Jenkins one morning to beg for food. Eula May shot him dead—she was skinning him, pulling the pelt off his bones when Faith walked into Eula May's kitchen to borrow flour for Lavidia. Thereafter, Faith never befriended squirrels again, nor had she given her affections easily, for fear that her loved ones would be snatched away from her by circumstances or, worse, by death. Somehow her affair with Maxwell was different: he could be replaced easily, as an object you loved could not; he could be Isaac Maxwell, Tom Maxwell, Dick Maxwell, or Harry Maxwell—and she wouldn't give a tinker's damn.

She could see Barrett's features in the window, frowning. Poor old foolosopher, she thought. Then she turned to Maxwell and said, "I've never cared about anybody but you." When he said nothing, she turned to him, her stomach knotting as severely as when she had the curse. Suspended like shimmering icicles on Maxwell's cheeks were tears. He was sniffling and rubbing his nose. Faith looked away; it was going to be harder than she'd thought.

He said, at length, "I can aw-aw-always be with you!"

Her head swam, and she really felt sick now. Thought, *What am I doing to him?* Then, *What am I doing to me?* To avoid looking directly at him she placed her arms around his neck, clasping her hands together between his shoulder blades, and buried her face in his chest.

"Yes," she whispered, "I *do* need you, Isaac."

"Faith, I'm nuh-nuh-NOTHING! I'm nuh-nuh-NOBODY, but I-I swear I'll work for y-you. I luh-luh-love you!" And he heaved a long sigh.

Good, she thought, very good. And she closed her eyes and clenched her fists. Her ear to his chest, she could hear his heart, a loud, throbbing, roiling thing in his breast: Tha-*bump, whir-rrr* . . . and the words were on her lips, had been there since the day she'd met him, and now, as he fought for breath and squeezed her tight enough to cause her pain, she could say automatically, quickly and without a thought:

"Be my good thing. . . ."

"Y-Yes!" shot from Maxwell's lips. His arms went slack with exhaustion. "Wuh-Wuh-Will you marry me?"

She opened her eyes, casting her gaze upward through the darkness to the round figure of a faded rosette in the center of the ceiling, then to the picture window where Barrett's disembodied hazel eyes closed in something like defeat. A shiver of triumph swept over her. The contest of wills. She shut her eyes again, relaxed.

"Yes."

aith Cross was among the dead living. We hear all the time of the living dead, those restless, glassy-eyed ghouls whispered of in a trembling voice by our white-haired elders—*dead*, because their bodies move only at the bidding of witchmen working black magic along the bayou, or in the swamps where, in the stench of black soil teeming with floral decay, their zombies wait, tight-lipped and reeking with age, calling for release—*living*, because their souls, freed like jinn from ancient, fire-forged urns, drift between our troubled realm and the netherworld. They wander through our world as elusive as smoke, peering through our windows while we sleep, gibbering. Snickering. They have no names now, so we call them IT's. Yet the elders don't tell the entire tale. Seldom is it pleasant. There are, as well, the dead living—their bodies grow, move, but their souls, alas! are as still as stone.

Now, Faith Cross was such a one.

Objects have no name. They are ITs, and this is what Faith saw reflected in her bedroom mirror on the day of her first wedding anniversary. IT was portly, IT stared with puffy eyes at her from the smooth glass, IT's body was well fed, but was losing IT's health; IT was lugubrious with a gleam along IT's round limbs, as swollen as a corpse in its seventh day. To tell the truth, Maxwell would have to hug her on the installment plan. Faith, dissatisfied and filled with disgust, turned from the mirror to glare at Maxwell, who had inspired her self-inspection with a smug remark about her widening derrière.

There were chintz draperies and valances framing the old iron bed Maxwell had restored, bracket tables on both sides of the bed, and old-fashioned pillow shams. At the cluttered bedroom dresser,

Maxwell tightened a triple knot in his tie, then folded the dimple in with his thumbnail. "Like I said, you'd just better get your fat ass in the kitchen and fix dinner. If I come back here with company and there's nothing on the table—"

Behind him, Faith frowned at his reflection in the mirror above the dresser. Said, "You'll *what?*"

Maxwell sighed and threw up his hands, turning to face her. She could see he was tired, and without his wig he looked old, old. The job, the exigencies of editing, laying out picture pages, and the almost one-year postponement of his prison column were wearing him a bit thin. You could see it in his chin. It seemed to grow smaller day by day.

"I don't want to argue," Maxwell said tepidly. He pulled his wig off the dresser, trying to remain calm, and dusted it off. He tugged it on—backward, and Faith bent down, doubled up with laughter. He began to color, and she came to herself, angry again.

"You never want to argue!" she shouted. "Well, *I* do!" Then she stormed after him as he hurried away from her out into the hallway, his palms pressed over his ears, into the living room. Maxwell's pickled-pine eighteenth-century desk was in one corner, a pair of blond beachwood Sheraton open arm chairs were situated on either side of a davenport near a Biedermeier satinwood table and two Italian fruitwood chairs. Pewter and Sandwich glass accessories were on the surfaces of things and, just above the sofa against the southern wall, was a print of Chirico's *Horses at Sea.*

There, trying to ignore her, Maxwell lifted flecks of lint off his sports coat, talking in a detached way, as though to the wood-paneled walls. "I *told* you what to do, woman."

"You expect me to jump whenever you say so, don't you?!" She stood in front of him, trying to fix her eyes on his. "*Don't* you?"

"I just expect you to carry the ball sometimes," Maxwell said sharply. "Is *that* asking too much?"

Nervously Faith chewed her lip. Thought: My life is *not* a football game. She wanted to tell him she was afraid to face company, not because of the trouble involved in fixing dinner and setting the table, or because it involved "carrying the ball" for the business guests he brought home, but because it would take her forever to make IT presentable. The fruit of her body had gone bad. Each day she looked in the mirror she saw deeper lines around IT's mouth and darker circles under IT's eyes. IT was beginning to lose IT's hair rapidly from overuse of a sizzling black straightening comb; IT changed clothes three times a day but still looked terrible; IT had spare tires around IT's waist that no amount of morning isometrics with that muscular man on daytime television could reduce. IT, she feared, was a hopeless case.

"You just get your fat ass in gear," Maxwell said with finality. He'd taken his favorite pose, his right leg slightly forward and bent at the knee, the left knee locked, and his left hand shoved in his pocket. A model's pose. Long ago he'd asked Faith, "How should I stand?" and presented several postures from *Gentleman's Quarterly* for her as she braided her hair—his arms straight at his sides, or crossed, his feet together or parted. "Which one looks best, honey?" To get rid of him she chose the one he posed now. "Did you hear me?" Maxwell said. He looked, or so he thought, like Harry Belafonte.

In the center of the living-room floor Faith began screaming. Maxwell's palms flew to his ears.

"That's not going to work this time," he shouted above her scream. He gave her his three-quarter view, said by some to be his best angle. "I won't *hear* it!"

She screamed louder.

"Faith, I'm warning you! When I bring this ex-con back, you'd better—"

A sound like splintering wood came from Faith's head. She collapsed.

There was a green meadow ringing with earth rhythms, stretching as far as her eyes could see; it was bounded on the north by the aurora borealis, on the east by the rising sun, on the south by the procession of the equinoxes, and on the west—by the Day of Judgment. It was a beautiful place. Birds darted through the air as fast as bullets. Knee-deep and dew-covered was the grass across this stretch of land, and here and there were trees. Faith felt the moisture of the ground beneath her and stood up. The grass rippled with a warm, unseen wind that sent the tops of maple trees swaying, like dancers, in the breeze. The area was inhabited with all the creatures Big Todd once told her about: ax-handle hounds who lived on wood shavings in lumber camps; the bearlike Gumberoos, usually found in burnt-out forests and who, it was said, were impervious to bullets. To tell the truth, Faith found herself in the mythical land of Diddy-Wah-Diddy. It's fairly hard to get to—the road leading to Diddy-Wah-Diddy has so many curves that a mule hauling a wagon-load of fodder can eat off the rear of the wagon while he's walking along; it's so crooked gnats have snapped their necks going around the curves. Faith discovered behind her a tall elm with hundreds of branches bearing thick green leaves. Those leaves rustled, showering her with dew.

And then the tree spoke: "My baby's blue. I can tell—"

Faith stepped back and shivered. "Daddy?"

"Uh, huh."

Faith caught her breath. "But how—?"

The tree rustled again. "It's simple, honey. I said, 'Uh, huh,' because that's one of the words the Devil gave us. I like it. Lucifer was down in Hell one day, taking inventory of his damned souls. He discovered that the number was runnin' pretty low in the fourth and fifth circles. So he flew up to Heaven and stole a few angels. He stuffed them into his mouth and nose and ears and under his arms. But when he was flyin' back to earth somebody on the ground said, 'You takin' alla them angels to Hell, Devil?' Lucifer opened his mouth and said, 'Right,' and all those angels fell right out and beat a straight line back to Heaven. So the Devil went back for more. That same fella said, 'You takin' a new batch to Hell, Devil?' Old Lucifer jes kept his mouth shut this time. He mumbled, 'Uh, huh.' "

"Not *that*," Faith said. "How can you be . . . a tree?"

The elm said, "Don't let that worry you none. We all become trees, phlox, and hydrangeas as soon as we die. That's only if you lived a righteous life, though. Ask your mother," the tree said. "She's right here." One of its branches gestured toward a weeping willow to its right.

Faith said, "Momma?"

"Don't ask me no questions," the willow whined, "I've got 'bout seven million gallons of carbon dioxide to move before I—"

"You *are* Momma!" Faith squealed.

The elm sighed through its branches. "She don't never wind down." Then, with one of its broader leaves, it stroked Faith's cheek.

Said, "Would you like to be a tree? Really, you're supposed to die first, but I think I can get it arranged for you."

She didn't hesitate. "Yes. Can I be a maple tree?"

"It's done," said the elm.

At first, Faith felt nothing unusual. She saw the lush meadow as before. But when she tried to move, she found herself rooted to the spot. She had innumerable limbs and could feel, where her toes should have been, the slow wiggling in the ground of worms and brown ants, as busy as businessmen. She felt so natural she concluded she'd always been a maple tree, that she had slumbered, as maples do, during the long white winter when her branches were encased in ice and the meadow was sprinkled with a film of snow that looked like talcum powder, and only dreamed she was a woman. Now she was awake. Spring birds were returning from their long sojourn South to reinhabit her uppermost limbs. Goofus birds flew backward, as was their habit, and settled in her leaves, as did Phillyvamos and the single-winged, storklike Gillyfamoo birds. Wiggywams (*Melancorpus dissolvens*)—beaverlike beasts who often dissolve in their own tears—settled to sleep against her trunk. They were joined by Tripodermae (*Collapsocorpus geomobilus*) who retreated their telescopic legs and lay back on their long kangaroo tails to rest in her shade. Some birds sang, and she understood their language, as well as the obscure tongue of the other trees and slumbering beasts at the edge of the meadow. The dream was over; she was going to be all right.

Then she woke up.

Faith looked down and realized she was stretched across her bed. Maxwell must have carried her into the bedroom. She called to him. No answer. She could have been angry again, but she fought that urge, wondering with absolute uncertainty if she was indeed Faith Cross who dreamed she was a maple tree, or a maple tree yet dreaming she was Faith. Somehow, not knowing made her peaceful again. She reviewed the last year with Maxwell, and decided it was neither real nor a dream, but a nightmare somewhere between life and death. She remembered the wedding ceremony at Mount Calvary Baptist Church on the South Side, and the grinning guests from Maxwell's office. Even Mrs. Octavia Beasley had come, dressed in white with an enormous pink peony pinned to her dress, crying as though Faith were her only child. Barrett, she remembered, had been absent, conspicuously so. He never plagued her again. It was just as well. He would have disapproved of the many tables of catered food in the church basement, her gown of ivory silk organza and imported lace. Maxwell, believing her story of being orphaned early in life, had agreed to pay all the wedding expenses. He had even seemed happy their first few weeks together, felt on top of things, and decided to rent an apartment for them by the lakefront. In the sky. He'd spent money freely, anticipating his hundred-dollar raise. Vividly she remembered the horror in his eyes the evening he came home a month after their wedding to announce that the prison column had been postponed until the newspaper's circulation picked up. All the Chicago papers were failing, he said, and *The Sentry* was failing fastest.

"It's television!" he fumed at the dinner table. "People think they can get their news off the television sets." He scowled and exhaled heavily, hurtling food from his teeth across the table at her. Looking around the room at the cause of their debts—a six-hundred-dollar stereo, expensive furniture, and Wedgwood-pattern wall-to-wall carpeting—enraged him. It brought on an attack; he grabbed at his chest and frantically pumped his respirator. "You've got to stop buying so much. Goddamn it, Faith! We'll go bankrupt!"

Then the fights began. They were all one-sided. "I don't argue," Maxwell said, which meant he turned his back to her and dammed his ears after laying down a law. In turn, Faith hurled furniture at his back, tore the gossamer-thin silk curtains from the wall, and started to break, one by one, their china. If all else failed, she could scream to shatter his silence. "If you don't care about *me*," he'd roar, "then think about the neighbors!" She would scream louder, and Maxwell, in frustration, would shake her until her teeth rattled. "Then think about the *landlord*!"

It was a nightmare. Faith climbed out of bed and went into their electrical U-shaped kitchen. Wainscoted wall cabinets formed a continuous line around the corners of the room, and here and there were electrical appliances which, she realized, saved her time but failed to tell her what to do with those extra hours. She pulled back the curtain of the room's single window and looked down the sixteen stories to the street. Pedestrians were below—as tiny as chinches on a pillowcase. And wasn't that view what she'd wanted, searched and lied for? Wasn't Maxwell, after all, the good thing Lavidia told her to find? The words turned sour on her tongue. She bent over the sink, feeling old, knowing that accusing him would be easy. Also, wrong. Maxwell wasn't evil, just disillusioned, not malicious, only disappointed. She knew she'd destroyed something important in him when she confessed her past in a moment of depression last Christmas. It had been a mistake. A sense of melancholy had enveloped her like a sheath, a nagging sense of dread that had no location, and she'd turned to him, spilling her memories of the hotel. The realization shook him horribly; he moved his pillow and bed clothing into the living room to sleep as far away from her as possible after that night. On the sofa. He slept there still, sulking, uncomfortably pinched between the armrests. She tried not to think about it. It wasn't her fault that no one had told him what life was about—the degradation, the death of great dreams.

Now she felt queer again, a muscle beating in her forehead, her hands burning on her wrists. Faith began to busy herself in the kitchen: she dropped two slices of diet bread into the toaster and removed a carton of eggs from the refrigerator. One she set on the counter to boil for her breakfast, then, remembering her daily struggle with IT, she took two, broke them in a saucer and separated the white of the eggs from the yolks. She took the saucer into the bathroom and smeared the white of the eggs on her face, staring at herself in the mirror until her skin began to tighten and draw up. Her thoughts slipped back and forth between memories, and though she faced the mirror she did not see herself for a while, not until the egg facial hardened and the surface of her skin appeared to crack, the lips turning white, the lines in her face becoming deep like those in clay baked by the sun. The facial made her look old and ossified, as brittle in her bones as Lavidia had been. She squinted, knowing she wasn't old, knowing her life was not already at an end, but unable to convince her uneasy stomach of this.

Came smoke from the kitchen. She hurried there, her face drawn up tight, and found the toast burning—it hadn't popped up and the room was full of the sharp smell of smoke. Now she wasn't hungry. Faith dumped the toast into a cellophane-lined waste can and stumbled into the living room, feeling raw; she left the curtains drawn and sat down in the middle of the floor, crying until the tears ran down her cheeks and washed off a good deal of her facial. Something had gone wrong a long time ago. It seemed that she wasn't out of bondage, not one bit. But that made no sense. What had been days of destitution and a destiny-driven life on the streets were now days of leisure. What had been a life of need was now a life of relative ease. Her closets were filled with custom-made clothing. She had more than ample food, a purse bulging with special plastic cards to purchase, on the spot, anything that caught her eye. She had everything, children, all the good things.

But Faith jumped to her feet, floundering around the spacious living room, afraid and pulling at her fingers. She wandered from room to room and finally stopped when she passed the bathroom again. For an hour she soaked herself in the tub, still feeling somehow unclean and uncomfortable at the pit of her stomach, thinking: Whenever she tried to pin this feeling down to a specific thing, such as something Maxwell had said or done, or anything that irritated her regularly, it escaped, slipping away as buoyant as the soap in her tub when it was pushed under water. As she toweled herself dry Faith knew she had experienced nothing like this until she came North. Yet it had nothing to do with locality. She and Maxwell had traveled through the Carolinas and had stopped for a few days in Georgia during their honeymoon. Even then she had felt it. Just to make sure the malaise was within her and not in the world, she coaxed Maxwell into driving through Hatten County. At first sight of the hills, the familiar scenery, she'd grown excited. She directed him to her parents' old farmhouse, pretending to be in search of a good fortuneteller in the backwoods who could foresee their future. The farmhouse was burned to the ground. Dark as satyr droppings. The stones that once supported it were strewn around the yard; only two walls, those on the sides, and the black stove of the kitchen kiln still stood, like lonely rocks at Stonehenge. Nothing remained of the furniture inside. All was ash. And around her parents' graves thick weeds had grown. In town she learned from a feed-store merchant new to the county that lightning had exploded along the farmhouse roof months ago and, within hours, the building was gone. It was so far off the road that the firemen had been unable to come within a hundred yards with their trucks and hoses. So blackened wood, skeletal foundations, and the stench of sulfur were all that remained.

When Maxwell left the store for a moment, Faith leaned over the counter closer to the proprietor and asked, "Do you know if Dr. Lynch still lives in town?"

"Lynch?" The proprietor rubbed his chin, then snapped his fingers. "Sure! You mean that loony old doctor that used to—"

"Yes," Faith said, wringing her fingers. "Is he here?"

"Nope." He yawned, his mouth as wide as a pit. "I heard tell he started research into plant life 'bout six months ago, and found out that rutabaga and philodendrons had feelings jes like people. Don't that beat all? It really shook him up—blew his brains out with a forty-four on Christmas Eve. . . ."

Faith's stomach sank. She thought for a moment, then said, "What about Oscar Lee Jackson?"

"We got us a new undertaker," the proprietor drawled. "Old man Jackson retired, went to California, I hear. . . ."

"Then Reverend Brown," Faith said, "do you know *him*?"

"Sho." He laughed. "At least while he was alive I did. That pain he was always havin' in his side finally got the best of him. He passed away right in the middle of a sermon 'gainst hoodoo and conjurin'. . . ."

Faith held her breath, staring at him, though her mind was miles away. "What about the Swamp Woman? Is she still here?"

"The Swamp *what*?" He removed his tiny silver pince-nez and stared at her. She dropped the question.

"What're you crying about?" Maxwell asked as they headed south for Florida. "You're always whimpering and whining about something." He craned his neck around and glared at her. "What is it *now*?"

She told him the change in climate was affecting her eyes. But the wreckage of the farmhouse never left her mind. There was nothing left of her old life. Nothing but tall tales. Perhaps Todd and Lavidia had become trees, which was well and good for them. Their release couldn't help her one iota. If she was to free herself from bondage, she needed help.

Faith drained the bathtub water, pulled on her bathrobe, and went to the kitchen to prepare for Maxwell and his guest. Children, this sister was low, lower than a whale's belly at the bottom of the China sea. And that's *low*. She fixed a soufflé with vengeance, knowing that Maxwell would never be able to help her. She didn't doubt for a minute that he was part of her problem, and that this was why she reacted toward him as Lavidia had to Todd, but in exactly the opposite way; whereas her mother chided Todd for dreaming, she lost no opportunity for riding Maxwell for not dreaming enough. The office party last Christmas had done it. She couldn't keep it out of her mind.

Before leaving for *The Sentry*'s Christmas party she'd tried to explain her quest to Maxwell. She hid nothing, not even her encounters with Tippis and Barrett, and the months in Hotel Sinclair. Maxwell listened in horror from the front doorway, his mouth open. He jerked his plaid muffler around his neck as though trying to strangle himself. Then he leaned in the doorway, wheezing, his head hidden in the crook of his arm.

A chill swept across Faith's shoulders. She wanted to hide, to take back every word. She was not ashamed of what she'd experienced; she had even thought there was a kernel of tragedy and strength in it. But her narrative, finally framed in her own words, had sounded shocking even to her own ears. Obscene. She was afraid to move or say more.

"How could you *do* this to me?" Maxwell whimpered. He jerked up his head and stared. His face fell away; beneath it was a grimacing demon deprived of its gold. "Are you trying to tell me I married a—"

"I couldn't help it!" Faith hurried toward him; she encircled his waist with her arms. Maxwell shoved her away, disgusted, and went into the long, quiet hallway where he began shouting at the top of his voice, "Did everybody hear that?!" He spread his arms as Christ had on the Cross. Unlike Christ, he laughed bitterly. "Does everybody know what life's done to Isaac Maxwell *this* time?"

"Stop it!" Faith screamed.

Maxwell shook. He assumed his arrogant stance again, right foot forward, left knee locked, his hand in his pocket. And already his underarms were moist and his face shiny with sweat. Down the hall a woman opened her front door and stuck a head full of grenadelike curlers out, gawking. Maxwell balled his fists at his side and groaned. "Let's go. . . ."

At the Christmas party, Faith's inner feeling of numbness was so great she couldn't drink. She tried, but found she was too tired to keep lifting her cup to her lips. Once inside the newsroom, decorated with a large, ornamented tree and blue-and-gold streamers hanging from the ceiling, Maxwell, though still in a pique, replaced his sour expression with a broad grin. He kept filling his cup, gravitated from Ragsdale to Cummings, and finally cornered Lowell by the tree. She could hear him pleading for the commencement of his prison column.

There seemed to be no way out of her bondage; her condition, her past were apparently a mark on her brow, because that entire evening people approached her with their problems. A young black from the circulation department singled her out minutes after she and Maxwell arrived, sashayed over to her, swinging his hips, and perched himself in front of her on the edge of a desk.

"I don't plan to be here forever, sister," he said, as if she'd asked. "I've got plans for my own business. . . ."

"Is that so?" It was very, very hard for her to stay awake.

"That's right." He leered knowingly at her, reeking with self-confidence, Brut, and alcohol. "I figure I can raise a little front money here, then invest it in a newspaper distribution service—just as soon as I learn the ropes here."

. . . five, six, *seven*. Just as soon as she'd released her smile, Ragsdale replaced the boy. Tilted to one side of his squarish head was a red, white, and blue party cap; around his neck was a string of Christmas-tree ornaments he'd made into a necklace. His breath, she noticed, smelled like a brewery.

"I'm a hippy!" Ragsdale roared.

"Sure." Faith reached for her drink. Though she didn't want it, she forced down its contents, and tried to smile. *One, two, three. . . .*

"Isaac's doing fine," Ragsdale said, trying to pull himself together. He blinked myopically at her through two glazed green eyes. "He makes mistakes sometimes, but over-all he's okay." His eyes wandered over her breasts, to her face, as he swayed back and forth on his heels. "Did I ever tell you what happened to the last black reporter we had?"

135

The sides of her face and cheeks were aching. Faith released her dimples, paused for respite, then forced them back. "No. . . ."

Ragsdale downed the rest of his drink in a single, rawthroated gulp. "He's with *The New York Times* now, I think. Oliver Lewis, our first bla—" He paused, narrowing his eyes and sucking at his cheek teeth. "Which do you prefer, Mrs. Maxwell—black, colored, or Negro?"

"For myself," she said testily, "Mrs. Maxwell."

Ragsdale lowered his eyes; his face colored. "Anyway, *he* ran off from us to the *Times*, and the other people we had of your, eh, persuasion, took choice government jobs. It's damned hard to keep a black newsman with competition like that!" Ragsdale sighed and studied the inside of his empty cup. "Do you think Isaac will stay with us?"

Her head was splitting; someone, she was certain, had split her skull with an ax and left it there. "Do you—do you want him to stay?"

"Of course! Why, if it wasn't for Isaac, the *Daily Defender* would have our coverage on the South Side beat by a mile."

"Then," she groaned, "he'll stay, I guess."

Satisfied, Ragsdale excused himself and crossed the room. Faith was certain she was going to be sick. The constant repetition of "Jingle Bells" on the scratchy record-player in the corner, the eruption of laughter from the blanched wives of the employees as they tottered around the room, and the slow but dulling effect of the alcohol—all this had her at her tether. Toward the end of the evening, Maxwell returned to her and led her to a corner of the room beside the sweet-smelling Christmas tree.

"Lowell's got his nose open for you," he said. He fished into his pocket and handed her the car keys. "I'll take a cab home," he said.

"What does *that* mean?" She had never seen him like this. He was so drunk his lower lip was hanging like an oven lid. He must have left and vomited somewhere, perhaps in the employee's bathroom, because gray kernels of undigested food—cheese crackers and chips—were caked in his skimpy mustache and spotted his white collar. His eyes, despite all this, were frighteningly clear.

"It means you're going to carry the ball for once." Maxwell hiccoughed and winced. He held his chest as though in pain. "You owe me *some*thing, Faith! And it doesn't make much difference since you're a goddamn wh—"

"Isaac!" She wanted to hit him, to tear at his red eyes and scream until the intensity of her voice or shame caused him to dissolve, fade away or disappear. She looked over her shoulder. The city room was almost empty. Crushed paper cups, some smeared with lipstick stains, were scattered across the floor between the even rows of desks and buzzing wire-copy machines. Standing by the door, sipping from his cup, was the old copy editor: Lowell—thin, with knobby, tree-limb arms. The lower half of his face, to tell the truth, looked like the impression made by a horse's hoof, sunken, shapeless, and slipping into the collar of his shirt as though his chin and collar were made in the same mold.

"I don't wanna argue," Maxwell said. "I don't wanna fight no more. . . ."

Neither did Faith. She took the car keys from his open pink palm and walked toward the door as Lowell turned toward her. He was incredibly drunk, his shirttail was outside his pants, and his trousers bulged with an erection as hard as Chinese arithmetic. He smiled.

Six-fifteen.

Faith sped up her preparations. Maxwell would be back at precisely seven. He was usually punctual, never a moment late unless he'd been drinking after work. There was really no way to hate him. For he, too, was dead living, and went through each day, not bumping into other things in the darkness of the cave, but swinging at them. The deferral of his column had nearly ruined his morale. The day after it was tabled indefinitely he came to work an hour late. He told her over dinner that night that the telephone on his desk had rung and he'd taken a story about the marriage of the daughter of one of Chicago's most powerful city officials. Lucius Bitch. Young Bitch Marries was the way Maxwell wrote the headline for the evening edition. Nothing came of that until the following morning when he arrived at the office to find every telephone extension in the building screaming. Ragsdale had already yanked out half his gray hair, Cummings was champing aspirin and tranquilizers like candy.

"Didn't you know we endorsed him last year?" Lowell shouted across the room from his desk.

Maxwell shrugged his shoulders. He'd already had three drinks that morning, but wanted another. "Yeah," he said, "I wrote the editorial, remember? SENTRY SELECTS BITCH, right?"

Lowell moaned; he buried his head in his trembling hands. "It's *Fitch*, Isaac! Lucius *Fitch*!"

That was hardly the worst of it. A month later Maxwell came to work and found a uniformed policeman standing beside his desk. He stopped in his tracks, dropped his briefcase, and looked at Cummings, Lowell, and Ragsdale. They kept their eyes averted from him, fixed on the sheets of morning copy strewn across their desks.

"What *is* this?" Maxwell shouted. He fumbled in his coat pocket for his plastic respirator. "What's going on here?"

The police officer stepped toward him. He had a round face and clear blue eyes. Dressed in blue, he looked somewhat like a robot and sounded like one when he said, "You'll have to come with me, Mr. Maxwell."

Maxwell jumped back three feet. "For *what*?"

The officer unfolded a sheet of official-looking paper. "The complainants state that yesterday you checked out company car number fifteen at nine hundred." He looked up at Maxwell. "It's still missing."

"I never touched any of those cars!" Maxwell shouted. "Fred," he pleaded to Ragsdale, "is that *your* complaint?"

Ragsdale looked up with a straight and sad face, then took a sip from the coffee on his desk. It was cold and covered with white scum. "The parking-lot attendant says he saw you take the car yesterday. He said he asked you where you were going, and you told him it was none of his damn business." Ragsdale looked away. "I'm sorry, Isaac. . . ."

The whole world caved in. The officer took Maxwell's arm and led him toward the front door. They stopped to let a wiry young black in a pink tank top and blue bellbottoms squeeze between them. Maxwell recognized the boy as the same one who tried to monopolize Faith's time at the Christmas party. Straightaway he went to the bulletin board where the company car keys hung on rows of silver hooks. Maxwell broke free from the officer's grip and raced to the board. He snatched the car key from the boy's hand.

"What car was taken?" he called to Cummings.

"Fifteen."

"This is it!" Maxwell shouted. He raised the key high in the air like a standard and looked at the confused boy beside him.

"I had to drop off some evening papers uptown," the boy said, a frayed toothpick stuck in the left corner of his mouth. "It was late so I took the car home with me."

Maxwell, almost sobbing, hugged the boy like a brother.

He was certain his editors were out to get him, just waiting for him to make some mistake. Faith remembered listening to his complaints at night. She guessed it was her ability to listen that kept their marriage together. That, and "carrying the ball." She turned off the stove and set the dinner table with their best, and as of yet unpaid-for, silverware. Then she went to her bedroom to sit in front of her mirror for half an hour, struggling with IT until she heard Maxwell's key turn in the front door.

He called, "We're here, honey!"

"I'll be out in a minute." Faith struggled with the zipper to her dress, checked herself once in her mirror, and stepped into the hallway. She could hear them talking in the front room, Maxwell and the ex-prisoner. Something slowed her steps, bringing her to a halt halfway down the hall. She listened. Alternating with her husband's voice was that of the other—warmer, slower, somehow more self-assured. It alarmed her, not because it rang resonant with more power than Maxwell's, or because it belonged to a man who'd spent, she'd heard, his last three years in prison. But because it sounded, strangely enough, of Georgia.

She entered the front room, stopping feet from them as they talked. Maxwell and his guest faced her, the latter stretching out his thick, calloused hand. Maxwell was in his favorite stance, his right hand playing with a loose thread on his jacket. As she reached for that rough hand hung in the air Faith felt her feet sinking through the thick carpet, through the floor, the earth, perhaps, down through its many-colored layers to the white-hot center of the world. Sometimes, children, you'll get that feeling. You'll be listening to someone and swear you've heard the same words he's saying sometime before; you'll be some place where you've never been, and swear 'fore God you've been there. You'll catch your breath like Faith did. You'll blink to clear your eyes. She did that, too. And if you're like Faith your lips will turn up in a smile, because you'll know reality is simply a rhythm, repeating itself, flashing the same faces into the world in different ages and different times and always—as far as your life is concerned—returning you, from time to time, to some touchstone from which your heart has tarried but to which it must always return.

Faith, as she shook the stranger's hand, believed it. She felt it in her blood even before Maxwell made their introductions.

"Honey," he said, "this is Alpha Omega Holmes."

olmes gave no sign. He took Faith's outstretched hand and pumped it until Maxwell frowned with impatience. "My pleasure, Mrs. Maxwell," Holmes said, grinning. Faith searched his face for recognition. Could he recognize her through IT? He winked. She almost fainted.

Maxwell cleared his throat. "Shall we get down to business?" He removed his sports coat and flung it across a rocking chair against the wall. "We can talk over dinner"—turning to Faith, "it's ready, isn't it?"

Faith quickly pulled her thoughts together. "It's on the table. . . ."

"*Ummgh*," Maxwell grunted, pleased but putting on a great show of indifference. Then he led Holmes into the dining room. It had a French Provincial feeling—yellow wallpaper with a brown motif, checked curtains, wire mesh in the cupboard doors, and French Provincial pottery, all designed to complement Faith's complexion. The light there was brighter than elsewhere in the apartment. Or so it seemed to Faith. She had put her best tablecloth, the one rich and green and pleated on its border, on their circular dining-room table. The details of the room stood out for her, and suddenly she felt awkward, as if her arms and legs were lead beams swinging through a room of glass. She moved carefully behind them, silent and staying in her place, recognizing Holmes's back as the image she'd seen in the Thaumaturgic Mirror. He seemed somewhat taller, more muscular than before, with bulging veins that moved under the skin on his forearms and neck like snakes. His clothes were simple—matching blue work shirt and trousers, low-cut leather boots the color of woodbark but a bit the worse for wear, and a brown corduroy jacket which she hung in the front closet. Anyone who dressed so simply, who disregarded his exterior, had to be rich inside, as complex and intricate as an old gold watch.

"As you know, there's an awful lot riding on this new feature," Maxwell said. He crossed his thin arms on the table, his head hunched between his shoulders as he played with his spoon. "I'll need to know as much about your background as I can to write a sidebar for the first column. . . ."

Holmes sat quietly, his big hands folded in his lap. His face was linear and lean-jawed. His hair, dark and moderately trimmed, was thinning on top. Faith watched him, almost able to hear the words forming in his mind before he spoke. "What do you want to know?"

"The Five W's," Maxwell said. "Who, What, Where—you know."

Holmes leaned back and cracked his knuckles, then sipped at his coffee cup to wet his lips. "I grew up in Hatten County, Georgia," he said. "If a man's from Hatten County, he'll usually say so right away. If he isn't," Holmes chuckled, "you shouldn't embarrass him by asking."

Maxwell frowned, bending his spoon out of shape, then back again. "Yeah. Right. What brought you to Chicago?"

Sighing, Holmes looked at Faith. "Work, mainly." He drew his lips back over two rows of square teeth. "All the mills and factories back home were layin' people off. My folks had a stretch of good bottom land handed down through the family since Reconstruction, but hit started goin' dry in the forties. Pa used to say hit was so bad, if he sold hit to a church, the congregation would have to fertilize the whole place just to raise a prayer. And the creek that run 'cross hit got so parched I once counted 'bout a hundred bullfrogs that never learned how to swim." Holmes laughed and slapped his knee. "Heh, heh, talk 'bout hard times, buddy!"

Faith hid her hands under the table. They were trembling.

"What kind of work did you find?"—Maxwell.

"I couldn't find a thing. Nothin'! Mind you, I ain't crazy 'bout work—hit didn't scare me none. I can lay down beside the biggest chore you ever seen and fall right asleep. Heh heh. But I was hungry —so hungry my stomach musta thought my throat'd been cut. I looked for months." He glanced at Maxwell, his eyes wide with humor. "Things got so bad at the flophouse where I was stayin' on the West Side that the rats were too weak to run or hide when somebody cut on the lights. And you could bile me for a sea horse if I wouldn't rather crawl into a nest o' wildcats, heels foremost, 'fore I did something like go on relief or start beggin'." Holmes started laughing again—it sounded like a hyena imitating a man. Faith smiled, then bit her lip when she saw Maxwell's incredulous eyes.

"What did they convict you for?" Maxwell demanded irritably.

"Stealin'," Holmes said. "I don't reckon hit was *really* stealin', though. I never took more than what I could use for food, rent, and a new canvas." As he ate, Holmes wagged his fork in the air reflectively, his jaws packed like a beaver's. "I don't suppose they would have caught me if hit wasn't for that. I had hit all figured out—I needed twenty dollars a week to live on, not a penny mo' nor less. So on Saturdays, if I couldn't win the money in a game of chance, I'd relieve somebody of exactly that amount. I stopped a guy down on Fullerton Avenue, liberated his wallet, and was in the wind. When I checked the wallet hit had twenty-*five* dollars in hit. Imagine! So I looked up his address—a Mr. Luther Langford, I believe—and took the five dollars back. . . ."

"That's when they caught you?" Faith said.

Holmes nodded. "A patrol car pulled up quicker nor a 'gator can chew a pup after I'd dropped that five-dollar bill in the mailbox!"

None of this sat well with Maxwell. He pulled at his left sock, which kept slipping down his leg, and ate carelessly, too quickly and with such huge mouthfuls that meat caught in his throat and made him cough. That upset his breathing. He hurried to the bedroom, found his spare respirator, and returned weakly to the dining room, wiping his eyes. "You aren't at all *sorry* for what you did?" he said.

"Sho am," Holmes drawled. "That twenty dollars woulda doubled the ante in the game back at the flophouse if I coulda made hit back in time."

Maxwell went silent, smoking a strange new product he'd found in a dime store. *Asthma Cigarettes.* They were filterless, twice the size of regular cigarettes in diameter, and filled with a green tobacco that smelled like hay. He smoked, coughed, but kept going until he'd finished three in a row. Faith opened the window to clear out the room and cleaned off the table as Maxwell and Holmes withdrew into the living room. In the kitchen, seated at the table with a fresh martini, she held her breath to catch snatches of dialogue drifting through the hall with Maxwell's green smoke. Holmes's voice, its tone and timbre, brought back, not with its words but its ring, that lost life in Georgia. It lifted her thoughts back to the time he'd saved her life. She'd be dead, she was certain, if Alpha Omega Holmes hadn't outfoxed Old Man Cragg.

(It was summer, one of those hot, sweltering days when your lips were so dry they cracked from the heat. Holmes suggested they steal into Old Man Cragg's east orchard and carry away a few peaches from his tree. She'd objected violently, because Cragg was second in awesomeness only to Big Todd. Children, he was so mean he gave his kids ten cents each every night if they skipped dinner, stole it from them during the night, and whopped 'em the next morning for losing it. Mean? Why, he was so mean and *low*down he had to reach up to touch bottom; he was so black his wife, Elsie, had to throw a sheet over his head so the sun could rise. No, you didn't mess with Cragg. Or his peaches. Faith demurred, but Alpha dragged her off to Cragg's farm. He rubbed chimney soot over their arms and legs and faces so they could sneak around invisibly at night. Then he shinnied up one of Cragg's trees and started tossing ripe peaches down into a basket while Faith kept watch. By and by, she felt something behind her.

A voice, like thunder, exploded. "You children better be baptized, 'cause I got yo' contracts fo' West Hell right heah!"

Alpha fell from the tree. He and Faith looked up and saw possibly the biggest man in the world—huge, and so dark lightning bugs flew around his head thinking it was midnight. He reached out to them with hands as big around as wheels on a hay wagon.

"You better not!" Alpha shouted.

"I better *what*?" Cragg boomed. "Boy, when I'm through, there'll be six men on either side of you; there won't be enough marrow in yo' bones to fill a thimble!"

Faith hid her face. She wanted to eat one of those peaches if this, indeed, was the end. But her throat was solid. It was hard to breathe.

"I'll take you on," Alpha said, "but you've got to let me pray first—"

Cragg grunted, and rolled up his worksleeves. "Tha's a good thought—you pray real good."

Still on his knees, Alpha raised his sooty hands, closed his eyes, and started rapping. "O God, you know I didn't mean to kill Stackalee and High John the Conqueror and John Henry, and Toledo Slim and Peg-Leg Willy, but they touched me and got a douse of this here terrible disease. You know that I told John Brown and Rip Bailey that this thing I got is terminal, that hit starts yo' skin to peelin' like old paint, and you start swellin' up with horrible boils and hit drives you mad and turns one half of your brain to pure crystal and the other half to water. You know I told them about hit before they touched me, Lord, jes like I'm tellin' this man Cragg who's gonna touch me and get hit and die all black and bloated in his bed like alla my relatives did. Don't blame me, Lord, if he turns to ashes even 'fore Oscar Lee Jackson can get his death wagon out to Cragg's house, or if his widow-woman and po', hungry kids come down with hit, too. . . ."

Alpha opened his eyes and stood up. He stretched out his sooty arms and started walking toward Cragg. Who trembled, spun on his heels, and ran like hell. Faith gave Alpha a big, sooty kiss, dug into the peaches, and ate herself sick.)

She left the kitchen table and hurried to the front room, where she'd heard the squeak of chair legs against the floor. Maxwell had Holmes's coat, and was walking with him to the front door.

". . . Next Friday, then?" Maxwell said.

"Sho. We can start any time you like." Holmes saw Faith and stuck out his hand again. "Mrs. Maxwell, that sho nuff was one of the most bodacious and tetotaciously pleasing meals ever to cross my lips."

"Thank you." She stepped back dizzily, closing the hand into which Alpha had pressed a folded note. Maxwell said, "I'll be back soon," and escorted Holmes out the door. Faith, when she was certain they were gone, opened the note: *Let me see you tomorrow*. He gave the time and place. She hid the note in her brassière and paced the apartment for an hour. Holmes was exactly Maxwell's opposite. Which made him identical to her. That broke Big Todd's maxim about marriage, but she knew she didn't care. Not one whit.

At ten, the front door flew open, and Maxwell came in. "It's not going to work," he said. He dropped his wig on the dining-room table on his way to the kitchen, then returned with a vodka and tonic. "The man's all wrong for this column!"

"What?" Faith's left hand went to her breast where she pressed down the wad of paper in her bra.

Maxwell settled into an armchair and kicked off his shoes. "I said Holmes isn't right for the column. He's not what I visualized for it. He's not angry enough—he doesn't show enough Will Power." He took a drink, gulped, and glanced up at Faith. "You can tell a man by that. You heard that bullshit he was babbling over dinner, didn't you? Je-*sus*!"

Faith sat down on the arm of the chair, looking straight down at Maxwell's bald head. "He has to be mad?"

"Damn right he's got to be mad! He's got to be representative of all the rage a prisoner feels, all the frustration and bitterness." He pressed his cool glass to his forehead and rolled it from his left temple to his right, closed his eyes, and muttered, "Holmes is too at peace with himself and the world. You'd think he'd lived in a fairy tale, or something—not a prison. . . ."

Faith slid off the arm of the chair to sit on a cricket stool in front of him. She rested her head in her hands, looking up. "What're you going to do?"

Maxwell groaned. "*My* hands are tied. I've got to select the right mouthpiece for the column. Holmes is on probation, and he's broken it already! They're supposed to report all their earnings, new possessions, change of addresses, and things like that every month the Lord brings. Holmes hasn't even called his parole officer once since he was released." Maxwell rubbed his eyes sleepily and stood up, stretching his arms. "I'll bet that they'll have him back behind bars in two weeks. I'll bet he hasn't enough Will Power to stay free a month!" Unbuttoning his shirt, he wagged his head from side to side. "I'll have to find myself another parolee."

Faith was on her feet, pulling at her fingers. "We won't see him again?"

Maxwell turned down the fold-away section of the living-room couch, dropped his trousers in the middle of the floor, and lay down. "I hope not!"

Faith slept not a wink all night. As she lay alone in her bedroom, her mind worked like machinery, a constantly churning instrument that focused upon Alpha Omega Holmes, moving around her memories of him like a lilting jazz improvisation, children—inspecting first this side, then that, reviewing him again and again from every possible perspective until her memories, like music, died away. She jumped out of bed when the warm sunlight of morning fell across her face, and fixed Maxwell's breakfast before he awoke. Maxwell, after stumbling into the bathroom in his sweaty shorts, came into the kitchen wearing his bathrobe, scratching his head.

"Damn," he whistled. "How come you're so happy this morning? What'd I do?"

She laughed. It was true; she hadn't been so happy in months. Her sleepless night had not left a mark on her beyond the pillow wrinkles now fading from the right side of her face. Too, there was lint from the bed linen in her hair. But she was wide awake, her irises the size of saucers. A healthy, ruddy coloring like that caused by sexual excitement spread across her cheeks. She moved about the kitchen so lightly on her feet that Maxwell was overcome. He grabbed her and kissed her neck.

"Am I still your good thing?" he asked, his voice hoarse before his first cup of coffee.

"Uh huh."

"And maybe," he offered timidly, "maybe we can still make it, eh?"

"Yes—maybe," Faith said, and she broke away from him to turn on the burner beneath a frying pan of bacon. Maxwell ate quickly, not quite awake, and—it was true—he looked somewhat wolfish at the table. His eyes were pink, his skin still blotched from sleep. He dressed and kissed her at the door. When he was gone, Faith took a quick cold shower, dressed, and started for the elevator. She stopped there, then hurried back to the apartment, where she pricked her left forefinger with a sewing needle and used the needle to write Holmes's full name backward in blood on the reverse side of his note. To add to her allurement she rubbed a film of rice powder along her breasts.

She rode the subway to his address in the lower sixties, reciting Psalms 45 and 46 to herself until she arrived. His neighborhood made her nauseous. Old brownstones with shattered windows, shattered doors, and shattered steps leaned forward as if about to fall into the street; clouds of yellow smoke rolled through the air from a chemical factory on the corner and settled on the cobblestones of the street as fine powder. She saw the heads of rats pushing through small piles of garbage in an alley, an old man still asleep under a blanket of newspapers—*The Sentry*—on the corner near a liquor store, and abandoned cars all along the curb. Down the street, whirling in a circle like a dervish, was a mad dog chasing its short tail, white foam like meerschaum filling up its mouth. Faith checked the address on her note again, anxious, smudging the paper with moisture from her fingers. Then she saw it clearly: the scene in the Swamp Woman's Thaumaturgic Mirror—this had been it. She crossed the street to a basement apartment on the corner, descended the steps, and knocked on an unpainted door, then waited, remembering that, in truth, there was no way to know with certainty if love and all she longed to believe about Alpha were real. Gestures told you nothing, nor did notes pressed into your palm by an old lover from home. It struck her that she'd been silly and was about to be made a fool. At the second she started to turn, to forget this affair entirely, the door opened, and Holmes stood before her in a pair of baggy gray pants and a wrinkled shirt open to his navel. He smiled. Features on a manikin. She parted her lips to speak, then simply licked them, unable to move as she wanted, unable to toss her arms around his neck. *How do you know he loves you?* Faith swallowed, a bit loud. She struggled for a moment, deep inside her head, then threw her arms around him. She listened, her ear to his chest, to his heart, and felt everything would be all right. She was certain. That was all.

Holmes looked down at her and chuckled deep in his throat. "We'd better stop, or your father'll whop my tail like he use to."

"Huhn?" Faith allowed him to direct her inside his single-room apartment. "I don't understand. . . ."

"Coffee?" he asked.

Faith declined. She took a seat on the corner of his bed—just a mattress, really, lying flat with half its white stuffings falling to the floor. Holmes walked barefoot to a hot plate across the room and started water boiling for instant coffee. A few groceries—unopened cans of butter beans, corn and cabbage, bottles of cheap wine and unopened boxes of instant potatoes—were stacked along the eastern wall behind a hot plate and beside a small refrigerator. His room reminded her of her own at the hotel: bare wooden floorboards with splinters sticking up like sharp needles, a low ceiling with a naked bulb in its center, and dingy walls. But the walls were covered in places with preliminary charcoal sketches. Half-finished canvases lay about and crushed tubes of paint were underfoot, their contents worked into the texture of the floor. The room had a feeling of presence and warmth that glowed behind Holmes's poverty. No— that word was wrong. It revealed not poverty but a sort of voluntary retreat from the world, similar to the atmosphere of a treehouse or a cave where children hide from their parents and talk about girls (or boys) and terrify one another with ghost stories. Beside it, her apartment was spiritual slum. Relaxing, she noticed an in-progress painting in the center of the room; she remembered the face well: the Swamp Woman.

Holmes poured his coffee into a tin cup, which he held in both hands, and sat down beside her on the mattress. Closer to her now, he seemed slimmer, shorter, and not at all like Big Todd. His sleeves were rolled up to his elbows, and she could see a tattoo around his neck with this legend beneath it: *Cut on dotted line.*

"Your daddy used to wallop me whenever I got funny with you, remember?" he said.

Faith searched her memory. She found nothing there. "Daddy was dead when I first met you. . . ."

"He was dead all right," Holmes laughed, "but his ghost could exfluncticate any man alive. Believe it." He sipped at his coffee, set it down, and rubbed his arms. "You 'member that time on your porch when I first run my hand down the front of your dress? And I flew outta my chair and ran off down the field, you remember?"

It was coming back. Slowly she recalled being seated with him on the wide farmhouse porch, late at night after Lavidia had gone to bed. The heaviness of the air returned to her. It was thick with humidity and smelled of rain after a short-lived sprinkle that left gleaming pools of water along the steps of the porch. She remembered the heavy moonlight floating in those puddles beyond the yard, the fluffy, drifting balls of fur from pussy-willow trees that moved around their heads like fairies, or daydreams. They had watched the rain, enjoying each other too much, had been driven closer together by the thunder, and then the stillness, the heat and oppression of night. They ran out of talk. Holmes wiggled closer to her on the top step of the porch, put his arm around her waist, and waited for her reaction. She could do nothing. She'd wanted him there, that close. Closer. But what of her reputation and pride? The trees were watching her, the summer moon and animals hidden out there in the bushes and trees. They saw her sit without protest as he dropped his hand inside her dress. They were jealous. She could feel it, because she felt she belonged to their world and not that of men, because she'd walked among them, her feet slipping on moonflower vines, her ears hearing and loving every birdsong of morning. They might never forgive her. But she let Holmes have his way until he'd been hurled away from her. He pitched forward off the porch and into the mud, where his head crashed and his arms flew out wild. Without a word, he'd taken off, stumbling through the yard, falling flat on his face, and eventually vanishing from sight.

"That was awful strange," Faith said. She found she could not look at him, especially into his eyes. It involved too much. "I thought maybe you had a nervous condition, and had an attack or something. That's why I never asked about it."

Holmes slapped his knee. "Hit was your old man! Soon as I lay my hand on you, he came along with a haymaker hot enough to set the Mississippi on fire." He imitated the move with his own fist, hitting his jaw, and fell back on the mattress. "He planted hit dead on my chin. Believe hit! I looked up from the floor, and there he was—all big and black and bristlin' mad, standin' between us on the steps. So I started travelin'. I ain't use to fightin' haints—no sir! I've fought some strange things in my time, but I wanted to be ready for him, to have hit out with him in the open. . . ."

"It was Daddy?" Faith shook her head and stared at the floor. "*I* didn't see anything."

"Swear fo' God," Holmes said, and he crossed himself once. "So I went out to the fields when I left you, and waited for him. Sho 'nuff, he came floatin' in toward me on the air. Like smoke. I swung at him, but my hand went right through his chest. Then he slapped me upside my haid, and stood over me, shoutin', 'You mess with my baby 'gain, and I'll whop yo' tail clean into next week!' Well, I figured I couldn't mess with nothin' like that. But I had to see you again, right?"

"Yes," Faith said. She pulled her lower lip, kneading it between her finger and thumb. He was lying—she could smell it (lies smell sweet, children: somewhat like a fresh biscuit), but she said, "That *does* sound like Daddy—"

"Yep," Holmes continued after finishing his coffee, "so I ran straight down to the swamps, and looked up that old witcher 'ooman."

Faith rose and went to the half-finished oil portrait. The outline of the Swamp Woman's head dominated the center of the picture; her yellow eye was shut tight, the green one shone as bright as jade. Faith turned to Holmes, her head pounding with pressure.

"I didn't have nothin' 'gainst your daddy," Holmes said, "but he was standin' in my way. You know how fathers are—they don't think *no*body's good enough for their daughters. Anyway, the witcher 'ooman heard me out, and gave me somethin' to overcome anybody that got in my way. I think I still got hit."

"A mojo?" Faith said.

"Just a minute—" Holmes stood up and fumbled for the frayed billfold in his hip pocket; from it he produced a square strip of white cloth bearing red and black letters:

A I K N

P R M C

D H T R

M M P M

"She wrote it for me during the full moon," he said, "and she told me to go straight to the graveyard where your daddy was buried— where his haint would be waitin' for me to have hit out once and for all. . . ."

Faith hurried to the mattress where Holmes had sat down again, picking at his toenails. "What happened then?"

"Oh, I got there at 'bout midnight. Hit was so dark I couldn't make out none of the headstones. I kept hearing noises, too. Laughter. They scared me. I wasn't but twelve years old then. This big wind came up, then a mighty grist of rain—noises flew up from the ground all around me, like chains were rattlin' somewhere. Honey, I wanted to run home. Believe hit. But you had my nose *wide* open. I woulda wrestled with the Devil and walked a hundred miles jes to keep on seein' you. Sho! But jes when I thought I couldn't stand hit no longer, when I thought my blood was 'bout ready to turn to water, I heard another sound behind me, turned around shakin', and saw your daddy behind me—whiter all over than if he'd jumped in a vat of milk, and twice the size he was when he was livin'. 'You ain't give up yet?' he said. The rain started 'gain, and hit got into my eyes. I could hardly see, and my legs and arms were as stiff as wood. I shouted, 'No!' and then he came at me, his big fists flyin' through the air. I shouted what the witcher 'ooman told me to: *As the eternal fires of West Hell burn, let my adversary twist and turn*! And he stopped jes short of hittin' me, his eyes popped open, and he started turnin' around in circles and screamin'—"

"He *did*?" Faith cried. "Daddy was hurt?"

"Naw, he wasn't hurt—jes caught in that old 'ooman's magic spell. 'Do you give up?' I said, and he cried, 'Naw!' But I knew he had, and was jes too damn proud to admit hit." Holmes looked up cautiously and said, "You don't believe me, do you?"

"Yes, yes, I do," Faith said. But she thought: Big Todd's grave was not in a cemetery but behind their farmhouse—Alpha had lied. But he'd lied well. . . .

"So," Holmes continued, "when he stopped turnin' he fell down, and started tearin' tufts of graveyard grass up with his fists. He shook his head, looked up at me real peaceful-like, and said, 'Ain't nobody beat me in life or death, and anybody who come as close as you did deserves to have my daughter.' Then he started laughin', and 'fore I could say 'nother word he was gone."

Faith fought a sinking feeling in her solar plexus and a chill that seemed to be not on her skin but beneath it. She felt like a bird ensorcelled by the eyes of a cat, and hung on Holmes's slow, melodious speech. "He *really* said that?"

Holmes nodded. Said: "Believe hit. I swore that nothin' was gonna keep Alpha Holmes from his honey if I could help hit, not even dead folks. I didn't count on your momma, though." He whistled through his square teeth. "Live folks can be a lot scarier than dead folks sometimes. . . ."

Faith stood up, returning to the painting of the werewitch, allowing her thoughts to move along its surface. Liar! she thought. But it stood to reason that if Todd approved of *any*one courting her, it would have to be a storyteller like himself. Someone strong, a giant, a Great Fool among frightened ones, a weaver of words and delicious little lies to woo other people and live by. She started, but remained still. Holmes had come up behind her, barefoot and silent, and folded his forearms around her waist.

"Hang me up for bear meat if I ain't been empty inside without you, Faith. . . ."

She hung her head, fighting the warm feeling that sprang between her skin and his. Who else could say something as silly as that—bear meat, indeed!—and make you believe in it? Like Todd, he was just an overgrown boy—long, apelike arms and hard black flesh hiding a mind that could create fabulous lies and believe in them. And, though it was wrong, she believed in them too. "Alpha, I'm married. I've been married for a year, and Isaac is good to me. . . ." She stopped, afraid to pursue that last thought any further. "It would be a sin—"

"Shoot! Life is short, sweetheart—you got to seize the day. Hit'd be a sin *not* to." He placed his rough face next to hers. "I wouldn't bet a huckleberry to a persimmon if you ain't the only gal that ever meant somethin' to me. . . ."

"Alpha, please—" She couldn't think. "Please—"

"I know you've seen lots of ripstavers since you knew me, but I'll be shot if I didn't pray like a horse to cross paths with you again. Without you I'd be as dead as a catfish on a sandbank."

Holmes tasted the inside of her mouth, and she his: warm, as she'd expected, faintly sweet, as she'd hoped. Then she was weightless in his arms, floating toward the soiled mattress. The thought of making love disturbed her. It had never worked out before. It had to be an exchange, give and take. With Arnold Tippis, Faith had felt the energy released between them stifled in this natural expression; rather, it had all come one way—she had been unreal to him, a thing in which to violently unload that energy, that tension Dr. Lynch spoke of; and Crowell had been hardly better with his hasty, mechanical approach to the matter. Maxwell, before they'd ended sex together and he moved to sleep on the sofa, had wanted passively to receive that energy, to be acted upon like soft clay. And with all the others—sheer horror. Yet now as Holmes's shadow fell across her it was somehow different; the energy was released, displaced, and sent shuddering back and forth between them, in the desired exchange. Alpha projected the image of himself in her, as she did within him until they seemed to exist, not as two people, but one. Or, stranger still, as nothing. It was crazy, but she thought of high-school math at the moment their images melted, drifted, and were transformed; she thought of herself, Faith Cross, as one lonely pole in the universe—FC, and Holmes as another—AOH with he a $+$ and she a $-$ when their rhythm touched its telos:

$$AOH: FC$$

Stillness.

Beside him, her pulse beats slipped slowly beneath his own, her chest fell as his rose, rose as his fell, and Faith refound just a bit of the enchantment of her childhood in being a woman. There was a twilight feeling like that of sleep in her body; and in her mind—the frieze of a frost-sprinkled earth, naked brown tamaracks twisting into a sky of milk-white clouds. Holmes, lying on his back, closed his eyes sleepily, flung his left wrist across his brow, and sang,

> "Here's to hit, the birds do hit,
> The bees do hit, too, and die;
> Dogs do hit and get hung to hit,
> So why not you and I?"

By and by he rose, pulled on his trousers, and started preparing dinner. He spread a tablecloth (really a large rag made from sewn-together work shirts) on the bare floor beside the bed, and within a few hours had it covered with plates of collard greens and baked bread. As they ate, Faith told Holmes of her search, its inception, its untimely end. For once her tale did not fall on deaf ears. As she unraveled it, he ate faster, as though it made him hungrier, and when she brought everything up to date, he reached across the table-cloth and held both her hands in his own.

"Things ain't hardly ever like they seem—not even me," he said.

"But they usually come out for the best." The muscles in his face grew slack, his eyes calm. He told a story:

When Alpha Omega Holmes was passing through South Carolina on his way North, he ran short on money and stopped to work on a tenant farm. The bossman looked him over, said, "You're pretty healthy lookin'—how long you wanna work?"

"Just a week," Holmes said.

And he signed up for just that long. Seven days later, he went to draw his pay. The bossman was in his shack near the fields where he employed about fifty men in picking cotton. He scanned his books and shook his head. "Ah been feedin' you for 'bout a week," he said, "and I figure that you et up alla your salary plus 'bout ten dollars mo'." He spread his hands, palms up, and grinned. "You've got to give me another week's work."

Since it was all there on paper and looked official, Holmes did not object. He went back out into the sun, back to his place in the fields, not suspecting anything until an old Negro named Junior collapsed right beside him. Holmes propped Junior up. The old man's throat rattled. He said, "You better run, boy. You'd better run *hard*, and hide y'self! That man's kept me here for five years—" And he died. Another worker stood beside Holmes, shivering. "Junior's the seventh one to die this month. You can't run 'way. The bossman's got a weak heart, but he comes after you anyway, with a gun and a whip and alla his dogs. He whops you, and if you run 'way, he won't give you no food."

The owner of the fields charged out of his shack and stopped beside them. He kicked Junior with the heel of his boot, rolling him over to see if he was dead. He scowled, wiped his brow with a red handkerchief, and thought for a minute. He turned to Holmes. "Bury him right here."

"I can't do no mo' work," Holmes said. "I got psychic powers." He bugged his eyes at the bossman and placed the tips of his fingers to his dark brow. "Ever now and then these spells come over me—I get visions, I get weak and see through things, and can't do a lick of work."

The bossman produced his whip, raised it, then looked curiously at Holmes. He dropped the whip and pried open Holmes's mouth to look inside. "You got blue gums," he muttered to himself. "Hit *is* possible. Blue-gum nigguhs can do 'bout anything when it comes to magic." Then his tiny blue eyes flashed. "You gotta prove hit to me. Tonight. And if you don't, I'll string you up to feed the crows."

That night, in the worker's shed, everyone prayed for Holmes. They knew he was lying. It occurred to Holmes that he was going to die. There'd be more vultures around him than women; they'd pick him dry. The bossman, certain all his workers were locked in the shed, went out and shot a coon, brought it back, and stuffed it into an old burlap sack. He entered the shed, the workers drawing back into the shadows; he dropped the bag at Holmes's feet and grinned.

"If you can tell me what's in that bag, you and me gonna make a lot of money." He rubbed his palms together. "Go 'head, we gonna be rich—"

Holmes circled around the bag slowly, then reached out to touch it.

"Hands off, Mr. E.S.P.," the bossman shouted. "You just tell me what's inside." He produced his whip and let it swing loose at his side. "You'd better not be lyin', Holmes! If you're lyin', I'll see you swing!"

You would have thought Holmes had been walking in the rain, so wet was his clothing. He stared at the bag this way and that, looked at it sideways, and every whichaway, until his eyes hurt. He couldn't figure it out. Cotton? Shoes? Corn? Finally, he gave up and hung his head.

"Hit looks," he said, "like you got this heah coon. . . ."

"What?" the bossman cried. His eyes strained at Holmes. "Tha's hit, tha's hit!"

Holmes looked inside the bag. He felt light as a feather, and turned to point his finger at the boss. "Yep, and I can tell the future, too. I can tell that in ten seconds your heart's gonna give out like a cheap watch. Believe hit! Hit's gonna draw into itself real tight like a spring, and BURST!" Holmes glanced at the clock on the wall of the shed and counted, "One, two . . ." and by the time he got to ten the bossman was stone-cold dead.

Faith was silent for a second. She ran her tongue along the inside of her mouth, then stared at the unfinished portrait on his easel. "But what about the Good Thing? You didn't tell me what it was—"

Holmes laughed. It sounded like barking. "You were good." He looked down at the tablecloth and their empty plates. "That story was good. The dinner was good. . . ."

Somehow it made sense. Faith went again to the Swamp Woman's portrait. She could almost hear it sniggering. The good things were the things of the moment, the things that had been felt and tasted and touched in the past, and might be tasted still. Kujichagulia should have stayed in the village of mountain vales. He should have loved and worked and lived to feel the Good Thing in its small reflections. He might have lived longer that way. . . .

Holmes stood up and threw out his arms. Stretched. She watched his easy progress to the portrait of the Swamp Woman. He took his palette from the floor, studied it, and, as he said something to her she would never recall, began squeezing paint from twisted, half-empty tubes of alizarin crimson and thalo green. What she felt about Alpha,

It was difficult to say, but she'd sensed something different about him as they made love, his weight smothering her comfortably like the curtain of evening on a weary farmer after a hard day in the fields. Unlike Maxwell and the Alpha of her youth, he had not asked if it was good: he'd changed. She could smell that change in his odor, no longer that of barley and cotton and Hatten County, but of turpentine and paint. Holmes walking through the dry weeds on the land behind his father's farm was not what she saw: but Holmes, his broad shoulders framed by the square canvas and his movements strangely ritualistic, merged, so to speak, with the canvas itself; Holmes to her seemed no longer a boy. But not a man either. An eternal child, perhaps. Yes. It came through now as clear as the lines in a wet leaf: when he created, he tried to create himself anew. She counted off long minutes while he spent preparing his tools—rusty palette knives, old brushes with cracked stems, waste rags, and a wide range of pigments, cleaning them with all the care a paraplegic might take to clean his added appendages. Thirty minutes. Then he began: the unfinished corners of the Swamp Woman's face were conjured beneath his brush, as were shadows and illusions of light, depth, and space in images as clear as those she'd seen on the blank pages of Barrett's *Doomsday Book*. Every inch of the lush, rolling background, every curve of the hills and angle of the farmhouse, every line of the fields crisscrossed with primitive industry was incredibly precise. But unreal. Holmes had no truck with describing the scene. He was, she realized, calling these things, changing, twisting, and transforming them into—what? Order. The scene puzzled her because there could be no doubt that Holmes, though he had no reason to be happy in his present situation, was, when he painted, freer, happier, and more whole than anyone she'd seen since she arrived in Chicago.

She was slightly touched, slightly saddened by the truth of it all. There was Holmes and his canvas, his object, but through his object, not in spite of it, he seemed to find release: the Good Thing. She envied him, then felt terrible, for since she could not create, how then could she realize her goal?

Almost in spite, she said, "That doesn't look like her at all. . . ."

Holmes looked over his shoulder, his grin more peevish than warm. "I gave up realism a long time ago—there's enough of that in movies." Seeing her jealousy, he smiled. "I started paintin' in prison. Durin' the day hit was the *only* time I was in control of my life. In the mornin's they led me to the machine shop; in the afternoons I sweated through exercises in the yard, but at night—when I was just a little tired and, therefore, alert—before they'd turn out the lights, I could paint." Holmes's eyes gleamed. "Hit was the only time in my whole life that I had something to say about what went into, or was taken out of, my world. . . ."

Completing a black boil on the Swamp Woman's nose, he dried his brush, then stood back to admire his work. "Hit made bein' in jail bearable," he said. "And when your husband convinced them to set me free, hit made bein' back in the world bearable, too. Hit ain't easy to explain—I tried to study up on hit to make hit clearer to me, but hit's still fuzzy." For a moment, he stroked his jaw and pulled at the wings of his nose; then he gestured at the canvas. "I ain't even certain what this thing *is*! A fellah in the joint told me hit was all a trick, that your eyes are fooled by the points and planes and lines. One guy told me hit was supposed to show life as hit *is*, another said hit wasn't no good unless hit made him forget alla his problems." Holmes frowned, bending toward the canvas, pointing at it. "A teacher in the joint said *what* I painted wasn't as important as *how* I did hit. A Muslim said my work was worthless unless hit was instrumental to his cause, and another guy—a damned fool!—said all that mattered was my puttin' alla my feelings in hit, like kids do, and forgettin' form." Holmes slammed his left fist into his right hand; he glared at the painting, then at Faith. "All I know is that doin' hit makes me feel good, the way goin' to Sunday meeting with Reverend Brown never could. In fact, if I paint on Sunday I don't even feel like I need to go to church!"

Now she knew she didn't know him. Yet what he said was familiar. She remembered the feeling of sanctity she'd felt when sitting under a tree, catching its hard sap in her hands on the Sundays she'd not gone to church but had felt—though she was miles from Reverend Brown's moaning bench—wedded with the warmth of the earth and the wind. Art, perhaps, was not confined to a canvas. Not at all. . . .

"See, I don't call *myself* an artist," Holmes said, slapping his chest. "That's a special word. A *real* artist doesn't play with colors like I do. He doesn't have to. It's as crazy as a coon dog with the tics, but it's true: a *real* artist is his own canvas. Me—I still need that empty surface. I ain't ready yet. But someday, when I've got hit all together, there won't be a dime's worth of difference between what I'm creatin' and myself—you won't be able to separate me from my work by space, or by a difference in materials, because—and I *know* it sounds crazy—my life'll be the finished work. . . ."

Holmes rubbed his nose, unconsciously smearing paint along his lips and, equally unaware, licking at it. Faith smiled to herself. He'd probably done that often—taken paint unconsciously on his tongue during the intoxication of creation, swallowed it, and sent it streaming through his system. He was that close to this thing.

"About the only real artist I ever knew was the Swamp Woman," Holmes said. "She didn't need no paints, or stone, or sheet music, and I swear I believe she could change herself into any damn thing she pleased. No paints, just ideas. That's what you work on the world with, right? But the trick's in not comparin' the ideas to the world to see if they're right. She compared them to other ideas." Holmes, cleaning his brushes, sighed. "The world'll never challenge your ideas—only other ideas can do that. . . ."

Without knowing why, Faith was alarmed. Something in her

rebelled against this. She gave it voice. "If you don't compare what you know, or think you know about the world to it, then how can you ever know if what you think is true?"

Holmes blinked stupidly, trying to unravel her question. "I don't—"

"You have to have something to compare things by, don't you? The Good Thing—isn't *that* the standard?"

He laughed. It did not sound wholly sane.

"There ain't no standard."

Faith said no more of this. Like so many ideas she'd been exposed to, she tucked this one away deep in her memory, refusing to dwell on it now and reserving it for those hours when she was alone, aching with wonder, and could inspect it like the contents of a lost purse one finds on the street.

Holmes changed the subject. "What're you going to tell your husband?"

"Isaac?"

"You've got more than one?"

Faith wrung her fingers. "What *can* I do?" The question seemed to pain him as much as it did her. He lit another cigarette, then pulled on his coat. Without speaking for a long time, he walked Faith back to the subway, then stood, his hands in his pockets, beside her on the empty platform.

"Alpha," she said, "what do I do?"

He shrugged his shoulders. "Be thankful that we had a good time —you can't ask for more than that." And he kissed her on both eyes as her El train roared up behind them.

Children, sweet Faith rode that subway train for hours, back and forth, from the West Side to the North Shore. Finally, to avoid going to the apartment, she walked around the block several times, paced the street, and looked up the sixteen stories to the lighted front windows where she knew Maxwell sat at his desk, working. Waiting. At the corner, she stopped in a bar, had three Bloody Marys for courage, then headed, coiled up inside, for home. The words were framed and well edited in her mind. "Isaac, this is *all* wrong! We've been lying to each other for too long. I've lost something, and I've got to get it back. I haven't been fair with you, but I want to settle all that now. You can have everything: the money, the furniture, *every*thing, but just let me go free." As she stepped from the elevator to her floor Faith thought of Holmes and added more to her confession. "Every life should be a kind of painting. We don't have that together. We keep slashing the canvas with lies and—"

"Honey, come in here!" She heard him the instant she'd thrown open the door. She entered the front room, her head erect, and found him hunched over his desk, papers scattered over its surface beside empty coffee cups and an ash tray overflowing with ashes and half-smoked cigarettes. His collar was open and stained black along its length with perspiration; both his eyes were red and pinched against the light in the room. Faith sensed her confession slipping from her. It wasn't going to be easy. Maxwell, despite his faults, despite the deadly chemistry destroying them, *could*—if she denied herself everything she valued—be loved. She admitted it: I love *some*thing about him. But not Maxwell himself. It was some general, vague thing about him that she knew she could love—the same thing she could love in a tree or a rock. Simply, that it was. But even that, no doubt, would be destroyed in the divorce courts. They might like, even slightly love each other when they went in, but the lawyers, to make a case, would have her and Maxwell at each other's throats. They would part in hatred. It wasn't right. . . .

"They loved my first column on Holmes," Maxwell said. Though tired, he was ebullient.

"They did?"

"Ragsdale said Holmes brought a kind of 'understanding' to the prison issue. Don't look at me! I just wrote down what your home boy said. The editors especially liked the stuff he said about being free in prison—spirit transcending confinement, and all that—like Boethius, Lowell said, whoever that is." Maxwell beamed. "They're going to run it next week, and feature it in all *The Sentry*'s sister papers."

Faith tried to remember the opening lines of her confession. "Isaac—"

"Ssssh!" he said, his left forefinger to his lips. He got up and went to the front closet, flung open its door, and let Faith look in. Side by side on the rack hung an ebony Persian lamb coat with mink trimmings and an ermine evening cloak.

She caught her breath. Maxwell grabbed her hand and led her

through the front door, down the quiet hallway, and to the freight elevator. Inside, as they descended, she regained her composure. "Where are we going?"

Maxwell chuckled, then handed her a set of silver car keys. Faith's hand shook as she looked at them. "These aren't ours."

"They're yours," he said. Downstairs in the parking lot beneath the apartment, he directed her to a sportscar so new there was hardly dirt on its tires. She knew little of these matters but sensed it was a foreign car, one of a limited line, and expensive. She felt her excitement building. And fought it. A car was merely metal, its chassis designed to cover as pleasingly as possible the ugly instruments, oil, and tubing inside. But the chassis was beautiful—long and sleek and silver like a newly polished bullet. The doors were cleverly concealed to give its surface the effect of uninterrupted steel, or an imporous surface like the robe of Christ, of power hidden beneath the hood.

"I got it all on credit, but the money's finally coming in," Maxwell said, "and I figure that it was mainly you, and what you did for me with Lowell, that turned the trick. He was raving about Holmes's column all morning long, and I know it's not *that* good!"

She was in a dream—a maple tree still slumbering through a nightmare that would evaporate at dawn.

"Don't you like it?" Maxwell asked. He sounded hurt; he waited nervously, his hands on his hams.

"It's beautiful . . ." Faith said.

"I knew you'd like it," he said. "It cost an easy ten grand, but that's just the beginning! I've been checking on houses out in the suburbs. There's a ranch house in Evanston, right near the lake. You'll love it."

"We can't afford that," Faith blurted. "You don't have the money—"

Maxwell laughed and led her back upstairs, the car keys burning in her hand. "As long as you carry the ball there's nothing we can't do together. In a year, maybe two, we'll have every damn thing we want."

He went to the refrigerator, mixed them drinks, and returned to the front room to click on the record player. Something old and blue by Billie Holiday came on. Maxwell plopped down beside her

162

on the couch, crossing his legs, feeling good, and nibbling at her ear lobe. Faith sat erect, as stiff as Lavidia in her casket, ice dripping from her drink to the thick carpet on the floor.

"Watch that," Maxwell said irritably. Then he grew warm again, whispering in her ear, "I knew we were going to make it—things just had to start happening." His lips curled with deep, trembling laughter. "You're a *great* ball-carrier, baby. . . ."

Faith smiled. Her *five* was sluggish, her *six* heavy on her tongue, and she never got to *seven* at all.

ome folks would say Faith was born without mother-wit, leading a deceitful double life like that. She stopped wearing her wedding band (the skin beneath it had turned pale, and *that* was some kind of omen), and, ultimately, pawned it along with a handful of her jewelry when Holmes's resources ran thin. He told her he didn't need much—just a bed, breakfast every now and then, and blank canvases until the time he could turn the creative process on himself. Most of his paintings, means to this end, he gave away, grunting, "Don't matter much, I got hit out." She insisted he sell them, that he try to associate himself with a gallery and make a living out of this thing. Each time he refused, and though it angered her, Faith was also glad that he could give his work away, and—especially—could make her feel brand new. She told him as much on the Indian summer afternoon they ate a late lunch in Lincoln Park.

Also this:

"I'm going to have a baby. . . ."

Holmes started choking, a whooping noise burst from his lips. He pounded his right fist on his chest, gagged, and coughed up a chicken bone. Tears ran from his eyes.

"You sho?"

Faith nodded. Timidly, she handed him a napkin.

"Lord, Lord, *Lord!*" Holmes whistled through his teeth. He looked at the half-eaten sandwich in his hand, frowned as though it held horse or stringy hippogriff, then flung it over his shoulder. He fell backward, spreading his arms on the grass, and groaned. "If that don't take the rag right off the bush! Me—a father! Hit don't make no sense. My works, *those're* my kids; that makes more sense." He reared up, his jaw hanging as though unhinged: "How long you known this?" Holmes's eyes half closed, became slits. "You sure hit ain't Isaac's baby?"

"It couldn't be." Faith shivered at the image of Maxwell sleeping on the sofa in the living room, afraid to approach her, uncertain what reaction would spring forth from their touch. She scooted close to Holmes, but he inched back instinctively. She started to reach for him, but her hand fell midway in futility. She blurted, before thinking, "Don't close me out, Alpha!" Then tried to pull herself together, tugging at the fingers on her left hand. "I saw a doctor yesterday. I'm almost five months along. . . ."

Grabbing his napkin, Holmes wiped furiously at his lips, so roughly she feared he'd smear them away. "Does Isaac know?" he said.

"I haven't told him yet. I'm afraid. . . ."

He grabbed her shoulders, held her upright, and thrust his head close to her. Again, she didn't know him. Holmes spoke slowly, deliberately. Making himself known. "I can't have no kids. I'm an experiment, y'see? Honey, I'm different—I can't settle down, or raise kids, or nothin' like that. I'm . . . an *artist*." His eyes narrowed. "I'm outside things, not 'cause I want to be, but because nature did somethin' strange to me—gave me a screwed-up nervous system so I see things different from most people, and have some slim muscular control that lets me paint." His breathing had become an ordeal, a painful thing to both their ears. "I've got to be free—to move around, to work, or loaf, but mainly to experiment with those goddamn paints, and finally with myself. See? I've got to see if a good idea *can* be made real. That means I'm going to suffer, hit means I'm going to be frustrated, and die inside, and wake up in gutters or in hotels with strange women, or—" In his eyes Faith saw him lose the thought. He wasn't seeing her, but something else, a vision that attracted yet repelled him. "That's what I am: a hypothesis. That's right, a theme. And I can't let nothin' tie me down until I see how far the damn theme goes. . . ." Holmes squeezed her harder, almost at the point of tears. "You're going to tell Isaac hit's his, *aren't you*?"

Watching him, she was amazed: full of wonder. "I don't want to lie—I don't want to hurt him, or you, or *any*body!"

"*Some*body's gonna get hurt," Holmes cried. His face flushed, tightened and released like a fist. "My life's the *idea* of what I can be, honey. I can't give that up!" Suddenly, calculation came into his eyes. Reason. "You've got a little money saved. You can get rid of hit—"

"No! I *won't!*"

She was on her feet, retreating backward. Holmes said, "I'm trying to be reasonable," and, with that, Faith started running, abandoning her shoes and purse to race across the park. By the time Holmes caught her both her feet were grass-stained and wet. Brown and green. And she was crying.

"I can't let this thing tie me down," he said. "I'm not being selfish. Hit's just that my life's not my own—hit's for art—the idea of perfection!"

She would not look at him. He shook her—hard.

"I'm *sorry*. I never meant for you to think I was free, that I could live like other men." His voice went flat and empty. "We'll think of somethin'. . . ."

Faith pushed him away and stood back, bitter, her voice husky and broken. "You don't *want* it!"

"Of course I do. I'm glad," he choked. "Hit's . . . the best thing that ever happened to me. . . ."

He coaxed her back to their original spot and, without speaking, began folding the checkered tablecloth and dropping their paper cups and cellophane wrappers into a metal trash can at the edge of the quiet park. As they walked spiritlessly to her new car, a sliver of bright steel by the curb, Holmes said, "We've got to look at this thing from every possible angle, take into account what we know can't give, like my responsibility to this idea. *That*'s got to go on, hit's my life—my *purpose!*" Inside the car he sighed. "Hit's all so tricky. . . ."

"You're *making* it tricky!" Faith cried. "What's more important to you—painting, or me?"

He didn't answer.

"I—" She could not find her voice; the silence was a boulder lying across her brain.

"Hit's not that simple," Holmes pleaded. "You don't understand." He kissed her with all the tenderness he could muster when she stopped in front of his building, then hurried out the curb door.

Faith called after him, "What am I going to tell Isaac?"

(*That we had a good time? That I met and gave myself to a man who had another mistress, a man as strange as a centaur who thought so little of his life and mine and this child's that he would forsake us for a daydream. God, no. . . .*)

"Don't tell him anything," Holmes said, returning to the car. He smiled down at her and stroked her hand through the window. "I'll go to his office before he leaves. We'll get this whole thing straightened out." Then he disappeared into his doorway.

As always, he put her at ease, but only slightly. She could watch him painting, her jealousy fading before the enchantment of the creative process—the painstaking application of paint, the corrections that brought to life something somehow beautiful and more real than all the things *out there*. He couldn't be blamed for his reaction. After three years of living away from the sunlight in a tiny cell he had a right to his freedom. Just the same, it disturbed her. From the moment she knew she was pregnant she realized that a portion of her bondage had come to an end. The thing moved inside her in some warm, deep place like sea depths where insects are spawned, or some immense vale so fertile your spit could make a thousand salvias burst like fireworks from their seeds. She could not hate him. Through him she was no longer apart from the mysteries of the earth, but involved in them. He had given her Big Todd's truth: only through the stranger, or one stranger than yourself, could you seize your own life's meaning. But he, like all men, was a stranger to her, to the earth, and was driven by a restlessness, a disease she only now understood. It had stricken Lynch and Brown and Barrett alike, had laid its heavy hand on Big Todd—suffocating them with a sense of fragility and foolishness before the rhythm of the world. She knew that was it—life was music and they could not dance, had no steps, so to speak, and stood there on the gigantic dance floor of existence, sulking and sneering at those who did dance. They could not be content as the humble caretakers of the garden of creation, could not create as she, or God, or a risible old witch woman could; they could not conjure beauty from the nothingness of all our lives. They were the dead living. Yet she had that connection with things, that capacity to dance if the universe said so, to sing if it demanded song. Unable to create, to conjure life from darkness, men railed against the world. Brown worshiped it to gain its favor, Lynch dissected it, Alpha painted it, Tippis—unable to change it—changed himself, Maxwell ignored it. Creation—conjuring, dancing to the world's grim *mi, fa, mi,* for all men was a queer thing—it couldn't be controlled, couldn't be bought, or captured on canvas, or bent to fit a desperate dream; above all, it couldn't be ignored. Then how did a woman—be she whore or housewife, shrew or saint, witch or virgin—seize that mystery? Deep within, Faith knew she harbored that secret. In a man's world she was denied so much. Conquest was forbidden; passion was forbidden; freedom was impossible: what remained? the biological superiority? creation? and how then creation? The child, in an odd way, was the answer—it was all history focused on a single point—a trillion amoeba, plants, and animals martyred by evolution to produce just this one child and no other, holding in microcosm all epochs, or so she believed; it pointed to every beast and tree and transformation of life, of that peculiar dance that had to be before it could be assembled. By her. She did this, created this new subject of the world. If it was a girl, she would know all this before her first words; if a boy—woe.

In her apartment she thought of this, prescinding the strange changes stretching and swelling her flesh and mind for reflection. Maxwell probably suspected. In the mornings he would watch silently from the bathroom doorway as she vomited into the toilet. Yet he said nothing. Five weeks ago she'd brought home four new dresses, all larger than the ones in her closet. He remarked about their size, but took his questioning no further. But if he suspected, why was he silent? Had her confession reamed out his feelings long ago? What she'd done to him, or failed to feel, came dangerously close to bordering on sin. Tippis hadn't mentioned the terrible rewards of taking another as one's object—the growing dependence, the loss of one's self-esteem. They had to be acknowledged; she lived with them every day; she saw the emptiness in Maxwell's eyes, saw the way his interest shifted from her and his home to the office, to overtime and drinking with his bosses, not because he coveted a raise or a successful column but because he could not bear to be home with her for long. And now? Would her bearing the baby break him completely? Perhaps it would be better to lie after all. But she had done enough, or not done enough, to Maxwell already. He was only a man. . . .

Seven-thirty.

Faith began to worry. He should have arrived hours ago. It was possible that Holmes, as disturbed as he was, had burst into *The Sentry* offices downtown and made a scene, had exposed Maxwell's marital problems for all to hear and so infuriated Maxwell that they'd fought. Faith chain-smoked. *If* they'd fought, inside the building or outside in some garbage-strewn alley, or on the street before dozens of onlookers afraid to get involved—and it was likely since Maxwell stayed at sixes and sevens with everyone—then Holmes would be arrested. He'd be sent back to prison. She'd be alone again.

Faith forced her worries from her mind and walked to her bedroom window. She looked to the dark lake below, to the waves plashing against stark white rocks along the brown, rolling beach. Two lovers strolled on the sand below, their fingers interlaced as they walked barefoot to sit on a large, blanched rock. Things *could* work out all right if Maxwell released her. It would be better for him. She remembered the last time—months ago—when he'd knocked on her bedroom door at midnight, his shorts straining with an erection as hard as Space-Age plastic. She'd risen, leaning on her elbows, pitying him, beckoning him into the bedroom with the hope that—*maybe*—things would work out. He'd kissed her full in the mouth, slid into bed with his respirator, and tried to rouse her feelings. But as he touched her arm he seemed to remember painful things—their arguments, her confessions, and his tool shrank completely from the occasion. She could smell his sweat as he lay beside her, whining. "You don't need me, I guess. You need somebody who can do you some good. I—" She'd pressed her lips to his, tasting the bitter fumes of his asthma spray, and he said, "Damn you," whom he meant, he didn't say; but he could hardly have meant his respirator. He cuddled up in her arms like a child, fell fast asleep, and not once during the night realized she had cried. He never approached her again. Not once. Faith lit another cigarette, certain that a break would be best for them. He could remarry someone more like himself, and she and Holmes could return to Hatten

County. They could rebuild her father's farmhouse, throw up a byre, work the fields, raise the baby. Big Todd's delicate dream of a bucolic life lived like a myth would not be lost, only deferred, not destroyed, but finally realized in her and the boy who had his favor. She swore to that, and decided to name the baby after Todd.

Before she could turn the sound of *Todd Holmes* over on her tongue, she heard a key in the door. It grated against the metal lock for a long time, like a cat or a demon trying to break in. It startled her; she imagined some long-dead thing covered with seaweed and brine, rising with blood-red foam from the floor of the lake, dragging its scaly form along the sand to the entrance of the building below, then slowly scaling the steps, oozing through the quiet hallway with a leer on its hideous three heads to claw at her door, burst in, and pluck her heart from her breast. The noise stopped. She heard a pounding on the door and wall outside.

"Open the god*damn* door for Christ's sake!"

By the time Faith reached the door she was out of breath; already the baby was stealing her wind. She threw open the latch, and Maxwell fell in, his head pitching forward. She caught him, coughed at the sickly sweet smell of whisky on his breath, and helped him to the davenport in the front room. Maxwell's head rolled back and forth on the back of the davenport—his mouth hung open, and his eyes were woven with red and blue veins of blood. His limbs seemed boneless. He leaned forward and tried to focus on her as she bit her nails. A chill ran up her spine as she imagined the course of his thoughts across the background of cocoa-colored walls, rug, and delphinium-blue draperies to the foreground where she stood, resting her hand on a straight-back chair, no more important to him than the cold furniture itself. They were obstacles to the tired tread of his feet across the room, even as she obstructed his progress through . . . She held her breath. Waiting.

"Your boy friend quit today!" he shouted in a whisky tenor.

She nibbled her fingernail, bit her forefinger, and winced, watching it bleed.

"Did you hear me?" Maxwell said. "Holmes came in today at closing time and said he wasn't gonna work on the goddamn column nomore!" He held out the fingers on both his hands and spread them as he pursed his lips. "*Pffft*! Just like that. He walked out on me. . . ."

She could hear her own heart hammering, as loud as a voodoo drum in a New Orleans swamp. It hurt her chest. Faith sat down on the chair to her left, holding her head. "What did he say?"

"He said he quit, that's what he said." Maxwell's mouth twisted clear across his face. "He said he was leaving town to take a goddamn job as a goddamn illustrator for a goddamn ad firm in New York City."

Something slapped her stomach, from the inside. Please stop swearing, she thought. She bent forward, felt her head swim, and tottered to the bathroom where she jack-knifed, vomiting into the bowl. Too weak to rise, she heard Maxwell's voice behind her.

"What do you think of *that*?" he said. "After all I did for him—"

There was a great claw flexing around her heart, crushing her insides. She dry-heaved, and this time she brought up black clots of blood. Maxwell dropped to her side, catching her around her waist before she fell forward. He carried her in his arms back to the bedroom, drew back the covers, and dropped her on the bed.

"I'm going to call a doctor," he said. He wagged his finger at her. "Uh *huhn*—I don't want to hear it! You're sick."

Faith sat up, shivering now. Sweating. He didn't know. He still, perhaps, loved her. There was still time.

Now.

"Honey," she said weakly, aware that her voice was hoarse, "come here." She had not called him that in months, not since his last visit to her bedroom. He froze in the doorway, his face full of doubt. "Come closer," she whispered, horrified by the hollow echo in her voice. Maxwell sat down on the bed beside her, his hands hanging heavy between his knees, his eyes vacant.

"We're going to have a baby. . . ."

The voice of the dead living was behind Maxwell's reply, a voice that has no mind, no sense, no emotion directing it. The larynx and vocal cords sound like taut strings wired in a small box located in the throat of a ventriloquist's dummy; the sounds grate from the lips like chalk scraping a blackboard, severed from thought: "A baby. . . ." His mouth shut with a snap.

All the air in her bedroom rushed to a single corner, far, far away from them. She heard a wheeze, a rattle deep in his throat. "*We?*"

She wanted to lie down. To wrap herself with the sheets, or in a shroud of dry forest leaves. To sleep.

Thought returned to Maxwell, coloring his words like blood slowly staining cloth. "We're—*we?*—are going to . . ." He sucked in his breath violently and stood over her, his palms pressed against his chest, his shirt collar, his legs stiff and head pushed forward. "We're going to have a *baby!*"

Do something, she thought. Why was it taking so long to sink in? She had to wait, motionless, for his move. It came. Like retribution, destiny, or a curse it came. Before her eyes his expression glided through a rosary of emotions—bemusement, suppressed rage—like a mime gone mad. The muscles around his mouth hardened; they stood out like tiny tumors burgeoning beneath his skin.

His voice grunted, sobbing from syllable to syllable. "You must think I'm a fool!" He tottered away from her bed, suddenly sober and choking for air. He searched his pockets for his respirator but only came up with lint. Maxwell swayed for a moment, snatched off his wig, and threw it to the floor. He whirled toward her. "*We* are going to have a baby?" he screamed. "Baby, we aren't going to have *any*thing! I can't even—" Maxwell closed his eyes and fought for breath; he turned from her on his heels and drove the flat of his fist against the wall. Once. Plaster rained from the ceiling to the floor. He looked at the gray shards from the ceiling scattered at his feet, and his face went slack. He looked at her, and she could hear him thinking, *Look what I did*. He seemed to be in control again. Said, "Bitch!" barely under his breath to define her, to frame her for the assault building in his mind. She could see his lips trembling under the exercise of his Will Power, his desire to not say a single word until he had thought it through. Then his face changed. He drew his lips back over his teeth, he narrowed his eyes at her, the wings of his nose went open, and his right hand rose, pointing a forefinger at her head like a pistol.

"Let me *tell* you something! I *tried* to play it straight from the first day I met you—I didn't ask any questions when it looked like you didn't want to give me an answer, but I told you everything about me. Didn't I?" He was shaking, remembering things he had said to her about his childhood, remembering his confidence. "Shit!" he swore to snap himself back. "I *trusted* you; I didn't think you'd lie to me, and even if I did catch you in a lie I thought you were doing it for my own good—our good—to keep us together. Even that insanity about the Good Thing, and the time you spent hustling in that goddamn hotel—it was all okay." Maxwell wiped away water from his eyes; he clenched his fists for control. "If you loved me I figured it was okay if you lied. And afterward I was glad that you told me . . . even though I didn't know how to act any more. I didn't know how to get next to you—to make you feel something for me. I thought buying you the car might do it. Or maybe if I could turn you on in bed—" He stopped, looking away, ashamed. "Maybe I was stupid—I've got less *feeling* than you, isn't that the way you put it one time, less feeling and faith. I ain't in tune with the universe! Well, I had some kinda faith, all right, because I believed in you, Faith! I lay there on that goddamn davenport in the living room night after night, believing that you'd make the next move, the *right* move—that you'd come in there and show me what I needed to do to keep us together." Maxwell bent forward, wringing his hands. "Do you understand?—you meant so much to me that I kept quiet when I saw you messing with that—that—that—*boy*! Yeah, I knew, but you meant . . . that much . . . to me—"

Maxwell rushed to her bedside, his left arm trapping her, his right squeezing a clump of her hair as he, then she, cried.

". . . and you *still* want to play me for a fool, a chump, a pathetic little clown." He brought his right palm against her face. Once. Twice—a third time. Hard. "You can go live with your barefoot boy for all I care. It's his, isn't it?" He waited. Faith could not answer. He slapped her. "*Isn't* it?"

"Yes!" She felt relieved. It was all out now; it was all over.

Maxwell pointed at her, lost his thought, frowned, and stood momentarily confused. Then he recaptured it. "Get out of here!" His hands dropped to his side. "I don't want to see you here in the morning—"

Blood running from her nose slipped through Faith's fingers, flowed to her dress and onto the bed. There was no stopping it, and she breathed huskily through her mouth. Maxwell crossed to her closet and ripped clothes from their wire hangers. He held her ermine cloak high in the air and muttered, "God!" then flung it to the center of the floor. He perfectly enunciated, "Go on!" carefully, slowly, like a voice on an English-language recording. All was stillness in the room. They were manikins behind a store's smooth glass window, he standing with his right foot forward, his left knee locked, and his hand in his pocket, she covering her face. Their lips were parted as though to say more, but neither moved, nor did breath break the perfection of their outlines and those of the bed, chairs, and dresser covered with cosmetics.

Click.

"You just lost your good thing," Maxwell sobbed, and he hurried out the open door.

Faith gave herself completely to her misery. Her face was wet and felt twice its normal size. She lifted her hands to her eyes and saw blood. As she stumbled to the bathroom she could hear him in the kitchen, tearing open the top of a beer can and talking to himself. More than ever she felt dirty, coated with the weight of her actions; but beneath that encrustation was a strange vacuum, an emptiness into which her thoughts plummeted. She gathered up her clothes and shoved them into a traveling bag. On the way out she passed the kitchen, where Maxwell, his head bent low over a beer can, sat at the table, smoking his asthma cigarettes and coughing, his mind shut up tight. He looked up at her, his eyes blurred and searching her face. *Who is this?*

And I? she thought. Faith wiped at her face with a tissue, and said, "I'm sorry—"

Maxwell's throat tore with a horrible sound. He threw back his head and stood up. She could bear it no longer.

"Good-by."

Chicago seemed darker than she could ever recall having seen it. The sky was deep purple and clotted with black clouds whirling west over a craggy skyline. On the El, Faith checked her purse and found close to three hundred dollars there. Instinct sent her to the South Side, to Sixty-third Street, where she returned to Hotel Sinclair. At the desk she rang the bell on the counter, and Mrs. Beasley appeared from a back room, her hair in yellow curlers.

"Child," she said, "you look like you were in a stick fight, and everybody had a stick but you!"

There was some truth in that. "It was more like a football game," she said. She set her bag on the floor and opened the register on the desk. Room 4-D was empty.

"I haven't been able to rent that room since you left," Mrs. Beasley said. "Folks complained all the time about ghost cats as big as Guernsey cows walking 'cross the floor all night."

"That's all right," Faith said. She knew she could sleep in a rat-infested sewer and not miss a wink tonight. "Can I have it back?"

"Sure, if you ain't afraid one of them spirits will take over that child."

Faith looked down at herself and smoothed her dress over the curvature of her stomach. "You can tell?"

Mrs. Beasley laughed. "You kidding? It looks like you've got a battleship and half the Russian army in there."

Faith could not laugh, not now; or in the days, the months that followed when Mrs. Beasley, who supported Faith in exchange for help around the hotel, tried to cheer her. Until the eighth month she was miserable, barely eating enough to keep herself, let alone the baby, alive. Being alone was unbearable. Could she, if another man came along, start again? For Faith the answer was obvious: there was nothing to live for but the baby who would rise Phoenix-like from her wreckage. Often, Mrs. Beasley caught her held by the spell of her round belly in the bathroom mirror on the hotel's fourth floor. Faith, naked to her waist, would look at the old woman's reflection without turning and say, "I'm ugly. . . ."

Mrs. Beasley slapped her behind and upbraided her. "There ain't nothing as beautiful as a woman about to give birth!"

That was comforting, but hard to believe. She saw herself with the detachment a stranger might have—the stretch marks extending from her sides to her navel, her swollen breasts too delicate to touch. "Will I look like I did before when it's all over?"

"Come away from that mirror," Mrs. Beasley said. "There'll be marks on your belly, 'course, and for a while you'll feel like a whole mountain passed through you. But that ain't nothin'. I raised seven kids and I was okay. It happens to everybody that way—"

Faith waited, marking her days. And as the time grew near she grew afraid, most afraid. Her breasts swelled even more, felt even more sensitive beneath her fingertips—from her neck down she felt clogged and clotted with life. It alarmed her. The thing was possessing her entirely, inhabiting her body like the vengeful spirits of the dead. It would come bursting from her as a chicken does from its egg, destroying its shell, stealing the last of her life to feed its own. Fine. Whether she died for it or somehow survived, whether it tore her apart or gave her new strength, or if—later, when it was grown —it came to turn on her, to deny her as Richard Barrett's children had done to him, then that, too, was all right. Just fine. She would love it—yes—even if it choked her dead in childbirth.

On the first day of snowfall in November, she lay across the moist mattress in 4-D, doubled over with labor pains quick enough to kill, she thought, a cow. They followed one another only minutes apart: it was coming—kicking itself free from her like a full-grown god bursting from the sea. She could see its brown face blurred under water, rising up with barnacles and slime to break the surface of her skin.

She screamed, her tongue caught in her throat. "Momma!"

"I'm right here," Mrs. Beasley said softly. "You lay back and fight it, y'hear. I'm right here. I've done this before. I had a pregnant woman without no husband down in room five-C once and—"

The room whirled around her head, bright like the eye of the sun at its center, dull at its dark edges. She was certain she could hear the child murmuring inside her, but she could barely make out its words. It was, she thought, calling her name. Mrs. Beasley brought pans of hot water beside her bed, spread towels beneath her, and talked in a cooing voice, the content of which was lost to Faith forever.

"Press your muscles down," she said.

There was no pain like this pain. Hadn't Lavidia said that again and again? There was no suffering like the suffering of creation. She could feel the strange pressure caused within her by the child's thoughts, its pulse; she could hear its tiny heart throbbing as loud as a gong. Life floated between feces and urine: what was it about?

"Bite on this." Mrs. Beasley shoved the wooden handle of a rusty kitchen knife between Faith's teeth, which sank in, clear to the metal beneath. She heard all sorts of breathing in an eerie concert—her own, quick and labored; the child's, soft and like that of a sleeping dog; Mrs. Beasley's, deep and as heavy as the wind.

The woman was exuding sweat, talking to herself in some crazy, sanctified, secret language of storefront churches until she shouted, "I see its head!"

Deep, silent screams rolled off Faith's tongue: a bolt of white lightning cut jagged paths before her eyes. Then there was darkness.

"The lights went out!" Mrs. Beasley shouted.

She was caught somewhere between life and death, this girl, the baby not yet born, but breathing in the air of the darkened room.

"Don't move," she heard the woman say. "I'll get us a candle from downstairs."

She *could* not move. She imagined herself dead, or at the bottom of the sea. The child was not completely free from her, and the image flashed across her mind of a huge momma cockroach dragging her egg behind her on the floor. The smell of blood and birth was everywhere. Faith was barely conscious when Mrs. Beasley bounded back into the room with a thick, homemade candle stuck in the neck of a wine flask. She placed it on the floor, then tugged at the baby's head; the rest slipped out into her hands.

"It's a girl," she sighed. There came then a slapping sound, and a burst of breath. "You hear that?" Mrs. Beasley laughed.

Faith smiled. She closed her eyes, and Mrs. Beasley finished her work. That done, she placed the baby in a dry towel, then into Faith's left arm. She held the candle close.

"I can hardly believe it"—Faith.

"Every birth," laughed Mrs. Beasley, "is a miracle, ain't it the truth?"

The child was as wrinkled as a head of lettuce, bluish in the flickering candlelight. Bald, its eyes were pinched together, and it fidgeted and wailed. Warmth rushed over Faith. It had her curious eyes—two brown dots set slightly asymmetrically on both sides of a small nose. There were a few indentations from Mrs. Beasley's hand on its head. Faith watched it cry, hugged it closer, and sniffled.

Mrs. Beasley rubbed her hands together like a craftsman after a chore, and stepped backward toward the door. "You hang on to her while I check the fuse box in the basement. I can hear the roomers bitchin' through the walls right now!" She left, closing the door with a slam that knocked the candle over.

Her eyes still shut, Faith pressed the child's soft cheek against her own, dreaming briefly of the life they might lead together. Then she felt a film of heat pressing against her eyelids, and opened her eyes slowly. The corner of the room where the candle lay was brilliant and crawling with iridescent tendrils of flame that licked along the dry wallpaper, the bare floor. A thick cloud of smoke rolled like a wave over Faith and choked the baby. She tried to rise, only to fall back, weak, watching the fire snake across the floor like a serpent to the bundle of dry rags and towels Mrs. Beasley had left behind; they burst—*fooom!*—sparkling like precious jewels. Flames of green, blue, and crimson fire surrounded the bed, each glowing like gems in the sand, in the dark, in the loneliness at the bottom of the sea.

Some unknown strength came to Faith. She scrambled to her feet, wrapped the baby in her blanket, and stood swaying in the hot film of heat. Where was the door? Her eyes were blind with water; the child was limp in her right arm. She stretched out her hand and stumbled, hoping to touch the door by chance. Her palm fell on the hot glass of the window. Her palm blistered; the glass was spreading red with flames, darkening at its corners with smoke. It shattered, showering hot shrapnels of glass across her face.

She shouted.

In the hallway someone cried, "Fire! Fire!"

"Is there anybody in there?" Another voice.

"Some woman," a third voice cried.

For an instant Faith stood wide-legged, wild-eyed, clutching the blanket. The bed to her left was as red as a drop of new blood. Fire blackened the blanket in her arms. She reeled forward, sucking in breath and holding a wail as old, as ancient as the swamps before it could hit her lips. She went mad for an instant, screaming and clawing at the door. A wall of flame seven feet high rippled across its surface, glowing, sputtering, and spewing like a senile old man, changing its outlines before her eyes and assuming a shape—tall, slender, eternal: Big Todd. She called to the trembling figure, reached for it through the heaving black smoke, and felt, without pain, her fingers dissolving along his fiery face. Flames crawled along her outstretched arm, slithered up her shoulder and face and into her dark hair, igniting it like the dry head of a match. . . .

"Want to be a maple tree?" Todd said.

"UHH *HUNH!*"

She dropped into the darkness closing around her like a stone down a well.

Sleep.

This, and for a long time:

She saw herself boiling in West Hell for her trespasses and troubled faith, whirling from burning cavern to cavern and finally falling headlong into a sea of fire. Reverend Brown had warned her, "You'll be annihilated," and the spirit man had prophesied her fall —"Flames from the pit will lick your bowels, your heart will explode!"

It was happening.

Demons, not philosopher-kings, swung from the stalactites, giggled and jeered as her flesh popped like grease in the fires; "You are nothing!" Her head was a crackling match, her blood shot out in a stream through her nose. Minotaurs and harpies danced around her and the other sinners who were immersed in filth and flowing seas of blood; serpents devoured men whole—the most fortunate there merely burst into flame. She opened her mouth, and from it shot a jet of steam: *Hisssss.*

"I don't think she'll need that oxygen any longer," a voice said.

"But," another voice replied, "she'll die before daybreak with that collapsed left lung. . . ."

"And *after* tomorrow?" a third voice said sadly.

Silence.

Faith opened her eye—her left one, because the right felt pasted shut. She was on her back, lying on something soft and yielding. She tried to arch her back and raise her right arm, but they stuck to the white bed clothing, their surface wrinkled and black as tar. She pulled her arm up again; it rose, but the skin remained.

"Try to be still," the third voice said.

The room looked warped through her single eye, blurred and distorted. As her eye began to focus, she made out a man's features— a thin nose, two eyes floating behind thick wire-rim glasses.

"It's me—Arnold. . . ."

"Arnnn—?" Faith caught her breath—flashing into the reflection of Tippis's glasses was a demon; a burned, hairless head half destroyed but, through some act of ultimate evil, allowed to persist, its left eye a discolored globe, its right eye closed forever. The nose was gone; in its place were two empty holes. It had no ears, only gaps along the side of its head. And the mouth—a gaping, lipless maw in which swam a bright red tongue. To her horror, the movements of that mouth exactly followed her own. She tried, but could not cry out, or move her gaze from that face so hideous it would have to sneak up on a glass of water. *Horrible*, children, *horrible*! A single dark tear fell from the demon's enormous eye. . . .

Tippis was dressed in white, his sleeves short and ending at the elbow. He lifted Faith's shoulders a few inches, adjusted her pillow, and took a seat by her bedside. One of the doctors opened the door to what Faith realized was a hospital room, and nodded at Tippis.

"You'll call if she needs anything?"

"Yes," Tippis said sadly. The doctors left. Tippis hunched forward in his seat, his head bowed, his hands held together between his knees. He looked at her from the corner of his left eye. "You're in Michael Reese," he said. "I'm a male nurse now—"

Once again the flames leaped across her vision. She saw the wallpaper in the hotel crimpling, the ceiling raining hot plaster. "Put it out . . . please . . . the baa . . . bee—"

Tippis looked away from her and took off his glasses. He pinched the bridge of his nose until it grew a dark color, then placed his hand on her arm, shuddering when strips of her skin stuck like soft, warm plastic to his own. "Do you want to hear the worst right away?" he said.

Faith did not answer. Her eye seemed transfixed on the sparkling acoustically sealed tiles of the ceiling. She thought of how Lavidia had looked in her casket, how she'd tasted when she kissed her, like an old wax candle. Would anyone, she wondered, kiss Faith Cross? Would the casket even be open?

Tippis exhaled and cleared his throat loudly. It sounded like an engine turning over. "They couldn't even find the baby," he said. "Mrs. Beasley's hotel is a complete ruin. The damn thing went up like a tinderbox. She's behind on her insurance. Won't collect a cent. . . ." He stopped, startled by a low, primeval moaning from Faith's mouth, some primitive sound of sheer animal sorrow. Tippis leaned back, exhaled, and gripped the arms of his chair. He pressed the heels of his shoes on the floor for strength. "The doctors said your right leg is just about burned to the bone. The report—I read it —it says you suffered first-degree burns on three-fourths of your body—you'll probably have to learn to walk with special therapeutic shoes and—" Sobbing ripped through Tippis's throat. His hands flew to his face. "They don't think you'll live. . . ." When he drew his hands away his face was wet. He put his glasses on, but in minutes they were steamed. He jerked suddenly to pull himself together. The glasses slipped crooked on his bulbous nose. He didn't seem to notice. "Faith, they're wrong! I'll help you climb back again!" He shook her hand, demanding a response. None came.

Tippis peeled his fingers from her forearm, rose, and crossed the room to the window. Her eye followed his movements; she heard every word he said. But the words were meaningless. She wanted to die, was thankful that it was a possibility. It made her laugh inside her head: there *was* freedom after all. Death was a peculiar thing, the boundary event through which all others were defined and delimited. You never believed it was going to happen when you lived; it only happened to others, and you went dutifully to their funerals, suspecting that you might escape their fate and live forever. Not now—she was going to become sand and stone, perhaps a maple or oak, or maybe she'd just be allowed to rest. . . .

"Are you afraid of dying?" Tippis said, his back to her. "It doesn't make any sense that suddenly we should be no more. Why should we *be* if we have to *not* be!" His shoulders hunched, pushing his head up like a jack-in-the-box. Behind him, laughter came from Faith. Fresh perspiration broke out on Tippis's face as he looked at her—a red open mouth of serrated teeth, a pink eye in a black head. He inched toward the door, his head tucked in, opened it without a sound, and slipped out.

With no one to hear, Faith attended to her own thoughts, aware of time mechanically clicking away in the wall clock near the door, not caring, comforted by no illusions of things to be done, no projects which, unless she completed them, might prevent the world from going on. A round sense of the void. But she did not want to die, although going on like this, trapped in a body that would not respond to her will, seemed like a curse. She was aware of it only by the painful itch crawling from her head to her feet, by the hardness of the plastic tubes inserted into her right side. Afraid, she wanted to pray, but suddenly could not recall a single verse. *Fine*, she thought, *just fine*.

The door opened. Her eye smarted with light from the hallway, then focused through a watery film on a man's figure in the doorway. He straightened the shoulders of his loud sports coat, touched first his bright pink bow tie, then his wig, and sat down with a frump on the bedside. It took a struggle, but she managed to turn her head toward him.

"I just heard an hour ago," Maxwell said. He leaned over, looking at her face, then winced. He closed his eyes, stood up, and backed away. "I'm sorry," he said. "The baby, too?"

Go away! she thought. Her head hurt now; something was flipping her brain over and over like a flapjack. *Please—*

Maxwell pressed his respirator to his lips thoughtfully and shifted from one heel to the other. It was almost pathetic; he was a writer, a worker with words for whom comforting words would not now come.

"Faith," he said finally, waving his right hand as if to pluck his phrases from the air, "I never knew it was going to turn out like *this*!" Air whooshed loudly through his throat; he puffed the respirator between his lips. "I tried to reach Holmes right after I heard, but he didn't leave a forwarding address with his parole officer. They're looking for him now. . . ."

He had deserted her. So Faith had expected. But why were they looking for Alpha Omega Holmes? Surely not for her sake, or the baby's. Such men as he and Big Todd could not be captured. Not really. You could chain that malleable, rough side of them that lay in history, but the rest was wind, a current that sometimes cooled you when you were dry, but broke you, as the wind did tar paper in a cabin window, when you got in its way. Somehow, it was just.

"If you pull through this, I'll make it up to you," Maxwell said. "I'm going to get you the best doctors that money can buy." He paused, his eyes narrowing on the silhouetted side of her head, his teeth bearing down on his thumb. "If you just show enough Will Power, honey—"

"*Go away*!" She got it out this time. It shook Maxwell. He started to speak but swallowed instead, then reached inside his suit coat. He withdrew his billfold and laid twenty dollars at the foot of her bed.

"In case you need anything tonight." He straightened his tie in the mirror above the sink in her room, and left without another word.

Time dragged on like a polecat mangled by a truck and hauling its dead rear end to the roadside. Each breath became harder for her to draw. Her body seemed already gone, but her mind was clear, as transparent as bubbling spring water with shiny stones visible on the floor of its stream. Side by side at the stream's bottom were stones for the respective stances she'd endured: Lynch, Tippis, Lavidia, Brown, Maxwell, Barrett, and Big Todd. Their voices tramped through her mind with the force of a hunter's bootheel—being and not-being, life cannot support itself, sublimation of instinctual drives, get yourself a good thing. . . . She had suffered, and what had she now? Ash on her tongue. The sides of her mouth drew together in a deliciously evil sneer, "*Faugh!*" Not one of them knew of the Good Thing, or even believed in its possibility—its necessity.

"*Faugh!*"

At that instant her eyes went cloudy, unclear, and ached from within—even the closed one, and when the left one again admitted light from her small room she saw crouched at the foot of her bed an extremely large white cat. Its eyes were like crystal, deep enough to lose your mind in, deep enough to suck her thoughts from one crystalline plane on its surface to another, and finally freeing her as it opened its mouth of razor-sharp teeth: "I can't do nothin' until you come, honey. You ready?"

Faith sucked in her breath and smiled faintly. It was a long way home.

**P**eople never tire of hearing Faith Cross's tale. An old farmer sitting before the kitchen stove, petting his rooter-dog, may make it an odyssey involving the fate of the world; harlequin-faced grandmothers will grin, giggle, and tell it as a gallyflopper spiced with the morals they want you to hear. It's said by some of them as far north as Chicago that Arnold Tippis returned to Faith's hospital room, that he started hollering for help. They say he cringed in her doorway, whey-faced and whimpering for a long, long time, staring at that charcoaled corpse—the mortal remains of sweet Faith Cross.

That ain't the truth.

Truth is, Faith took hold of herself, grabbed the bills Isaac Maxwell left on her bedside, and rose from her bedsheets—minus a lot of skin; she stole down the empty hospital hallway of Michael Reese, and out through the receiving room. Quiet as a ghost. You didn't need a Navajo guide to follow her trail—it was marked by the line of frightened faces of folks who saw her creeping wraithlike from corner to corner through the streets of Chicago. Clear down Michigan Avenue: horrified folks holding their hearts. The old man in the ticket booth at the train station saw her—he's in a coma to this very day. Faith rode the rails for hours, asleep with the Swamp Woman's cat on her lap, and—at Hatten County—climbed off. Without a word, children. Don't you believe Lem Hastings when he says his hair turned prematurely white from worry. The last murrain that killed his mules didn't do it. It was fright. Sheer horrification at seeing Faith's wreckage hauling itself down the back roads past the black hole where her father's farmhouse stood. Passersby said they saw *some*thing as white as snow, swaying, whispering to itself in the farmhouse ruins, moaning, and meandering from room to room.

Touching things. Wailing, they say. Then it moved on, across the fallow brown fields to the mephitic bogs. The mud was as high as her hams when she crossed the bottoms. Late autumn winds winnowed rotten leaves around her head. Anguish welled within her; her thoughts were red-tinged, burning her eyes until they watered. It was as if she'd made the transition from the dead living to the living dead (think sharp now), but was back in the world on a temporary visa. By nightfall, Faith could barely break through the tenebrous, twisting barrier of naked trees and thorny bushes bordering the swamp. Everywhere was the septic, intoxicating, sweet smell of seasonal decay. She kept on stepping.

Clutching vines and fronds fell away from her path at a clearing, and in the distance, surrounded by the roundel glow of moonlight and its reflection off the stagnant waters of the bogs, was the Swamp Woman's shanty. All else in Hatten County might have changed—calamity might have leveled its houses, families might have been swallowed whole by time—but the shanty still stood, half submerged in the swamp like a ruin, or the white rib of a mastodon, or a cow skull sunk in the sand. Right. That she was dying Faith had no doubt. And of all the people in the world, probably only the Swamp Woman had a way with death: an understanding. The cracker-barrel philosophers at the feedstore in town often told how Casey Fudd, after the death of his first wife and four children in the great epidemic of '29, wanted to throw in the towel. So aggrieved was he that he asked the Swamp Woman for a herb to end his life as quick as possible. She refused. "Then," Casey swore, "I'll do hit m'self." He found enough courage to buy himself an old .45, a gallon of kerosene, a long rope, and an economy-size bottle of rat poison. Brother Casey was going to do it up right. Folks say the Swamp Woman wanted Casey to persist, though, and ensorcelled him right on the spot. Not knowing this, Casey tramped down to the river, sat himself upright in a rowboat, and pushed off, floating down the river until he came to some low-hanging trees on the bank. There, he tied the rope around a tree limb, doused himself with the kerosene, swallowed the bottle of poison, raised the pistol to blow out his brains, and kicked the boat out from under himself. What happened? Old Casey pulled the trigger, but the bullet broke the rope, the river doused the fire and, when he got a lungful of water, he gagged up every drop of that rat poison. Old Casey pulled himself up on the riverbank, vowed to make a new man of himself, and ran for Commissioner of Hatten County. And he won, too.

Weak, ready to give up the ghost, Faith pulled herself hand-over-hand along the swaying bridge to the shanty. There was still hope if, before she drew her last breath, the Swamp Woman would clear up the mystery of the Good Thing. The glowing lights within the shanty blinded her left eye as she crawled through the Door of the Dead. The werewitch was there, hunched over one of her workbenches amid open Black Books, a gilded copy of *De Novum Candarus Salomis*, the *Kitab-el-Uhud*, *Clavicle Keys of Solomon*, and *The Grimoire of Pope Honorius II*. Her three forefingers marked her place in one of these as she peered, cackling, through a microscope.

Faith's voice cracked. "I've come again. . . ."

The Swamp Woman glowered, spun around on her stool constructed of old gray skeleton bones, and lifted her fingers to the place where her lips should have been.

"*Shhhh!*"

Faith, swaying on her feet, her head bent low, despaired. The werewitch, it seemed, had no time for her. As the Swamp Woman returned sniggering and squinting her green eye through the microscope, Faith turned away, hobbling to the door. She passed the full-length mirror in front of the pallet bed, looked. Shuddered. "Nice looking," bubbled bitterly from her lips, yet she did not cry. There was almost something aesthetic about her ugliness—her round, hairless head, the cockleburs and mud caked on her tattered white gown. The fire must have destroyed one of her breasts—only that could explain the concave area running from her right shoulder to her hip. Bones forked up through her skin and all over, her body looked as crinkled and black as a soft marshmallow left too long in the fire.

"You're looking good, girlie," the Swamp Woman laughed. She turned away before Faith could respond. Whatever had the werewitch's attention must have been of epoch-making importance. She kept her eye to the lens, whispering to herself, ". . . *Tausend ein Million* . . ." and wrote furiously with her free hand. Faith stumbled across the slanting floor, only half aware of the Swamp Woman's remodeling of her shanty. A new cabinet of alchemical cookbooks and peeling tomes was in the eastern corner beside a shelf of bottled toadstones, molting boar skulls, and growing plants: satyrion, henbane, and sea-blue lungwort. Faith fingered a healthy monkshood for a moment, trying to lose her thoughts in its gristly, hirsute texture. It didn't work. Emptiness weighed heavily upon her, wrought ruin with her frail attempts at self-regeneration. Only inches from her feet was the Thaumaturgic Mirror. She stepped close, touching the waist-high urn, peering over its rim.

"And *now*?" she whispered.

Electrified water in the urn bubbled briefly and shot before her eyes a single, ancient image: the bogs.

"*C'mere*!" shrieked the Swamp Woman.

Slowly Faith hobbled to the side of the werewitch. Who clapped her hands gleefully and tossed back her misshapen head. "I've got it, girlie!" She winked mischievously and giggled. "I've been workin' on the solution to this problem for goin' on a century now!" She leaned forward, peaceful repose sagging her features, and sighed. "I guess I don't have to be a werewitch no more—when the fish is caught, you toss away the net, right?"

"You don't!" Faith said. It was unthinkable. No more Swamp Woman? It was like saying the sun had burned out, and there would be eternal night. "I thought you'd always be around—"

"Nope!" The werewitch wrinkled her nose. "Don't ya think I'm *more* than a werewitch, just like *every*body's much more than whatever they have to be at one given time? It's like this: everybody looks for the Good Thing in different ways, right?"

"Yes," Faith said. "I understand—"

"*Do* ya, now?" the werewitch grumbled. "Do ya *really* understand that a man or woman or werewitch has a thousand 'n one ways to look for what's good in life? Do ya see that ya have to start with the limitations that ya find y'self in, say, as a preacher, then follow the preacher's path as far as that'll take ya—like the Russians say, *vynoslivost*, 'living a thing out'; then, ya take a scientist's path 'n see how far that'll take ya?" Across the Swamp Woman's face was a seriousness and intensity Faith had never seen. "Ya take every path: the oracle's, teacher's, the artist's, and even the path of the common fool, and ya learn a li'l bit from each one. That's life, girlie. Ya keep right on steppin' and pickin' up the pieces until ya gets the whole thing—the Good Thing. As for me, werewitchin' is pretty played out." Seven gnarled forefingers reflectively stroked her crooked jaw. "I think maybe I'd like to try a young girl's way—innocence, faith, and all that. Might be a lot of laughs—"

"But you've got the 'answer'?" Faith gestured at the microscope, the hope of a final solution to her quest sticking, like a chicken bone, in her throat. "You said—" She stopped, noticing that the Swamp Woman seemed puzzled and had cocked her head like a hound. "Child," she said, "this is *one* answer (and a damned good one at that). It's about the only kind of answer that somebody on my path can provide." She shoved the microscope across the table and said, "Look in there."

Placing her eye to the lens, Faith focused and saw an enormous silver globe floating in white space. The head of a pin. And clustered thereon like ants on a sweet apple were thousands of people— more black folks than you can find at Vicksburg on a circus day, all dressed in full-length robes with holes in the back for ebony wings.

"Two hundred million, seven hundred, and sixty-nine angels," the Swamp Woman giggled, "*that's* the answer—in an average case, that is, just countin' Virtues, Thrones, Dominions, Powers, Principalities, and Archangels. If you throw in them li'l cherubim, the number will rise to the third power. . . ."

Disillusioned, Faith removed her eye. The Swamp Woman slapped her knee and howled; she sailed off her seat, crashed headfirst on the floor, and commenced to rolling around, kicking up her heels, laughing, pointing, and signifying on poor Faith, "Oh, look in the mirror! Hee hee! Look, oh, oh—look, *look*!"

Faith hurried to the mirror and saw, encircling her one good eye, a sooty ring. She wiped it off. Shouted, "You're *terrible*!" Her throat convulsed with humiliation, and she started to cry, letting it all come out—the misery, disenchantment, and, now, a deep and certain longing for death. "You're an evil, heartless old witch!" she cried.

That brought the Swamp Woman to her feet; she erupted every now and then with snickers and hid the smile on her face with both her hands. After she had calmed down she placed her right arm around Faith's shoulders and said, "Girlie, I didn't mean no harm. Categorically, that trick proceeded from the Good Will. That's right!

It didn't involve no means-end relationship whereby I said, '*If* I want to poke fun at girlie, *then* . . .' *Uhn, huhn*. I tricked ya 'cause I had to act in such a way that a maxim based on my action might itself become a universal law." She patted Faith tenderly on the head, then palmed it playfully. "Wouldn't it be nice if everybody did that to everybody else?"

Weariness had its way with Faith. She felt numb and insulated from the world. Her good eye, though it had no lid, began to darken, slowly, like fermenting wine. "I only came to say good-by before I die. . . ."

The Swamp Woman jumped back and stomped her foot on the floorboards. "You're giving up? Child, you'd better stick your brains back into the stove—they ain't done yet!"

"The quest is over," Faith whispered, more to herself than to the werewitch. "I failed. I was a fool—"

"Over? How can it be over when ya only been on *one* path—and a silly one at that?" The Swamp Woman's face blackened with rage. "There ain't no beginnin' and there ain't no end." She stroked her chin in deep meditation. "There ain't nothin' but searchin' and sufferin', too! To be human *is* to suffer, child—to feel, to be sentient, y'see? And, if nothin' else, ya can do what that sweet gal Imani, Kujichagulia's wife, did." A smile spread across the Swamp Woman's face. "Haven't ya figured out, after all this time, who Imani is?"

Faith was alert now. "*You!*" She was furious and, since furious, quite alive, her spirit reviving with violence. "You lied to me! You didn't tell me the whole truth! You said the Good Thing was lost." Faith trembled with anger. It had all been a great lie from the start. "You *lied* to me!"

Her accusation so angered the Swamp Woman that she spat upon the floor. The fluid, landing at Faith's foot, burst into black flames. Dark tears fell from the werewitch's eyes. "It was lost to Kujichagulia, girlie, not to Imani. Not to me! Did Plato lie when he told Phaedrus that love was a god, and then denied that very same thing before all those folks in the *Symposium*? Dialectics don't hold to no single truth, child; it reaches out for the Good Thing, affirming and negating itself until the Good Thing's regained."

Faith held her breath; her words hissed through her teeth. "Did Kujichagulia—did he or did he not find the Good Thing, and then come to ruin?"

Sheepishly the Swamp Woman smiled. "Yes!" She cackled and danced across the room to a corner. There, as Faith simmered with rage, she rifled a box of old rags and produced a doll. "I made this mojo for ya," she said. "Figured ya might—"

"I don't want it. I don't want to see any more of your tricks and Bourbon Street shenanigans ever again!" The doll, Faith realized, was a nearly perfect likeness of Alpha Omega Holmes. It even had a tattoo circling its neck. "I just want the *truth* about the Good Thing."

The Swamp Woman dropped the doll onto her bench and narrowed her eyes. Smirking. "The *logical* truth?"

"Yes," Faith said wearily.

"Got ya 'gain!" the werewitch squealed. "There's Aristotelian logic, transcendental logic, phenomenological logic, dialectical-materialist logic, symbolic logic, instrumentalist logic—"

"No!" Faith screamed. She balled her fists and, with them, hit her head.

"Then," the Swamp Woman said craftily, "ya wants the *non*logical truth, eh?"

Exhausted, Faith supported herself by leaning against the workbench, sick deep inside her stomach. "Why are you playing with me? Haven't I suffered enough already?"

"Girlie, ya ain't suffered nothin' until ya suffer *the* truth. But I reckon you're ready for it now. You're 'bout done with the path of the pristine young innocent, ain't ya?"

Faith could not answer. She wanted to sleep away the sound of all these confusing words. She looked up toward the Swamp Woman and received a shock she was not, nor could ever be, prepared for. Before her eyes the werewitch proceeded to remove her boil-ravaged skin. She snared two of her sharpest talons in a fold at the nape of her neck, lifted off her face like a cowl, and slipped from the rest as though it were long underwear.

Faith swallowed. "God!"

"Glad you mentioned that," the Swamp Woman said. " 'Cause, like God, the Good Thing's governed by what's called the Docta

Ignorantia—that is, knowin' it always implies negativity, 'cause it's beyond, in the final analysis, everyday understanding." Skinless, and vigorously scratching her dark liver and spleen, the Swamp Woman lurched across the room to a hook near the door. There she hung her skin and smoothed it out, removing flecks of lint, here and there, from its surface. Her naked white skull turned to Faith and laughed. "Did I tell ya that Kujichagulia left that gal Imani, left me that is, and started climbin' Mount Kilimanjaro, the elements arisin' to bring him down, and all that?"

Unable to look directly at the werewitch, and still trying to swallow, Faith lowered herself onto the nearby pallet bed. Said, "Uhh, huhn...."

"Well, that's true. Must be. That's the way I always tell it. It seems to me that after Kujichagulia died in them mountains things got real hard for Imani. She managed to raise her kids and keep life and limb goin' until they was all grown up, outta her hut, and married. And when that happened, she decided to climb that mountain herself, to die beside her husband (he was confused—lemme tell ya!—but I loved that fool). That night she was climbin' was as dark as All Hallow's Eve, child, and it took a long, long time for her to climb it, 'cause she was old, almost crippled, and just a li'l outta her mind. But she kept right on steppin', just like we all got to do, and on a moonless winter night she got there. Under her bare feet were Kujichagulia's dry, bleached bones. In the air was thunder, and right behind that—lightning. She thought the Good Thing was gone for good, girlie, hidden by them wrathful, thick-necked gods. But they took pity on this child. Her eyes were innocent, her heart —bless her soul—never once questioned the good things like Kujichagulia had (I ain't braggin' now, that's *why* I was called Imani). So the gods dropped down a lightning bolt that lit up the whole sky like the aurora borealis, honey—it twisted around in the shape of the Sign of Solomon and spelled out the words *In This Sign Conjure.*

" 'Cause that's about the best way there is for callin' up the Good Thing: conjurin'. Imani took only one path, child. She became a midwife to mystery, y'see? Her hair was as white as hoarfrost, and she started conjurin' day and night, invokin' spirits from sweet-gum trees, dredgin' up demons from the most common things of all. You was like Kujichagulia, girlie, the kind of child who'd forgotten how to play, to sing, and trembled in the darkness instead of enterin' into it; you clung desperately with both arms to the belief in certainty, and screamed at the wind, the shadows—you were the child whose throat is dry when everyone else's is filled with song. Y'see, the worst part of restlessness and questionin' is not insecurity and fear, but just this: insensitivity; the worst part of insensitivity is not torpidity, but loneliness; and the worst part of loneliness is not the lack of friends, but the lack of intimacy with the world, the lack of unity. You was born in the winter of the Age of Reason—an ugly age (or so it is and seems to me), filled with disillusion, rife with conflictin' theories that bend and fold and mutilate men like a computer card to explain them completely and, through all that, deny their freedom to create. To conjure. You started out as close to the world as the baby is to its momma's tit, you *were* it, you felt oceanic feelings so deep they sometimes made you want to cry but, by and by, you got smart. Sho! The tit wasn't you, after all. *Was* it, girlie?"

"I guess not." Faith shook her head to clear it. "But—"

"Quiet! I'm conjurin'!" the Swamp Woman shouted. "And you looked a li'l bit further, and saw that *nothin'* in the inner or outer world was you; it was all outside of you, separated by space and time and primary qualities and *Ding-an-sichs* and—hah! It made you wonder what you *were*, didn't it? Don't answer! Yes! Instead of bein' one with every object, every object became a thing apart from ya—ya even became a thing to y'self! So ya broke your bonds with the world when ya got smart. That's part of bein' smart, ain't it? Object-ivity: standin' back away from the world to check it out. Don't answer! It's true: ya broke 'em, sweetheart, 'n ya couldn't live a good life no more until ya found out what the universe was doing. Sho! That made sense—find out what the universe was doin', *then* get in harmony with it. Yes, *yes*! But how? A pineal gland? The negation of the negation? Faith? Christ on the Cross? Back to Nature? *How*, girlie?"

Faith cringed. The Swamp Woman was making it appear hopeless. "I don't know! You're right, you *do* have to know what the Good Thing is before you can get right with it—"

"*Nonsense*!" The werewitch cackled. "Ya think too damned much!" She sneered, poking her pointed tongue through the left side of her skull. "The Good Thing. What's *that*? Hee hee. I'll tell ya:

when the struggle with synthetic systems has been fought out and the battle seemin'ly won, when the mind has categorized animals, vegetables, minerals, and all the rest, when the levels of reality have all been systematized, taxonimized, and bled dry in the antiseptic laboratories of a reason loosed from all restraint, *then* and only then does the mind grow weary of system—it grows blank and cool and clear and capable of conjurin' not only what the categories and tables of judgment can't contain, but also that in which the heart of men, beasts, and birds revel: love."

"The Good Things's love?" Faith cried.

"Don't pin me down!" the werewitch wailed. "If you ask me 'gain, I'll say it's hate. Ask me thrice, and I'll say it's neither, 'cause the Good Thing's spontaneous; it's *absolutely* nothin', but *particularly* it's everythin'."

Faith did not take her gaze from the wooden floor. "So all I did was for nothing?"

"*Nothin'*?" The Swamp Woman roared. "You mean I've been wastin' my breath? Wasn't that story 'bout Kujichagulia good?"

"Yes, but—"

"And wasn't it—well, you *know* the rest, girlie. I see I can't explain nothin' to ya when ya wants demonstration." She snickered, "Damn fool empiricist," and pointed behind Faith to the window. "Just look outside."

Confused, Faith pulled back the thin curtain to the window (it *was,* she realized, made of skin—great strips sewn together with human hair). Light burst in thin blue beams that caused her to blink, opening and closing her eyes quickly until she could see. It was dawn, a time that had always taken hold of something in her blood; dawn, a new beginning; dawn, a moment both still and serene, suggesting that her long night of questioning had been quite unreal. Around the shanty, coming in waves from the swamp, was the sustained orchestration of songbirds: hooting, cooing, chirping, squawking, and crying on the unseen undercurrent of the wind. There rang out a melody from a wren, and somewhere in the wild bush a bullfrog answered; and with each call another came, louder, competitively as if the birds and bullfrogs, wise as philosophers in their own way, were in a contest to celebrate the coming of day when dull mankind slept and only the sensuous, long-suffering trees could hear. She saw an elm towering over the other trees in the distance, waving its highest branches in the breeze. Todd Cross. She was certain. Certain of everything. Certain the air was cool and scented with the clean smell of dew. Certain the wind pushed on, and the birds swung into the empty sky like sleek arrows, no destination, no duty, no destiny in mind. Daylight came, their sweet lays drifted away. . . .

"Hee hee! Systematize *that*!" The Swamp Woman laughed. "It makes ya feel stupid, don't it?" Then she was dead serious. "Who says ya gotta understand the universe to love, to conjure it, girlie?" As ghastly as a corpse freshly unearthed from its crypt, the werewitch returned to the box from which she'd taken the mojo of Alpha Omega Holmes. Grumbled: "On every path you take you'll find a li'l bit of the Good Thing and vexations as well. Try *my* path, why don't ya?"

Faith, for the first time, understood.

The Swamp Woman removed a fresh suit of skin from the box. She slipped it on, tugging at its loose seams, then zipped up the back. Faith held her breath: the hair on the suit was formed around its head in a full, mushrooming natural; the skin was creamy and the color of caramel, the eyes in the head were slightly asymmetrical, and the breasts—small.

"Ya feed the manticore out back for me," the Swamp Woman said, "and don't let the cockatrice outta its cage." A devilish glint exploded in her dark eyes. "I ain't never been a foolish young girl, ain't never tasted the Good Thing in quite that way." She started toward the door, young again, smiling, and emerged into the glare and promise of day.

"Watch out for Arnold Tippis," Faith called. But the werewitch was gone. Faith almost knew what she would encounter, could predict it, because she'd been there herself. That awareness made her feel like an oracle. It convinced her that prescience was not so much a gift of magic as it was the product of experience. Flipping a dry toadstone over in her palm, she wondered if other magical feats were also at her command. The only way to know would be to start a new path. To step into the Swamp Woman's abandoned skin. Faith left the toadstone on the workbench and walked to the boil-marked skin by the door; she examined the manufacturer's label sewn on the inside of the collar (Elysium) and, finally, slipped it on.

Nothing immediately came of that.

The skin fit perfectly around her body, but was slack at her fingers like an oversized glove. The fingertips swung empty at her sides; the rest was as tight as hosiery. And creeping through her mind were the most marvelous thoughts: formulas for elixirs and potions flashed before her single eye, and faraway she heard the moaning of dead spirits on the wind, the chilling *mi, fa, mi* of the earth. She knew, in an intuitive, immediate way freighted with love and hate and, somehow, neither, whether Plato was *really* Socrates; how to concoct love potions from lion powder; how the pineal gland linked *res extensae* and *res cogitantes* but left the problem of mind-body dualism unresolved; the cryptic runes for raising the dead and parting waves; and the meaning of pre- and pronormative ethics on the methodeutic measure of Firstness, Secondness, and Thirdness. Her mouth pushed forward with glee:

"Hee hee!"

She'd suffered several roles: the innocent, the whore, the housewife. And now, the werewitch herself. There would be others. There had to be. She was more than any one path, or the total of them all. She would glean from each its store of the Good Thing, would conjure it up: the enthusiasm and naïveté of youth, the self-sacrifice of the streetwalker, and the love that even the most miserable housewife received—exhausting them, moving on to another path, and another. That was life, children. And when she'd traveled the existing paths, she would create a new, untrodden one. That was progress. If she discovered X number of paths and traveled them all, then she, before she died, would leave X-plus-1. That was responsibility: factoring the possible number of paths to the Good Thing, but not becoming fixed, or held to those paths in her history, or the history of the race. Moving always on. . . .

Faith stopped, still as a mummy, her ears straining at a slushing sound from the swamps. Snorting, she yanked back the tarpaulin to a window and saw two timorous, barefoot children crossing the bridge. She giggled, rushed to the machine in the corner, and shouted, *"Faugh!"* The Gila monster awoke running in place on its treadmill (what good things lie in a serpent's way of being-in-the-world? Someday she would have to try that one, too). The shanty filled with mournful music. Quickly she reshaped her nose into a sharp cone and seated herself cross-legged on the floor. She decided to tell them first about Aristotle's Illusion (cross your first and second fingers on one hand, then rub a pencil between them; it'll feel like two pencils, not one, scraping your skin), and then the tale about Stackalee's great battle with Lucifer in West Hell. It made her laugh:

"*Hee hee!*"

But she was ready, children, because there always was and always will be an old Swamp Woman cackling and conjuring in the bogs (someday it might just be you), just like there'll always be the Good Thing for folks willing to hear and hunt for it. But you've got to believe in it. Don't be interrupting to ask if the tale is true.

Was it Good?

Was it Beautiful?

All right.